Christie [...] [...] [...] bestselling
romanti [...] [...] eart Lane

The item should be returned or renewed by the last date stamped below.

Dylid dychwelyd neu adnewyddu'r eitem erbyn y dyddiad olaf sydd wedi'i stampio isod.

Newport
CITY COUNCIL
CYNGOR DINAS
Casnewydd

BETTWS

To renew visit / Adnewyddwch ar
www.newport.gov.uk/libraries

THE NEW DOCTOR AT PEONY PRACTICE

CHRISTIE BARLOW

One More Chapter
a division of HarperCollins*Publishers* Ltd
1 London Bridge Street
London SE1 9GF
www.harpercollins.co.uk
HarperCollins*Publishers*
1st Floor, Watermarque Building, Ringsend Road
Dublin 4, Ireland

This paperback edition 2022

1

First published in Great Britain in ebook format
by HarperCollins*Publishers* 2022
Copyright © Christie Barlow 2022
Christie Barlow asserts the moral right to
be identified as the author of this work
A catalogue record of this book is available from the British Library

ISBN: 978-0-00-841315-6

For Julie Wetherill,
A woman who matches my level of craziness.

Loveheart L

Primrose Park

The Lake House

CLOVER COTTAGE ESTATE

The Old Bakehouse

Bumblebee Cottage

The B

Starcross Manor

Scott's Veterinary Practice

THE GREEN

Primary School

HIGH STREET

Post Office

H

Peony Practice

Callie's apartment

Solicitors Office

Dolores' apartment

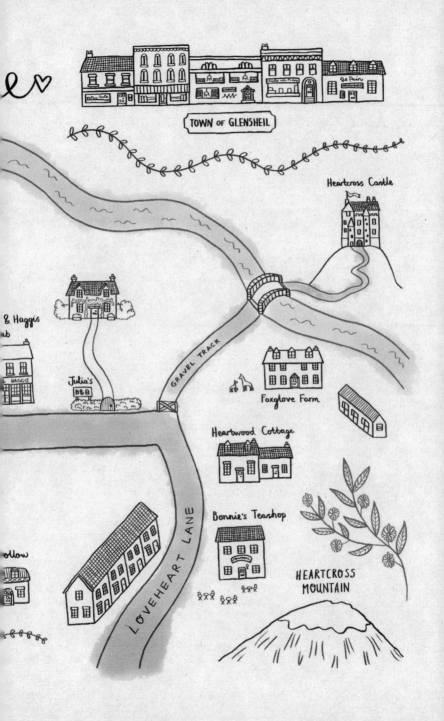

TOWN OF GLENSHEIL

Heartcross Castle

& Haggis
ub

HAGGIS

GRAVEL TRACK

Julia's
B&B

Foxglove Farm

Heartwood Cottage

Bonnie's Teashop

ollow

LOVEHEART LANE

HEARTCROSS
MOUNTAIN

Chapter One

No one likes Mondays. All day Ben Sanders had been run off his feet at work and couldn't quite believe the number of patients that had walked through the door of Peony Practice. The phone hadn't stopped ringing and as soon as the clock struck six-thirty, Helly, his reliable receptionist, switched on the answerphone and turned the sign on the back of the door to closed before slumping into the reception chair. She stared at the huge mound of filing that Ben had placed on the edge of her desk.

'What a day!' she said, exhaling and looking over towards Ben, who was taking a breather and standing in the doorway of his office.

'A hell of a day,' he confirmed, blowing his hair off his forehead. 'I thought birthdays were meant to be relaxing and fun.'

Helly placed her hands on her desk and slid backwards

in her chair. 'I nearly forgot,' she said, standing up and pulling open the drawer of the filing cabinet. 'Your present!'

Helly had been the receptionist at the doctor's surgery since Ben had arrived. She'd applied for the job on a whim after not knowing what direction her life was going in and had been quite surprised to discover she loved being in charge of the office. Each day brought its own challenges, but with her brilliant organisational skills and kind nature, the job suited her just as much as she suited the job.

'Happy birthday to you! I'd break into song but maybe that's not the best with me being tone deaf and all that. Do you think there's any sort of medication that could help?'

'I'm really not sure there is but it's the thought that counts,' Ben said, taking the oblong present wrapped up in Christmas paper.

'Sorry about the paper.' She grinned. 'It's all I could find in the dark depths of the dresser at home.'

Ben raised an eyebrow. 'There's nothing wrong with a little bit of Christmas spirit in the middle of July.'

'And what do you get a doctor who has everything?' Helly gestured for him to open the present. 'It was a tricky one. I trawled the internet for hours.'

'Really?'

'Don't be daft, I saw an advert on the TV and thought… that's it …that's exactly what you get a doctor.'

Ben laughed as he began to tear open the Santa wrapping paper.

Ben Sanders had arrived in the village of Heartcross six

months ago. His adopted parents were Irish but had moved to Edinburgh due to his father's job when Ben was a baby. Ben had a burning ambition from an early age to become a doctor and through sheer hard work and determination, Ben had attended medical school at St Andrews and his dream had come true. Having always been a city guy, he loved the hustle and bustle of the bright lights, but he'd begun to enjoy the slower pace of life since arriving in Heartcross. His two-bedroom apartment was above the practice, so his commute to work was a flight of stairs. For his last job, his commute had been a hectic hour and a half, which had included the Tube, a bus and a ten-minute walk.

'An Ancestry DNA test…every man's dream present,' mused Ben, scrunching up the wrapping paper and tossing it in the wastepaper bin. He knew the smile had slipped from his face for a second as the tiny pang in his heart returned once more. Ben had actually considered taking a DNA test on numerous occasions, but he knew the results could change his life for ever. 'A very unusual present.'

'I just thought it was very doctorish,' replied Helly, not noticing the suddenly serious look on Ben's face. 'Not that that's even a word, but you never know what you might discover or who you're related to – could be royalty or even Harry Styles. Could you imagine?' Helly took the box from Ben and slapped it lightly against his chest. 'I think I need to do one of these. Interesting stuff.'

'I really couldn't imagine being related to Harry Styles.' Ben shook his head in jest.

'Free tickets for all of his gigs.' Helly gave him a knowing look. 'It'll definitely be worth taking the test just for that. It could open up a huge list of possibilities.'

'Or a huge can of worms.'

'Is this what it's like reaching the grand age of thirty-five? You just become cynical?' she teased. 'I've got all this to look forward to.'

'It's called being a realist.'

'You are no fun. I hope you're going to up your game for your birthday party tonight.'

Ben really wasn't one for making a fuss about his birthday, but his new friends Drew and Fergus were not going to let it pass without a beer in the local pub, which had escalated to a party with a buffet and now a local band had been added to the mix. But he knew he mustn't grumble. Since arriving in the village, everyone had made him feel so welcome. Just to know he could walk into the local pub after a hard day's work and have a chat with anyone that was propping up the bar was welcoming in and of itself. It had been a different story in the city where everyone seemed to avoid eye contact and conversation.

'Of course I'm going to up my game,' he said, making some weird movements with his arms and body.

'Woah! Just stop!' Helly ordered, shielding her eyes from the embarrassing chicken-like dad moves. 'Do not dance like that tonight. If you do, do not let on that you know me,' insisted Helly, with a chuckle.

'The youngsters of today have no taste. And thank you

for this,' he said, holding up the DNA test. As Ben walked back to his office, he glanced towards the blank name plate on the office door next to his.

'What do you think they are like?' asked Helly, picking up the pile of filing but following Ben's gaze.

'It's not long until we find out. They arrive in the morning. Here's hoping they're just as laid-back as us and fit in nicely.'

Six months ago, Dr Taylor had retired from being the village doctor and Ben had stepped into his shoes. It wasn't until Ben had been in the job three months that he realised that Dr Taylor must have been superhuman. He was a one-man medical machine who had done the job of two doctors. It just wasn't possible for Ben to carry on that way. He had contacted an agency, and now help was arriving to lighten the load.

'And at least we might get home at a decent hour. Leave the filing until morning.' Ben glanced at his watch. 'The birthday celebrations will be starting in just over an hour.'

Without question, Helly dropped the filing into her desk drawer and picked up her bag. 'I'm not going to argue with you, boss. Catch you later, alligator.' Within a blink of an eye, she was gone and the office door closed behind her.

An hour later, Ben had showered, changed and was on the way to the Grouse and Haggis pub. The sun was still high in the sky, providing a welcoming warmth with only a few clouds sporadically dotted about. As he stepped inside, he paused to take in the view. The pub was heaving. Happy birthday banners hung from the wooden beams that crossed the ceiling and at each end of the bar, a cluster of colourful balloons danced. There were curled streamers dangling from the light fittings and confetti scattered across the tables. The party was already in full flow.

'Here he is: the birthday boy!' Fergus bellowed above the chatter. Everyone turned and cheered.

'Just look at this!' Ben said with a grin, gesturing around the room.

Allie was working the bar alongside her parents Meredith and Fraser and waved in Ben's direction. 'Drink?'

'A cold beer. Thank you.' Ben turned towards Drew and Isla. 'I'm feeling so humble. All this trouble just for me?'

'Any excuse for a party,' teased Isla. 'How's your day been so far?'

Ben blew out a breath. 'Honestly, run off my feet. I'm looking forward to the new doctor arriving tomorrow, believe me.'

'That bad?' replied Isla. 'At least you can let your hair down now. Have a drink and grab something to eat.' She gestured towards the fabulous buffet that was laid out at the far end of the room on long trestle tables adorned with crisp white tablecloths.

'I am starving,' admitted Ben. He had missed lunch that day.

Walking towards the buffet table, Ben was surrounded by his new friends wishing him happy birthday and patting him on the back. After everyone had suitably piled their plates with mounds of food, Meredith took to the microphone.

'Welcome, welcome!' She left a little pause until everyone was looking in her direction.

'It's not your usual quiet Monday night in the pub, but tonight we have a birthday in the house. It's been six months since Dr Ben Sanders joined the village of Heartcross and a very welcome addition he is too. Please do join me in wishing Ben a happy birthday.'

Everyone held up their glasses and mirrored Meredith's words. Ben nodded and tried to make eye contact with as many of the well-wishers as he could.

'Please do enjoy your food,' continued Meredith, 'and let the celebrations begin. Without further ado, please put your hands together and welcome our band for the evening.'

Three men and a woman walked onto the makeshift stage at the front of the pub and picked up their instruments. 'I believe we have a birthday in the house,' the lead singer bellowed into the microphone.

Ben nodded his appreciation and gave a thumbs up. The drummer banged his sticks together and the band began to play. Within seconds, Isla dragged Drew in front of the band and began to dance. Other partygoers followed suit.

Ben felt a tap on his shoulder and turned to see Helly

behind him. She gave him a mischievous smile and gestured towards the bar. There were six shots lined up.

'Shots?' exclaimed Ben. 'It's a Monday night!'

'And? It's your birthday!' replied Helly, pushing him lightly towards the bar and taking his plate of food from him.

'We have work in the morning!'

'And…?'

'We have a new member of staff arriving. We can't be breathing alcohol fumes all over them.'

'Just give your teeth an extra brush.' Helly handed Ben the first shot glass. 'Tequila! Come on, don't be a party pooper. One…two…three.'

Ben threw back the shot and scrunched up his face. 'Yuk,' he said, not liking the taste, but before he could protest more, Helly crookedly balanced a party hat on his head and dragged him off to the dance floor. Within seconds, Ben was in the centre of a circle and dancing like no one was watching. The mood was jovial and everyone was enjoying the night. At first, he'd had reservations about working as a village doctor in a close-knit community, but as soon as he arrived, his social life had increased tenfold.

A couple of hours later, the lead singer announced there was only one song left, so everyone gathered on the dance floor in anticipation. He gestured for Ben to join him up on the stage and the band began to play 'Happy Birthday.' The whole pub erupted into song. Helly walked on stage with a cake made by Rona from the teashop. When everyone stopped singing, Ben blew out the candles. Whilst everyone was still clapping, he took hold of the microphone.

'This morning, I really wasn't a fan of Mondays, but my day has certainly got better! I have to admit this is one of the best birthdays I've had in a long, long time. Thank you to the band, Meredith and Fraser, Rona for this magnificent cake and to you all for coming out on a Monday night and welcoming me to Heartcross and for doing all of this for me. You are all just brilliant.'

'Three cheers for my boss!' bellowed Helly, holding up her drink.

The cheers rippled around the room and Ben put his hands in a prayer-like stance. He knew the grin on his face was wide. His gaze began to span the room, acknowledging all those standing in front of him, and just at that very moment, all the joy of the evening evaporated as his eyes fixed on someone standing straight in front of him in the middle of the dance floor.

Surely not. They just stared at each other. Ben was dying on the spot, opening and closing his mouth like a goldfish. She looked real. She was definitely real and Ben's birthday had just plummeted to an all-time low. There she was, the woman he loved to hate and the one woman he never expected to see again in this lifetime: Katie O'Neil, his nemesis from medical school. What the hell was she doing in his local pub in the middle of a village in the Scottish Highlands?

'Surprise!' She flashed him the biggest white smile as

she tottered towards him on the highest of heels, wearing a well-tailored suit. Her jet-black blouse matched the colour of her nails and her graduated blonde bob had been blow-dried to perfection.

This wasn't a birthday surprise he'd anticipated. Ben opened his mouth to speak but nothing came out.

'You're catching flies, Mr Average.'

Ben shook his head. Mr Average, a name she'd called him at medical school. Throughout their university days, they'd been in fierce competition, their rivalry in the classroom constantly at an all-time high. They'd been super competitive, pushing each other to the max, always trying to come out on top, which made them stand out from their peers. They were named the power couple, always top of the class, leaving the rest of the students behind.

Katie O'Neil had always been confident within herself; she knew exactly who she was, and with the perfect family life and her natural intelligence, she was someone Ben was a little envious of. Ben's story was different. He hadn't been confident in his own skin, feeling like he never really fitted into his family life. It wasn't as though his adopted parents weren't kind or encouraging, but he always felt there was something missing.

With the sweetest of smiles, Katie placed both her perfectly manicured hands on his elbows, kicked her leg up behind her and planted a kiss on both his cheeks. Ben was in shock, frozen to the spot. He wasn't quite sure if he'd passed out from the shots or was hallucinating.

'How long has it been? And your birthday too.' Katie stepped back. 'It's so good to see you. You seem to be lost for words.' Her eyes ran up and down the whole of his body. 'Toned abs, too. You have been working out.' She gave him an approving look.

Ben was speechless. His heart was pounding. He noticed Drew and Fergus watching him from the sidelines and as Ben cast a glance around the room, he locked eyes with Helly, who raised an inquisitive eyebrow. It was only then he became aware that the room had fallen silent. Everyone was aware of the tension in the room and all eyes were on them.

Once Ben realised this wasn't a dream and he was standing on the makeshift stage with Katie holding his gaze, he gave himself a little shake. 'What are you doing here?' he managed to say.

'I'm your knight in shining armour…so to speak.'

Puzzled, Ben shook his head. 'What do you mean?'

'Partner in crime…Peony Practice…the new doctor. Me and you are going to be seeing a lot more of each other. In fact, every day. Just like old times!'

Ben's mouth fell wide open again. Feeling like he'd just been hit by a high-speed train, the only word that he could muster up was 'shit'…and he was really hoping that he hadn't said that out loud.

'Happy birthday!' trilled Katie.

It was official. Ben really didn't like Mondays or birthdays.

Chapter Two

Ben's sleep was unceremoniously interrupted when he heard a car horn sound outside his bedroom window. Stretching out his arm, Ben fumbled for the glass of water that sat on his bedside table before swilling back a couple of headache tablets. It was as if a group of Irish dancers had taken up residency in his head. He prayed the throbbing would soon ease. He blew out a breath and prised open his eyes, the vivid red numbers on the digital display of the clock resonating in his brain slowly. He'd overslept and was now late for work.

Bolting upright in bed, the movement was way too quick and, immediately, Ben allowed his body to sink back down, every effort causing his head to throb even more. He had the hangover from hell. How had he even allowed himself to get into this state on a Tuesday morning? Then everything came flooding back... Katie O'Neil.

He was beginning to dislike Tuesdays too.

Last night, Katie had disappeared after dropping the bombshell that she was the new member of staff that would be working alongside him at Peony Practice, leaving Ben propping up the bar with Drew explaining how they brought the worst out in each other. He remembered Drew laughing, claiming the picture that Ben was painting couldn't be that bad, and if it was, all he had to do was be the bigger person.

'A bit of healthy competition never hurt anyone,' Drew had added.

'You should have seen the smug look on her face every time we got an assignment back. Her marks were usually top of the class, with me coming in a very close second. Then she always made the same comment about me being Mr Average,' said Ben as Drew handed him another drink.

'Was that before or after you slept with her?' joked Drew.

Ben remained silent.

'Oh my God.' Drew's eyes were wide. 'You did sleep with her! You love to hate each other.'

'That was a mistake. A huge mistake. Once. A mistake that will never be repeated.'

'I just knew it!'

'And, for the record, that is the not the reason she calls me Mr Average. Stop staring at me like that.'

Drew was grinning. 'But you slept with her. Which means there was something between you once.'

'Believe me, there is nothing between us; that woman can be so annoying,' Ben said to Drew, draining the dregs of his drink from his glass.

'What you need to do is clear out all that negative energy and think of her as a blessing in your life,' encouraged Drew.

Ben raised an eyebrow. 'A blessing?'

'If she was always top of the class, she's going to be a good doctor, which means your workload will become easier.' Drew slapped Ben playfully on the back. 'And you know what? Kill her with kindness! She will be like putty in your hands.'

That night, six years ago, was firmly implanted in the back of Ben's mind. There had been a heavy downpour in the early hours of that Saturday morning. It had been the last night of the term and Ben had been standing on the edge of the pavement trying to hail a taxi after a party. When one finally arrived, Ben was just about to open the cab door when Katie appeared from nowhere and slid herself into the seat.

'I was here first,' she'd said.

'No, I was. Everything doesn't need to be a competition, you know.' Ben was never going to leave her out in the cold, waiting on the pavement in the rain for another cab. After all, their flats were right next door to each other.

For the whole journey they'd sat in silence. Ben had glanced in her direction on numerous occasions only to find her smirking at him. He couldn't deny that night she'd turned heads, dressed to impress; every single man in the room was hoping she'd look in their direction. Once they'd stepped out of the cab, their bodies had been drenched with rain within seconds, and it was at that point they both ran towards their front doors dodging the puddles. It was only then that Ben had realised he'd locked himself out.

'Damn. I'm locked out.'

Katie hovered in her doorway. 'Well, you only have one choice. You'll have to stay here.'

Ben was momentarily thrown by her suggestion. He looked up the road, but the cab had disappeared, and he knew his flat-mate Eddison wouldn't be back until the morning.

For a second, he toyed with the idea of finding a hotel, but with the weather as it was, he really didn't want to be venturing out again. With lightning striking and a boom of thunder rolling out across the dark sky, he made his way back down the path towards Katie's flat. The girl he loved to hate was standing in the wide-open doorway with a smile on her face. 'Even I couldn't leave you out in the rain.'

Ben's entire body was drenched with his curls completely flattened and the rain dripping off the end of his nose. He swiped the water from his bare arms and looked up at Katie, who was soaked through too.

'Look at the state of me,' uttered Ben as Katie took a

cautious step back and her eyes swept over his entire body. Then their eyes locked.

'I'm looking,' she replied, biting down on her lip with a glint in her eye.

Ben looked down at his shirt, every inch of wet cotton clinging to every muscle of his chest.

Then his gaze swept down to her blouse, her wet top clinging to her breasts. They just stared at each other in silence. Her body was so damn perfect. Everything about her was so damn perfect. His heart started to thump a little faster, and for a moment, he forgot she was Katie O'Neil, the girl who drove him insane.

'That's not a bad sight for a late Friday night, early Saturday morning,' she teased. 'I think you need to take off that shirt before you catch pneumonia, and I couldn't have you dying of hypothermia on my watch.'

'For a second there, it sounded like you cared,' replied Ben, her suggestion taking him completely by surprise.

'Don't kid yourself,' she replied with a flirtatious smile. Without warning, Katie had crossed her own arms and pulled her top over her head. 'Come on, don't be shy. Take off your wet clothes.' She jokingly began to pull at his shirt. The girl he loved to hate was now standing in the hallway semi-naked, and all of a sudden, there was a surge of electricity between them. Before Ben knew it, they were kissing passionately, their hands all over each other. One thing led to another, and the next day Ben found himself waking up in her flat by himself and she was gone. The next

CHRISTIE BARLOW

time he saw her, she froze him out and there was no mention of the night they'd spent together, leaving Ben totally bamboozled by the whole encounter.

And now it was the morning after and Ben's head was throbbing just like it had done that morning six years ago. He sighed. Ben knew working with Katie O'Neil was going to be the biggest challenge of his career so far, and it wasn't one he'd ever anticipated. Going to work had actually been a joy until now.

Finally lifting himself out of bed, Ben gingerly made his way over to the window and parted the curtains to view the rest of the world, which looked in a better state than he felt. Throwing the window wide open, he welcomed the breeze. He knew he needed to message Helly, even though she would have already ascertained that he was running late and know the reason why – he had the hangover from hell.

After switching on the shower and waiting until the water ran warm, he checked his phone. Big mistake. Ten missed calls and umpteen texts from Helly, telling him to wake up and get his backside into gear. The surgery was full. Patients were sitting in the waiting room tolerantly waiting for his arrival. Stepping under the warm spray of the shower, Ben let the water cascade down his body, and attempted to pull himself together as best he could. Within ten minutes, he was dressed, and as he hurried down the stairwell towards the office, he threw his tie around his neck.

Walking into the surgery, he forced a smile, and the first thing he noticed was the distinctive aroma of a perfume he knew so well from the past – Katie O'Neil was in the office. Annoyingly, Helly looked as fresh as a daisy sitting behind the desk with a huge smile on her face.

'Good morning,' sang Helly, pushing a pile of files over the desk towards him.

'Good morning,' replied Ben. *How is it that this morning, of all mornings, everyone decides they need to see a doctor?* he thought, looking around the waiting room at a sea of faces looking back at him.

'You've no time to waste,' urged Helly. 'Too many patients to see.'

Ben nodded; how he was going to get through the morning feeling like this, he had no clue. With his briefcase in one hand and the files in the other, he took a deep breath and walked towards his office door.

'You're in room two today,' shouted Helly, tapping away on the keyboard.

Ben stopped in his tracks and turned back towards her. 'What do you mean, I'm in room two? Room one is my office. It's *always* been my office.'

Helly looked at Ben. 'I didn't think you'd mind, and after all, we want Katie to settle in quickly…don't we?'

'Of course we do,' he replied, knowing he sounded abrupt, but his hangover really wasn't helping.

With a glance towards his office door, he saw the name Dr Katie O'Neil in bold lettering on the door plaque. His name had been moved to the door of room two. Of course he felt agitated – that was his room – but the waiting room was full of patients and they were his first priority. At that very second, his office door swung open and a patient left. Katie appeared in the doorway. She walked straight up to Ben and straightened up his tie.

'Good morning! You look kind of green. Can I get you anything?' asked Katie with concern.

Ben was thrown by her kindness; he was expecting some sort of sarcastic comment about finally turning up to work. 'No thank you,' he replied.

'I hope you don't mind. Helly suggested I make myself comfortable in room one, and she's already set me up on the computer system. I'll start working my way through the appointments, if that's okay by you?'

Ben found himself nodding at Katie, but glancing in Helly's direction, who was smiling back at him.

'You don't mind, do you?' asked Helly. 'I just thought it would be nice if Katie had the lovely view on her first morning and room one is a little more spacious.'

'Of course, what a lovely idea,' he replied, still a little miffed. 'Whatever makes it easier for you to settle into Peony Practice. Welcome! We are one happy family, aren't we?' He glimpsed over his shoulder at Helly, who was looking at him with amusement.

'One happy family,' Helly repeated, cocking an eyebrow, wondering why Ben's voice had just risen an octave.

'One happy family. I like that. I think I'm going to like working here.' Katie gave Ben a warm smile before calling in the next patient. She disappeared back into his old office.

Opening the door to room two, Ben felt confused. Katie was acting relatively normal; this wasn't her usual sarcasm or put downs like he remembered. She'd smiled at him, offered to help him, and whilst he initially thought she'd marched in and taken over his room, that wasn't quite the case. However, Ben knew leopards didn't change their spots. Maybe Katie was just lulling him into a false sense of security.

With his head still pounding, the door swung shut behind him and he stumbled on the cardboard box that had been left in the middle of the floor. It was full of his own stuff from the other office.

'Ha, I knew it,' he murmured under his breath. Katie might be playing nice on the outside, but if the past was anything to go by, on the inside, she was still trying to get one over on him.

Hurling the cardboard box on top of the desk, he took out his mug, his pen and a notepad. How the hell had she only been back in his life less than twenty-four hours and already he felt like he was playing second fiddle? Still, there was nothing he could do about it now. Sitting down on the old battered chair behind the desk, Ben switched on the computer, but it immediately clicked and made some sort of whirling sound. It was slow to boot up this morning, just like Ben was. He exhaled and raked his hand through his hair. Could his day actually get any worse?

His office door swung open. Katie was standing in the doorway. 'Are there any patients today that you wish to see, maybe follow-up appointments?' she asked.

'No, just go for it,' Ben replied.

'Honestly, if you don't feel up to it, I can—'

'Of course I'm up to it,' he replied curtly.

'Okay, I was just saying. If you need anything, I'm right—'

'Next door,' interrupted Ben, as if he could forget.

Katie smiled as she left the room.

Ben knew he was acting like a bear with a sore head, but that's because he did have a sore head. He'd hardly had time to get his thoughts around Katie working in the same practice and having a hangover really was not helping his mood.

As soon as the door shut behind her, Ben couldn't help himself. 'Urghh! How the hell has this happened?'

Almost immediately, the office door swung open again, Helly waving at him frantically. She hurried towards the desk and budged his elbow out of the way. By mistake, Ben had pressed down on the intercom button that called the patients to the office. The whole of the waiting room had heard his frustration.

Ben pressed the intercom again. 'Sorry, sorry, just testing the intercom was working.'

Helly looked at him. 'You are going to get yourself into trouble. You should be smiling. The calvary has arrived and your workload is about to lessen.'

'This morning, I really don't feel like smiling.'

Helly looked amused. 'Wait there.' Within two minutes, she returned holding a mug of steaming coffee and a packet of headache tablets. 'Get these down you and please put a smile on your face. Goodness knows what Katie must think on her first day of work. I've never actually seen you moody. You look worse than some of the patients sitting out there.'

'I'll do my best, and thanks for the coffee,' replied Ben, beginning to look through the files.

'Ben, call it a gut feeling but I'm getting the impression that you don't like Katie much. I can sense a little tension.'

'Past history, in one form or another. We met at medical school. St Andrews.'

Helly's eyes widened. 'Really? Interesting. History as in university or history as in *history*?' The intrigued look on her face didn't go unnoticed.

There was a lot Ben wanted to say about the past, but that would be unprofessional of him and Helly now worked for them both. They had both stood out at university, and sometimes not for the right reasons. Ben had an uneasy feeling in the pit of his stomach about Katie's arrival, but there wasn't a lot he could do about it right at this moment.

'No comment,' he replied, shaking his head lightly and taking the coffee from Helly's hand.

'No comment always means there's something to hide.' She gave him a cheeky grin. 'Oh, and here's your post.'

As soon as Helly left the office, Ben took a huge swig of coffee and somehow managed to miss his mouth and spill it down the front of his crisp white shirt. 'Christ on a bike.'

Damn, it just wasn't his day. The only thing that was going to get him through the next few hours was the thought of snuggling back under his duvet and falling fast asleep at the first opportunity. 'Here goes,' he said to himself, picking up the first file of the morning and pressing the intercom to call the patient's name.

Surprisingly, the morning passed quickly and, three hours later, the long queue of patients that had seemed never-ending had finally dwindled. Ben felt like he'd dealt with what seemed like every ailment possible. Taking a breather, he stood up and looked out of the window. The view from this office was not as stunning as the other. This office looked down on the yard of bins. He exhaled. Deep down, he knew he was struggling with a number of issues in his life, but he did what most people did: brushed them under the carpet. Katie had resurrected some of those unwanted feelings he'd tried to bury.

He picked up his empty mug and walked into the reception area, where Katie was perched on the edge of the desk chatting away to Helly. She threw back her head and laughed. Slowly, she tucked her hair behind her ear. Katie was striking: her skin smooth with a hint of a tan and minimalistic make-up, her huge blue eyes framed by long black lashes and a light blush across her cheeks. As they spotted him, Ben looked around the reception. There were pictures on the walls, certificates sporting Katie's name, and a new noticeboard with the names of the doctors at the practice. Of course, Ben's name had now been moved down to second place. She'd only been here a morning and already Ben felt like she was completely taking over the practice.

'What do you think? Everywhere seemed a little cold and clinical before.' Katie gestured towards the pictures. 'They give a warm, welcoming feeling, don't you think? Oh, and the plants in the waiting room too.' Katie swept her arm outwards, highlighting the new jungle that had sprouted in every corner. 'They've brightened the place up. It just needed a little warmth and an inviting area—'

'I'm not sure we should be inviting people to be ill,' interrupted Ben.

Katie laughed. 'You always had a good sense of humour. I can't believe you've not attempted to spruce up this place a little, give it some character,' she trilled, ignoring his lack of enthusiasm.

'If plants and pictures make you happy, who am I to stand in your way? And your new office, is it to your liking?'

'It's lovely,' she replied.

'Good, because we want you to feel welcome, don't we?' Ben looked towards Helly, who nodded.

'Of course, just one big happy family,' Helly replied.

'Exactly that. Who's putting the kettle on? After such a busy morning, I could do with another coffee.'

Helly and Katie slid their mugs across the table towards him.

'That'll be me then,' he said. Ben picked up both mugs and walked into the kitchen. Ben was feeling a little tetchy, even more so when he placed the mugs down on the worktop and read the words in bold black capital letters plastered across Katie's mug: THE BOSS.

Taking a deep breath, he switched on the kettle and opened the drawer to reach inside for a teaspoon, only to discover that the drawer was now empty. Where the hell had the teaspoons gone? Who'd stolen all the cutlery and why would anyone want to do that? He checked the sink, but that was completely empty, so he opened up the next drawer. Last night, that drawer had been full of useless random stuff that had no set place in the office and now there were numerous tea towels that looked so neatly folded that Ben suspected they had been ironed. Who in God's name irons tea towels? He muttered under his breath, already thinking he knew the answer to that question.

Finally, after relocating the cutlery drawer and making three drinks, he reached for the tray that was usually behind the old rusty tea canister which had now been replaced with a brand-new set of floral canisters for the tea, coffee and sugar. The sugar bag and coffee jar had been disposed of. Ben was bewildered. What time had Katie actually arrived at work this morning? Nothing was in its normal place.

Feeling riled by Katie's immediate reorganisation, he straightaway emptied the tea towels from the drawer and put the cutlery back in its original place. Then he swung open the bin lid and lifted out the empty sugar packet and coffee jar.

'What are you doing?' asked Helly, standing in the doorway. 'Rummaging in bins?'

Ben spun round; he knew he was acting irrationally, but he just couldn't stop himself. He held the items up then gestured towards the new floral canisters. 'Everything has changed.' He pulled out the cutlery drawer. 'Nothing was in its normal place, so I've put it back exactly where it should be.'

Helly was watching him with amusement.

'And where is the tray that has lived in the same place for the last six months?' asked Ben, his eyes flitting around the kitchen.

Helly walked over towards the microwave and held up the tray that was resting on top of it.

'It doesn't live there, it lives here. It's always lived here.' He took the tray and slid it back in place behind the canisters. 'It lives there,' he repeated. 'And look at this, she's taking over. There's floral stuff everywhere and who irons tea towels?' Ben knew he was over-reacting. Even though Katie wasn't in the room, she was still managing to push his buttons. Ben took one of the ironed folded-up tea towels and shook it open like he was a magician, then scrunched it up in both hands.

'Child,' said Helly, rolling her eyes. 'It's just a tea towel.' She bit her lip to stifle her laughter. 'This has nothing to do with Katie. I changed all this and brought in the new canisters. They brighten up the room and I washed the tea towels. What has got into you?'

Feeling a fool, Ben pointed at the door but couldn't express himself any further and blew out a breath.

'I know something is winding you up, but let it go. Past is past. Katie seems lovely.'

'Competitive, arrogant, confident…' Ben's voice rose slightly, then realised he was out of order expressing his personal opinion in front of Helly, especially when she was waving her arms, encouraging Ben to keep his voice down.

'I know I'm out of order and I'm sorry, but you didn't have to endure years of that woman at medical school. Always had to be top of her game and every time I joined a club, so did she.'

'Maybe she just wanted to join the same clubs? There's nothing wrong with that.'

'You just don't understand.' But Ben knew he couldn't say any more. In the past, he'd felt like he was playing some weird game of Top Trumps with Katie pushing him so hard yet still coming out on top.

'People do change,' suggested Helly.

The look on Ben's face said it all.

'Crikey! She really does get under your skin, doesn't

she? Or you actually find her attractive.' Helly cocked an eyebrow.

'Behave! I'm not even dignifying that with a response.'

'You don't have to. I can see it in your eyes. But how about this for a theory – maybe she likes you too.'

Ben rolled his eyes. He wasn't going to admit that the first time Katie O'Neil had walked into a room, she'd taken his breath away. She'd caught him off-guard and wasn't like any other girl he'd ever met. She immediately stood out from the crowd. Katie had confidently walked into that lecture room and had taken a seat next to him, her honeysuckle perfume distracting him from the lecture as his thoughts shifted to the two of them winding through the English countryside, holding hands and warmed by the sunshine. To this day, he could remember what she had been wearing: a pale-blue headband in her smooth blonde hair that bounced just below her shoulders, a white blouse tucked into her jeans and blue ballet-type shoes. She had been the vision of gorgeousness and had left Ben mesmerised.

Ben had initially gone out of his way to impress her and had feigned a level of competence he didn't have, but which he thought she wanted. This amused Katie to no end and backfired completely, as this made them super competitive with each other. Usually, it was Ben that came out second best, and at times became a less authentic version of himself just to prove a point.

But that was the past and Ben knew he was now wiser

and more experienced. He was not going to feel intimidated by her. His goal used to be to rise to her challenge, continually putting himself under pressure to impress her, but that was all going to stop. Ben knew he didn't want to feel those pressures again. He was just going to be himself. He thought he'd once wanted Katie O'Neil's validation, but now he just wanted to contribute to his community and Katie could take him as she found him. Ben was feeling settled in Heartcross with a good job, a place to live and friends. He was in a different place now, and he decided there and then just to see how working in the same office with Katie panned out. What was the worst that could happen?

'Can we all just try to get along?' suggested Helly.

Ben nodded, knowing that Helly was right and it was the only professional option.

'I'm hoping that nod means that everything is going to run along smoothly. Oh, and I came in to get you as Stuart Scott has just popped into the surgery. Nothing medical, he said, but would like a word with you, if that's okay?'

Stuart Scott was the village's retired vet, his empire taken over by his son Rory who'd opened a new state-of-the-art veterinary practice and animal hospital on the Clover Cottage estate.

'Something about a fund-raiser,' continued Helly, placing the mugs of coffee on the tray.

Ben pointed at Katie's mug. 'And look at that mug: T-H-E B-O-S-S.' Ben strung the word out.

'It's just a mug,' replied Helly, putting her hands on his shoulders and spinning him around, gently pushing him towards the door. 'I'll bring the drinks through.'

Ben walked out into the reception to see Katie and Stuart sat down next to each other in the waiting room. Katie was looking enthusiastic, chatting away to Stuart as they looked over the notebook in Stuart's hand. Stuart's smile broadened. 'I think it's the perfect idea.'

'What's the perfect idea?' chipped in Ben, walking towards them. Katie retrieved her mug from Helly's tray and held it up towards Ben, discreetly pointing at the wording.

Ben smiled at her, then turned towards Stuart. 'Hi, Stuart, how are you and Alana? Helly said you've popped in to see me.'

Stuart stood up and shook Ben's hand. 'We are all good. Some days are good, other days are difficult,' admitted Stuart. 'In fact, more days are difficult. And that's why I'm here...and this wonderful doctor, Katie, has just come up with the best idea.'

Katie had a huge beaming smile on her face. 'Stuart's just been telling me all about Alana's dementia and about his plans for raising awareness for National Dementia Day in a few weeks' time. And you wouldn't believe it, but I'm actually an ambassador for that charity!'

Ben could fully believe she was an ambassador. During their university days, Katie had her fingers in every pie. She was captain of the quiz team and involved in everything from chess to netball to water sports, and of course she aced everything. She was constantly giving speeches or in the pages of the local newspaper. Back then, it was rare that Katie was out of the headlines.

'Good for you,' replied Ben. 'With your knowledge of the charity and the best ways to promote awareness, it looks like Stuart has come to the right place. And what is your idea?'

'You are going to love this…and it was the first thing that popped into my head.'

'And I think it's a brilliant idea,' added Stuart.

Ben noticed that Katie had bitten down on her lip to supress her smile. Whatever she was about to suggest, he knew she was waiting for his reaction. He braced himself.

'A boat race down the River Heart. Thirteen kilometres of two teams battling it out. The whole community can get involved with fund-raising and we can raise awareness. We make a day of it – a community day! We can contact the local TV news and have a social media presence too. You know how much you love a boat race. Remember, Ben?'

'Thirteen kilometres,' cut in Helly. 'Why thirteen?'

'Because it's going to be unlucky for some, isn't that right?' Katie was looking right at him. 'There's only one team that can win. A little competition never hurt anyone, did it?'

Ben remembered all right. How the hell could he ever forget the humiliation?

'It'll be just like the university days.' She gave Ben a

32

wink. 'You know how those lovely toned abs of yours look good in a wetsuit.' Katie raised her eyes suggestively, leaving Ben to roll his.

The university boat race had taken place along the River Eden and Ben thought he'd been stitched up something rotten. Of course, he had come last. The paddle had fallen off his oar and a hole in the rowing boat had caused the boat to slowly start to sink, which meant by the time Ben had reached the mid-way point, he was going nowhere fast. But he passed the finish line by sheer determination and swam most of the way to discover Katie and her pals had finished the race more than an hour before.

'Such a brilliant idea,' he replied, knowing that the previous boat race had been posted all over social media. He also knew the amount of training that Katie had put in to win that race and if this was a rematch, her competitive edge would be out in full force. But all he could do was remain optimistic about the boat race for Stuart's sake and pray that history didn't repeat itself.

'As long as all is fair in love and war,' he said, holding Katie's gaze.

'There's nothing like a bit of friendly competition,' said Katie, grinning. 'A rematch it is!'

'Please,' interrupted Helly, 'play nicely!'

'Of course,' replied Katie. 'I'm just thinking…'

'What are you thinking?' asked Stuart.

'How about I'll be captain of one team and Ben is the captain of the other. Let's call a meeting and get the whole

community involved. The pub would be a good place. I can picture it now: local stalls selling produce, maybe music, tourists can flag wave from the banks of the River Heart, and we can raise funds and awareness for dementia. This could be fun. What do you think, Ben, are you up for it?'

Ben thought about it for a second and had to agree getting the whole community involved was a good idea. He thrust his hand forward. 'Challenge accepted.'

Katie gave him a warm smile. 'Thank you for agreeing. It will be brilliant to raise money and awareness for the charity.'

Ben was not only taken by surprise by the sincerity in her voice but was momentarily thrown by the strength of her gaze. Did Katie just thank him? Usually, Katie would be full of herself and making sure Ben knew that she was going all out to win, but there seemed to be a sense of calmness about her. As her hand brushed against his, Ben felt himself tingle with a tiny flutter in his heart. What the hell had just happened here? Giving himself a little shake, he released her hand.

Helly was standing beside them. 'I think it's best if I appoint myself as referee,' she declared, 'I think that is the safe option and, if I'm truly honest, I'm not that fond of water. What's the plan of action now? A meeting in the pub to pick the teams?'

'Exactly that,' replied Ben. 'Don't worry, Stuart, I'll arrange the meeting, the teams and publicity. We need sponsor forms too.' Ben was getting into his stride.

'We'll sort everything together,' corrected Katie, linking her arm through his. 'It'll be a good way for me to meet and get to know the villagers.'

'Thank you, thank you,' replied Stuart, looking pleased with the suggestion. 'This is going to be brilliant.'

The three of them watched Stuart leave. As soon as the door shut behind him, Katie turned to Ben and slapped him on the chest. 'You better put in the training. There's not a cat in hell's chance I'm letting you win.' She gave him a lopsided smile.

There she was, the old Katie he loved to hate. He knew she couldn't hide the competitive streak for long.

But then she added, 'Honestly, I'm joking. It will be a good way to bring everyone together to support Stuart.'

Ben knew he was staring. There seemed to be a softer side to Katie, a more sensitive side to her than before. The confident, arrogant and competitive woman he once knew was standing there, still with passion in her heart, but dimmed somewhat.

'Why are you looking at me like that?' she asked, narrowing her eyes.

'No reason,' he replied. 'The win here is raising funds for a good cause and community spirit. It's not about crossing that line first.'

'Exactly that, but still with a little competitive spirit.' She winked, pinching her thumb and forefinger together.

Despite Katie playing it down, Ben had every intention of putting in the training. Twelve months ago, his fitness routine had been rigid. Every morning he'd be up and at it with at least a 5k run through the park before work, followed by weights and a swim. Tonight, first thing after work, he was heading down to the old boathouse and upping his stamina whilst perfecting his rowing technique. It couldn't hurt to put in some training.

He finished his coffee and Katie's phone sprang into action. She moved herself into the doorway of her office and Ben watched as she talked animatedly on her mobile.

'So come on.' Helly nudged his elbow. 'What happened last time you two hit the water together? I'm sensing it wasn't all plain sailing.'

'I'm saying nothing,' replied Ben, still watching Katie.

Within seconds, Katie was back in the room with a smile on her face. 'I'm so sorry, I need to nip out. That was the estate agent. They've just lined up a property for me to view.'

It hadn't even crossed Ben's mind where Katie was living, but she soon filled in the blanks. 'I checked into Julia's B&B long term until I found somewhere, but I really need my own space. Do you mind?' she asked, thrusting the boss mug into Ben's hands.

'Not at all,' he replied. 'See you back here at 2pm for afternoon visits followed by evening surgery.'

Katie waved above her head as she disappeared through the surgery door. Ben took a deep breath in. Yesterday, life had been chugging along nicely, but now it looked like Katie was here to stay – for a while at least. He looked over at Helly, who was sitting on the reception desk, swinging her legs back and forth. She was staring intently at her phone. With a mischievous glint in her eye, she glanced at Ben and threw her head back, laughing wholeheartedly.

'Oh my!' She turned her phone towards Ben. The crimson blush rose up Ben's cheeks as he watched the YouTube video that had come back to haunt him.

There he was, clambering out of the River Eden, gasping for breath an hour after everyone had finished the race. He rolled his eyes and shook his head. 'I believe my boat was somehow sabotaged.'

'Really?' asked Helly. 'And why would someone do that?'

'You don't understand how competitive Katie was at university.'

'But to sabotage someone's boat seems a little far-fetched, surely?'

Ben shrugged. 'I'm not actually sure,' he admitted, even though it felt like that at the time.

'And over one hundred thousand views,' observed Helly, playing the video again. 'You are YouTube famous!'

But Ben didn't answer. He was already back in his office with the door shut firmly behind him, thinking about the last boat race. Katie seemed a lot more laid-back now, but he wasn't sure it was a good sign.

Chapter Three

The evening surgery had been just as busy as the morning, but thankfully, by the late afternoon Ben had started to feel human again and his hangover had finally begun to wear off. He went home, pulled the shirt from his back and changed into his loungewear. Thankfully there was nothing on the agenda except to take it easy and hopefully get a good night's sleep.

Pouring himself a glass of wine, Ben walked out onto his tiny balcony. There was a small bistro table, a couple of chairs and a handful of potted plants. It wasn't the largest of outside spaces, but he loved sitting out there and although his flat was modest, the view from the balcony made it the best end to a hectic day at work. It was simply breath-taking and Ben couldn't wait to see how it changed through the seasons. Heartcross Castle was towering in the distance, the

River Heart tumbling over the rocks, and the town of Glensheil standing on the other side of the bridge.

Sitting on the chair and his feet resting on the balcony rail, he balanced his laptop on his knees. On the table was a pile of post he'd not yet opened. Ben had begun to research the dementia charity for which the boat race would be raising funds. As soon as he clicked on the website, Katie's face appeared on the page as an ambassador for the charity. According to the bio, her fund-raising for the charity had generated tens of thousands of pounds. 'Good for her,' said Ben out loud, knowing that was no mean feat. He was actually impressed. Katie had thrown herself into treks, skydives, bungee jumps, diving with sharks – the list was endless and now another boat race was going to be added.

Next Ben googled The Old Boat House. He'd only wandered down to the river a couple of times to take the water taxi across to The Lake House and had vowed to undertake some water sports in his spare time, but being the only doctor in the practice, that spare time had been practically been non-existent. There was a booking system online, so Ben booked himself a rowing boat after tomorrow's evening surgery. Then he rifled through his post – there was the usual mail that went straight into the recycling bin, but right at the bottom of the pile, there was a square cream envelope with gold type. He slipped his finger underneath the lip and opened it. Inside was an invitation to a medical school reunion. It had been six years since everyone had parted company. Here was an invite to bring them all back together for one night only, back where it had all started in the town of St. Andrews. The reunion was to take place in a hotel close to the university. He thought about Katie. No doubt she'd received an invite too and he wondered if she would be going.

The following morning, Ben was feeling as fresh as a daisy and up with the larks. Getting ready for work, he checked his watch and buttoned up his shirt. Then he heard a loud thud, taking him by surprise. He stopped in his tracks. He walked from his bedroom into the living room, but all was quiet. Puzzled, he slid his tie around his neck as he wandered into the bathroom, where he squirted himself with cologne. Then, walking into the hall, he picked up his briefcase which was waiting by the front door. He knew he was early for work but after arriving late yesterday, he wanted to be on the ball today. He had plenty of time to look over the patient's bookings for the morning and make sure he was up to speed with their medical history. This was something Ben liked about living in a close-knit community – he could take a real interest in people's lives and get to know the patients. In the city, it was rare he ever saw the same person twice in six months. If he passed them in the street, he'd have no clue who they were. Back then, he'd missed the personal touch.

With the apartment keys in one hand and his briefcase in the other, Ben stepped out onto the small landing outside his flat and paused beside his front door. That was indeed strange. He immediately recognised a perfume that he knew belonged to Katie. Had she been standing outside his apartment? His eyebrows pulled tightly together as he looked over the stairwell. There was no mistaking that scent. Had she been up to his flat? Why? He took in the silence all around him.

Then Ben thought he heard the TV coming from the flat next door, which was slightly worrying as it had been empty since he'd moved in six months ago. He put his ear to the door and listened. There was definitely someone inside. Surely, he would know if he was to have new neighbours. Nothing got past the village telegraph and someone would have said something, but it appeared that wasn't the case. Still, it was too early to knock on the door and introduce himself. Maybe it was better to wait until after work.

Ben had been looking forward to having someone live next door – maybe another young professional like himself with whom he could socialise and have a late-night beer. He was just about to walk away when he heard the bolt slide across the door and a key twist in the lock. Then the front door swung open and there stood Katie. She stepped onto the landing. Her eyes sparkled and her smile grew. Ben was fully aware his mouth had fallen open.

'You are catching flies, Mr Average.'

Ben pulled himself together. 'Please tell me you aren't squatting.'

'Don't be ridiculous. In this suit?'

'Then why are you coming out of the flat next door to

42

me?' Ben's question slowed towards the end as the penny dropped. 'You are my new neighbour...'

'Exactly that!' Katie replied, her voice rising an octave. 'Can you believe it? We are going to have so much fun living next door to each other. What is it neighbours do? Pop around for a cup of sugar?'

'Thankfully, the office always has sugar.' His sarcasm wasn't lost on Katie.

She linked her arm through his. 'Shall we walk to work together?' She put her manicured hand on the arm of his shirt and gave it a slight squeeze. The way she stared at him was hypnotic. Leaning in closely to his ear, she said, 'Just don't you go forgetting your keys. You know what happened last time.'

Ben felt a sudden burst of jitters and his thoughts switched back to that night when their hands had been all over each other, ripping at each other's clothes off in the hall of Katie's flat. Ben had never felt passion like that night and hadn't felt it since. But Katie had never mentioned it again, so Ben had tried his hardest to push their time together out of his mind. Although he had to admit, from time to time, she'd crept back in there.

They walked in silence down the one flight of stairs, but the door to the practice was already open. Ben had been the last one to leave the office the night before and he always triple-checked the door. He stepped forward and pushed the door open to find Helly already sitting at her desk.

'Good morning,' she chirped. 'What took you so long? Some of us started work at least half an hour ago.'

Ben raised an eyebrow. 'If we keep coming to work this early, there may be a possibility we will never go home.'

'And how is home? And the new neighbour?'

Ben's eyes widened. If Helly knew that Katie had moved in next door, why hadn't she warned him?

'I know where your loyalties lie,' he murmured to Helly as he walked past her. He was heading to his old office when Katie coughed and pointed to the other one.

Ben quickly changed direction and shut the office door behind him.

Ten minutes later, there was a knock and as he looked up, he saw a white tissue being waved around the door, followed by Helly's head. 'You okay, boss?'

'More than okay, but I am still wondering why you wouldn't give me the heads-up. She's moved in next door and you said nothing.'

Helly looked a little sheepish. 'I didn't know what to do and you two living next door to each other could be a good thing.'

Ben raised an eyebrow. 'How do you make that out?'

'I'm not quite certain, but surely there will be some advantages. Anyway, I'm going to do a breakfast run up to Bonnie's teashop. Bacon or sausage sandwich?'

Before Ben could answer, Katie appeared in the doorway juggling numerous oblong boxes. 'DNA test kits. I found them stuffed in the back of the filing cabinet,' shared Katie, dropping the boxes onto Ben's desk.

'They look exactly the same as the one you bought me for my birthday.' Ben picked up a box. Helly was now looking a little shifty. 'Where have these come from? Helly?'

'Mmm, busted!' she joked. 'I didn't exactly buy yours. We kind of got these for free.'

Ben shook his head in jest. 'You are unbelievable! No expense spared on my birthday present. You gave me part of a job lot after convincing me you'd put so much thought into my present.'

'Oh I did. I saw these and thought "bingo! That'll do!"'

Katie suddenly looked pensive as she turned over the box in her hand. 'These things can open up a right can of worms. I've watched lots of programmes on TV about this sort of stuff. It can actually be quite interesting.'

'It's cutting-edge stuff,' replied Ben. 'The world's largest online family history resource to predict your genetic ethnicity and help you find new family connections.'

Ben knew exactly how cutting-edge stuff this was. He'd struggled with his own family history all his life and had come close to taking a test on many occasions, but he was scared about what he would actually uncover. Even though Ben had loving adopted parents, there was always a niggle in the back of his mind which intensified around his birthday and Christmas time. Why had his biological parents given him up for adoption? Why hadn't they wanted him? He'd often lay awake at night torturing himself with every possible scenario. When he asked his adoptive parents, they weren't forthcoming with any answers, which only made the situation worse for him.

Now that his parents had passed, Ben had once more been battling with the decision to uncover his past. He wanted to know about his real family. Who were they? Where were they? But he didn't know if he could cope with the pain of being rejected a second time.

'I think it's really fascinating,' added Helly. 'Just imagine all those people it's brought together that were looking for their family. Lots of happy endings.'

'And just think of all those that never knew and all those family secrets that have been hidden for years and then suddenly wham bam, all hell breaks loose,' added Katie.

'I think we should all give it a go…all three of us.' Helly waved a couple of boxes in the air. 'What's the worst that can happen?'

Ben could feel his heart beginning to thump faster. Was this the time to take the gamble and play emotional roulette with his heart and past?

Before anyone could object, Helly had opened the first box and was already reading the instructions. 'It's easy! All we have to do is take a sample of our saliva, pop it in the tube and place it in this envelope. It costs absolutely nothing.'

'Just like my birthday present,' teased Ben, a little pensive as he picked up one of the boxes.

'You really need to get over that,' replied Helly with a

grin, handing a box to Katie. 'I think this is so interesting. I would love to know my geographic origins. Just imagine if it identifies potential relatives.'

'I'm just not sure,' said Ben.

'Don't be a spoilsport. You may have hundreds of cousins out there.'

Ben looked between them.

'Stop putting a downer on it. If it confirms what you already know, then so be it, but if it turns up a long-lost relative in Barbados, then just think of the free holidays.' Helly tipped her head to one side and gave them both a knowing look.

Katie laughed. 'You may actually have a point there. I'm game,' she said, opening a box and taking a sample of her saliva. 'There...easy.'

Helly followed suit, then they both looked at Ben. He knew there was a possibility it would throw up more than a long-lost cousin in Barbados. His stomach was churning as Helly began to question him further.

'Why the hesitation?' she asked. 'Come on, it's going to be time to open up soon and I wanted to nip to Bonnie's teashop for some breakfast rolls before those patients walk through the door.' She pushed the test into his hand.

'No hesitation,' replied Ben, swallowing down a lump. Maybe this was the push he needed. He could feel his palms sweating as he mirrored their actions and took the test.

'But just so we agree, if any of us turn out to be related

to someone famous or are really a prince or princess, then we all share the wealth,' joked Helly.

Ben smiled at Helly's enthusiasm, but his excitement was mixed with trepidation as he put the sample inside the tube. There was no going back now. 'There. All done. Now all we have to do is await our email. Now can we have breakfast and get on with our working day?' asked Ben, still staring at the box. It was possible that the unknown could soon become part of his life.

Oblivious to what was going on, Helly chirped, 'Yes boss! Bosses! I'll pop these in the post box on my way to pick up breakfast.' Slipping the three envelopes into her bag, Helly disappeared out of the office.

'Let's see what can of worms that opens up,' said Katie, walking out of Ben's office towards her own. She hovered in the doorway. 'Did you receive your reunion invitation?'

'I did,' replied Ben, holding her gaze.

'Well, we may as well travel together?' she suggested.

'You want to travel with me?'

'It makes sense, doesn't it?'

'I suppose,' he replied, a little surprised by the suggestion. When they had lived next door to each other before, Katie never suggested travelling anywhere together, even walking to lectures together.

'Why say it like that?'

'You seem to have mellowed in your old age.'

Ben dodged her playful swipe. 'Oi, less of the old.'

Katie's phoned beeped. She glanced at the screen. 'Heartcross village WhatsApp group.'

'You're in the village WhatsApp group? How do you even know there's a WhatsApp group? I've been here six months and I've not been invited to join any.'

'Well, what can I say, Mr Average? You either have it or you don't.' She gave Ben a wink. 'There's a meeting Friday night in the pub regarding the boat race. We need to firm up the date with everyone and pick the teams. I hope you don't mind but I've already contacted the local press to give us some coverage and they are fully on board. I've been thinking we could make a day of it, with stalls along the riverbanks, music, food, beer tents...a bit like a riverside summer fair. This is going to be so much fun. I bet your life was dull before I arrived in the village,' she said with a glint in her eye.

'I like dull,' replied Ben with a little sarcasm. He couldn't quite believe how quickly Katie had got involved in village life. She'd not been in the village more than seventy-two hours and she already had her fingers in so many pies. Just like the old days.

'You don't like dull, and if you do, then you need a re-think. Life is for living...you need to go and get life more.'

He watched Katie walk towards the door. She stopped in the doorway and turned around. 'That colour shirt really suits you. In fact, you look pretty good.' Katie ran an approving eye over him, taking Ben completely by surprise.

'And you fit into that shirt better than you did at uni,' she said with a cheeky wink.

The door shut behind her.

Where had the old Katie disappeared to? In the past, she would have goaded him that he would have no chance of winning the boat race; she would be spouting about training plans and trying to influence the strongest people to be on her team. And that cheeky wink – was she actually flirting with him? He gave himself a little shake. Of course she wasn't flirting with him. She was trying to distract him. Katie loved nothing more than winning and she would do anything to make Ben think about something other than the race.

Ben leant back in his chair. He knew the boat race was for charity, but that wasn't going to stop him from trying his best. Never mind row, row, row the boat – he was going to row, row, row and gloat. History wasn't going to repeat itself. All he had to do was train hard for the next few weeks and make sure he crossed the winning line first. How hard could that possibly be?

Chapter Four

'For all those who haven't met me in person yet, let me introduce myself. My name is Dr Katie O'Neil and I'm working at Peony Practice.' Katie smiled and cast a glance around the pub, trying to make eye contact with as many people as possible. Ben was sitting next to Drew at the bar, taking a sip of his pint. He was watching Katie closely as she addressed the room.

He couldn't help but be mesmerised; she knew how to work a room, engaging everyone. Katie looked over in his direction and her eyes locked with his for a moment. Ben felt his pulse quicken. He had to admit there was something about her.

'Penny for them,' Drew nudged his elbow. 'You're sitting there gawping.'

Ben rolled his eyes. 'There's something different about her.'

'What do you mean?' asked Drew.

'She seems to have mellowed a little; has a more sensitive side. I've never seen that before.'

Katie looked very much at home with the microphone in her hand, her voice warm as she talked sensitively about the dementia charity. At one point, Ben thought he saw her blink back a tear, her voice faltering, but he couldn't be quite sure.

'And if the whole community could support this event and charity, we are very much on to a winner,' said Katie, looking towards Stuart sitting at a table next to Allie and Rory. There was a pile of sponsor forms in front of him. 'As well as raising as much as possible, since we know this charity is close to many hearts in this room, and after talking with Stuart, we've decided to host our very own boat race on the River Heart. We would love to hear your thoughts on it.'

There was a ripple of excited murmurs around the room.

'What we are proposing is two teams, with Ben and I as the two team captains.'

Everyone turned towards Ben and gave a small round of applause.

Drew leant across and whispered, 'Paddy Power odds is that you haven't got a cat in hell's chance of winning.' He thumped Ben's back playfully.

'Don't count your chickens. You have no idea the effort I'm prepared to put in to win this.'

'You have a pint in your hand – you are not taking this training seriously at all,' teased Drew.

Ben looked at the pint in his hand, finished the beer and placed the empty glass on the table. 'Not another pint will pass my lips until this race is won.'

'I'm impressed,' replied Drew.

'And let's turn this boat race into a community day. In fact, we could make it an annual event. It will attract all the tourists, who can line the banks of the river, flag wave and cheer us on from the bridge.' The enthusiasm oozed from Katie as she carried on. 'We can have buckets for extra fund-raising, hot dog stalls, etcetera. Can we have a show of hands for everyone that would like to be involved in the actual race?' Katie looked around the room and smiled as numerous hands shot up in the air. 'Fabulous!' she trilled, turning towards Flynn who was standing at the bar next to Julia. 'Are we able to borrow kayaks from The Old Boat House?' she asked.

Flynn gave Katie the thumbs up, 'Absolutely you can.'

Then Katie swung a glance over to Ben and gestured for him to come and join her.

'Please can we give a warm welcome to our other team captain, Dr Ben Sanders.' Katie's voice carried across the room and the bar erupted in applause as Ben weaved his way through the chairs and tables towards Katie.

'Has anyone got any questions or would like to share their thoughts about the race, the day or the charity?'

Martha was the first to express her opinion. 'I hope we

aren't going to be penalised for our age.' She was quick to point out that she'd kayaked down the world's longest river and the best way to explore the River Nile was on the water itself.

'Absolutely not. Experience is always welcome and a winner,' replied Ben, impressed by Martha's previous kayak adventure. 'This may technically be a race but it's not about the winning. It's all about increasing awareness, raising funds and the community coming together for a fabulous day out.'

'Poppycock! Of course it's about all those things, but it's definitely about the winning!' replied Martha.

Katie nudged Ben. 'Martha's got a point. We need to decide who picks first.' She pulled out a coin from her pocket. 'Heads or tails?'

'Heads,' replied Ben, watching Katie flip the coin up in the air.

'Bad luck! Tails! I'm picking first.'

'Mmm, I think there is a fairer way to do this. I think we should put all the names in the hat and each pull one out,' suggested Ben.

'I agree,' said Stuart, looking towards Meredith who was standing behind the bar. She began to tear strips of paper from an order pad and then wrote the willing participants' names on the paper.

'And you can actually have my hat to pull the names out of,' chuckled Wilbur, taking his hat from his head and handing it to Ben.

With the names written down on the paper and then folded up into squares, Drew made the sound of a drumroll with his hands on top of the bar. Ben held the hat up high whilst Katie reached in and pulled the first name out.

'We need a team name,' declared Katie, looking pensive for a second. 'The Unsinkables or Seas the Day! Pier Pressure or...'

'Rowing Dirty or In Deep Ship,' murmured Ben, tongue in cheek, thinking about the last race.

'I think I'll go for "Seas the Day" as our team's name,' confirmed Katie, pleased with her choice. Then she read out the name on the piece of paper. 'My first team member is... Martha!' Katie turned the paper around so everyone could see. 'Come on up, Martha.'

'And look what we have here.' Katie reached inside a bag next to her and pulled out a bright-pink T-shirt with the charity's logo printed on the front. 'We'll get your name printed across the back too. Oh and we have a cap!' Katie handed over a matching bright pink cap.

Martha looked chuffed as she held up the T-shirt against her body and placed the cap on her head. 'Got to love a freebie,' she declared, looking more impressed than Ben did at this moment.

They hadn't talked T-shirts and caps – now what was he going to hand out to his team? This was the sort of stunt that Katie used to pull all the time to get the upper hand. He raised an eyebrow at her.

'And don't think I've left you out.' She was smiling as

she handed a bag to Ben. He was pleasantly surprised to see exactly the same T-shirts and caps in blue. Feeling a twinge of guilt for thinking the worst, he thanked her and held up a T-shirt.

'My team will be called Making Waves,' announced Ben, thinking fast on his feet. He caught Helly's eye, who looked amused as he pulled a name out of the hat. 'The first person on my team is Allie!'

Once the crew were picked for both teams, Ben gave Wilbur his hat back and Katie quietened down the excited chatter. 'We need to confirm the date for this race, so a show of hands will be great and I think it's best we go with the majority. Do you agree?' She turned towards Ben, who nodded.

Katie fired out numerous dates and when everyone agreed to Saturday in four weeks' time, Stuart began to hand out the sponsor forms. 'We also have a JustGiving page. The details are on the bottom of the form and for my race team…' Katie handed them a slip of paper. 'Here's the training schedule. Please attend as many as these sessions as possible.'

'See, she's organised a training schedule already. Of course she wants to win.' Ben was perched on the bar stool next to Drew, who was trying to stifle his laughter.

Drew spoke in a hushed whisper in the style of a commentator. 'The intellectual jealousy and competitive streak stretched back years between Dr Katie O'Neil and Dr Ben Sanders. The catalyst, a previous boat race when Dr

Ben Sanders claimed his boat was sabotaged. He could be seen clutching his boat, swimming along the Scottish water and finally clambering out of the river, hours behind the winners – much to his own embarrassment. But that has not deterred the doctor, who has taken up the challenge of a rematch and is competing again for academic superiority, having completely lost the first round. Don't worry, I'll make sure all is fair in love and war this time. I've got you a pint with a whisky chaser. I think you are going to need it.' Drew pushed both drinks towards Ben.

Ben's eyes were wide. 'How the hell did you know about the first boat race?' He picked up the whisky and took a huge swig. The amber liquid burnt the back of his throat.

'I thought you weren't drinking until this race was won?'

'You just bought me the drinks.'

'It doesn't mean to say you have to drink them! And this is a village, mate. Everyone knows everything.' Drew was grinning from ear to ear and winked at Helly.

One last time, Katie took to the microphone. 'Making Waves and Seas the Day will go head-to-head four weeks on Saturday and our adjudicator and referee will be Peony Practice's one and only fabulous receptionist Helly. The race will be thirteen kilometres down the River Heart – obviously unlucky for one team but lucky for the charity. All details and updates will be posted in the village WhatsApp group. Remember, this is for charity so please spread the word, get fund-raising and come and join in the fun.'

'She's even in the village WhatsApp group. I'm not even in the village WhatsApp group,' protested Ben, looking at an amused Drew.

Drew held out his hand. 'Give me your phone. Let me invite you…there you go, invited…accepted…part of the fam! It really is no big deal. You need to chill out more. Take a leaf out of Katie's book.'

Katie was sitting at a table with her team and laughing heartily.

'You'll be putting yourself in an early grave if you carry on like this. She really doesn't seem as bad as you think.' Drew patted Ben on the back, his smirk hidden as he drank his pint. 'Honestly, she seems okay to me.'

Ben was still glancing in her direction, but maybe Drew was right. Since she'd arrived in Heartcross, she hadn't been quite as bad as he remembered. 'She's even got the better office and has moved into the flat next door to me.' Ben blew out a breath. 'I must have been so bad in a past life.'

'You doth protest too much,' said Drew with a grin. 'Give me one of those sponsor forms. I'll sponsor you – Meredith, can you pass me that pen by the till?'

After writing the first signature on Ben's sponsor form, Drew stood up. 'I'm up early milking the cows and I suggest you start eating superfoods and make that your last pint.'

Once Drew had left, Helly slipped onto the bar stool

next to Ben. 'That went well, didn't it? Everyone is on board…and I hope that's where you stay: on board. It wouldn't look good for the team captain to be coming in last.'

Ben didn't rise to it but leant in towards Helly. 'So tell me about Katie's training schedule.'

'I can't do that, I'm the neutral one!' exclaimed Helly. 'But I'll share with you that it's intense.'

'I just knew it.'

Before Ben could question Helly more, Stuart was at his side. 'I can't thank you enough for this. This is great support for the charity and I can't wait to tell Alana all about tonight. I'm sorry she couldn't be here, but there don't seem to be many good days at the moment.' Stuart's voice faltered a little.

Ben knew exactly how difficult and emotional it was to watch a loved one suffer with abnormal brain changes. He'd supported so many families in similar situations and it was indeed heart-breaking.

'Katie has arranged for local TV news to film a small report tomorrow. Hopefully that will increase awareness. Fingers crossed that on race day, the tourists will line the banks of the river too. It is going to be amazing.' Stuart cupped his hands around Ben's and shook them wholeheartedly.

'You don't need to thank me,' replied Ben warmly.

From across the room, Katie was calling Stuart's name, which gave Ben the opportunity to turn back to Helly. 'And what I want to know is how do the villagers know about my previous boat race?' He stared straight at Helly, who was now looking a little shifty.

'It's getting late,' she declared, standing up.

'Helly!'

'I can neither confirm nor deny,' she replied. Her eyes twinkled as she gave Ben a cheeky sideward glance, then nudged him in the ribs before disappearing out of the pub.

With his eyes back on Katie, Ben watched her flitting between the villagers, introducing herself and shaking everyone's hand. She really did know how to hold someone's attention, but Ben couldn't help but feel that Katie was overcompensating for something. She always threw herself into every situation and wanted to be part of every group. It was like she was always willing people to like her.

In the pit of his stomach, Ben knew that life was going to be a lot more interesting with Katie around, and in the last forty-eight hours she had been constantly on his mind. Dr Katie O'Neil had started to scratch an itch that Ben hadn't even known needed scratching and he couldn't get her off his mind.

Chapter Five

It was Friday evening and the banks of the river were heaving with tourists. The weather was still glorious with the sun looking like it wasn't fading anytime soon in the cobalt sky. The Old Boat House was doing a roaring trade. The bay reminded Ben of a mini St Tropez, with boats and yachts bobbing all around on the river. It was easy to see the charm of the Scottish village of Heartcross that attracted tourists in droves. The scenery was stunning, the pretty harbour housed colourful wooden masts, and spectacular white cliffs lined the river while the purple heather mountains and lavender fields swept over the rolling hills in the distance. With The Lake House and Starcross Manor, this place offered the millionaire lifestyle for the average person with a twist of French Riviera chic thrown in.

Wilbur was standing outside The Old Boat House and

waved at Ben as he headed towards him. 'Shouldn't you youngsters be out on a Friday night instead of kayaking?'

'That's not good for business, Wilbur, encouraging us to spend our money elsewhere,' Ben replied. 'You are doing a roaring trade! I've never seen so many boats on the River Heart.'

'It's been the busiest season yet and now the villagers are out in full force, thanks to the boat race. I'm assuming that's why you're here, to get some practice in?'

'Absolutely. There's only going to be one winner, Wilbur,' said Ben confidently.

'You're not the only person to say that,' shared Wilbur with a smile. 'I've never known such competitiveness for a fund-raiser. There's hours of training time already booked in.'

'Really? How many exactly?' quizzed Ben, wanting to know all about Katie's schedule.

'That's more than my life's worth,' replied Wilbur, still smiling.

Ben stepped inside The Old Boat House and glanced at the rails of wetsuits hanging up. 'The question is, do I hire one or buy one?' Ben was weighing up his options.

'Definitely buy one,' trilled a voice as the changing room curtain opened and Katie revealed herself.

'What are you doing here?' asked Ben, unable to take his eyes off her. How the hell did she even manage to look good in a wetsuit?

'My guess is the same as you,' she said. 'If you could

book me in for a single kayak session in the morning, Wilbur, that would be great, and I'll take this wetsuit.' Katie shut the curtains and within seconds reappeared, carrying the wetsuit over her arm. She stood next to Ben, who was trying to pick out a suit for himself.

'Are you thinking of renting or buying one? Why not add a little colour to your life?' She reached for a black wetsuit with bright-red arms. 'This one will suit you. It'll brighten you up a little.'

Katie was giving him the once-over. Ben looked down at his clothes. There was no colour to his clothes – only his cheeks – as Katie playfully pinched his arm. 'Mmm, Ben Sanders in a tight wetsuit showing off those abs. Every woman's dream. Don't forget to pick a solid bright colour for your kayak, like yellow or orange…they particularly stand out in low light sky. It's more helpful if you get lost or capsize.'

She turned and paid Wilbur before giving Ben a beatific smile and headed out of the shop back along the riverbank.

Wilbur looked amused. 'I think she likes you.'

'I disagree,' replied Ben, feeling flustered. He didn't know why he was feeling flustered – he didn't have anything to feel flustered about – but somehow Katie always made him feel that way.

'Would you like to purchase or hire a wetsuit?'

'Hire please,' replied Ben, handing over his debit card and taking a wetsuit from the rail.

'The lockers for your clothes are over there, the kayaks

63

are down by the edge of the water and pick up an oar on your way out,' advised Wilbur, swiping the card and handing it back to Ben once the transaction had gone through.

Fifteen minutes later, Ben walked down to the tiny rocky bay with his oar. The river lay silver in the light of the evening sun and the rippled water ran right into the crevices, washing over the rocks time and time again. The kayaks were lined up at the water's edge. He looked at all the different bright colours and punted for a bright-orange boat. In his mind, he'd already mapped out his route and was heading to the tiny sandy bay downstream.

The front end of the kayak was planted on the shingle and the rudder joyously afloat as he found a rock-free area to enter the water from the shore. The cool water splashed against Ben's legs as he waded in and his feet squelched inside his now-soggy trainers. With the drag marks already half erased by the waves, the carrot-coloured boat was now bobbing in the water. Ben tightened up his life jacket and strapped his helmet under his chin. He scooted slowly into the cockpit, extending one leg at a time. Ben began to use sweep strokes to pivot the angle of the kayak and soon he was heading out into the middle of the river. Despite the horror of the last time he was in a boat, Ben felt surprisingly relaxed. He soon got into a rhythm and was picking up speed. The water was a little bumpy at times, but nothing that he couldn't handle.

He thought about his team: Allie, Rona, Drew, Meredith

and Flynn. Having never been in a kayak before, Rona might need a little coaching, but just like Katie, Ben had put a training schedule together. The race was a relay race. Each crew member would paddle their kayak a little over two kilometres to a certain place along the river with the next team member taking the baton, so to speak, at certain points. Ben and Katie were up against each other in the last leg of the race. Already donations were flooding into the JustGiving page, which was amazing to see.

Ben knew that over the last six months, Stuart had found it difficult to cope with Alana's dementia. The person Stuart knew was slipping away. Some days, she didn't even recognise him. Her hallucinations were also increasing. Ben had often looked out his office window to see a fire engine outside their cottage with the siren whirling after Alana had claimed there was a fire when there wasn't. But despite all the challenges, Stuart kept going with a zest for life, doing the best he could. Thankfully, with the support of his friends in the village, he was never on his own. Ben admired him and it was commendable of Katie to help increase awareness and raise money considering she had only just arrived in the village. The more Ben thought about it, the more he was actually beginning to think that Katie was indeed not like he had remembered.

Ben continued to pick up speed. The view was stunning from the water and he admired the truly striking Heartcross Castle and the mountainous terrain as he continued to paddle. Up on the bridge, he noticed a film crew, which had become a regular sight in the village of Heartcross since the celebrity chef Andrew Glossop had arrived and filmed his successful TV show from the magnificent kitchens at the castle. There was a crowd gathered and as Ben paddled closer, he looked up and spotted Katie. He narrowed his eyes and noticed she was being interviewed by the local TV news.

He continued to watch when suddenly there was a loud crack that boomed over the water.

'Shit!' Ben shouted as the kayak hit a rock in the water and bounced backward with force. Ben tipped upside down. He gasped for breath as he swallowed a mouthful of river water. The oar fell, now out of reach, and the kayak was travelling fast down the river.

'Double shit,' Ben muttered to himself, treading water. Thankfully, he had been spotted by a passing speedboat which slowed down and cut its engine. Ben began to swim towards the boat. At first, he didn't dare to glimpse up at the bridge but knew it was inevitable he was being watched and he wasn't wrong. He grimaced and looked in that direction. It was his worst nightmare – everyone standing on the bridge was staring and pointing in his direction alongside the TV cameras. Of course, amongst them was Katie, who waved at him as he was being hauled onto the deck of the speedboat. Why was it she was always there to witness his cock-ups?

Chapter Six

'Christ on a bike,' were the only words that came out of Ben's mouth. Feeling mortified and with his head in his hands, he was now sitting safely on his settee in the comfort of his living room and cringing in front of the TV. He was plastered all over the local news.

The headline was dramatic: 'Local doctor in boating accident.'

'For God's sake, how over the top,' Ben murmured, watching the embarrassment unfold in front of his eyes. This was the second time he'd watched the news report as he played it back. Of course, the TV crew had filmed the whole of the unfortunate escapade. There was Katie being interviewed about the up-and-coming boat race and, in the distance, Ben was being thrown from his kayak. He shuffled to the edge of the settee and stared at Katie. He couldn't deny she lit up the screen. For a second, he forgot his embarrassment and couldn't take his eyes off her. Then, on the TV screen, he heard a loud gasp from the spectators on the bridge as Katie swung round to witness his kayak capsizing.

'There seems to be an incident happening right here at Heartcross,' claimed the interviewer.

Ben was shaking his head in disbelief; the news reporter was making a mountain out of a molehill.

'Dr Sanders in kayak accident, here on the River Heart. He is now being pulled to safety by a passing boat,' continued the reporter.

Ben couldn't stop his huge sigh; he knew Katie was going to take great pleasure in his misfortune.

Knock…knock…knock.

That's all he needed – Katie coming to gloat at his misfortune. He didn't move. Hopefully she would think he wasn't in and go away.

'Open up, I know you are in there.' Helly's voice filtered through the door. 'I can hear the TV.'

Reluctantly, Ben opened the door and took a quick look over Helly's shoulder.

'Who are you avoiding?' asked Helly, looking behind her.

'I know exactly why you're here.' Ben rolled his eyes as Helly bounded past him and bounced her backside on the settee with an almighty grin on her face.

'Sit down, why don't you.'

'I thought you'd never ask,' she replied, grinning. 'The talk of the town you are.'

'And for all the wrong reasons,' replied Ben, sitting in the chair.

'Dr Sanders in dramatic rescue.'

'There was nothing dramatic about it.'

Helly leant forward and squinted at the paused TV. On the screen was Katie looking like a Hollywood movie star, dressed in a designer polka dot dress wearing Audrey Hepburn-style sunglasses and ballet-type shoes. Helly grabbed the remote control from the coffee table. 'And why have you got the TV paused on Katie?' Helly gave him a cheeky, knowing look.

'Because you knocked on the door.'

'That's your excuse and you're sticking to it. She is very stunning, isn't she?' Helly twisted her head to take a better look. 'Attractive, brains and lives right next door. A match made in heaven.'

'Did you want something in particular?' Ben wasn't rising to the bait.

'I'm just seeing how you are after your ordeal.'

'There was no ordeal and I'm absolutely fine.'

Helly was gazing at him. 'You couldn't write it, could you? There's Katie on the TV talking about the up-and-coming boat race and then there you are making a complete—'

'All right,' interjected Ben as Helly clicked on the remote and the news report carried on.

'It's this bit now.' Helly pointed at the TV. 'Boom! Tossed out of the kayak into the river.'

'Thank you for the running commentary, but I have already seen it.'

Helly's eyes widened. 'Blimey! Are you playing it back? You are, aren't you, eh?'

It was at this precise moment Ben was wondering if he could break his 'no alcohol unless he goes out' rule and the answer to that was yes. 'No, I'm not playing it back.'

'Umm, are you sure about that?'

Ben rolled his eyes. 'I need a drink.' He stood up and walked over to the bookshelf in the corner of the room which housed his alcohol supply. He poured himself a whisky and swigged it back, then exhaled.

'Drinking whisky? That will be the shock,' chipped in Helly.

Just at that moment, Ben's phone vibrated on the table. There was no way he was even going to look at that phone. He knew he was most probably going to be a laughing stock.

'Your phone is pinging,' she observed.

'I know.'

'Aren't you going to take a look?' She leant forward and glanced at the screen. 'Village WhatsApp group.'

'Feel free to take a look,' he said. Helly would see it anyway since she was part of the same group.

Without hesitation, Helly picked up the phone from the table. 'It's Drew! "Call yourself a captain".' Helly sniggered as she read the message out loud. 'He's wondering if it's too early to jump ship…' Helly laughed out loud. 'Did you see what he did there?'

Ben didn't pass comment. He took another swig of whisky.

'He's wondering if there are any spaces on Katie's team.'

'It's nice to know he's concerned about my well-being. I did just nearly drown, you know.'

'So dramatic!' replied Helly. 'Oh, and a message from Fergus, and one from Rory. The village WhatsApp group is pinging out of control.'

Now Ben really wished he hadn't kicked up a fuss about being in the WhatsApp group. At least before, he wouldn't have had a clue about the jibes everyone was writing about him. Helly continued to read out the messages while Ben rolled his eyes.

'Isn't it nearly your bedtime?' asked Ben with a hint of sarcasm.

'Funnily enough, I'm over the age of twenty-one and tend to stay up later than…' she looked at her watch. '8pm.'

'Shame,' murmured Ben under his breath.

Helly was just about to put the phone down on the table when it let out a trill. She looked at the screen, then a wide beam spread across her face. Ben knew exactly what that sound meant but it was too late. Helly did now too.

'You have a new match! What are you doing on dating apps?' Helly's grin was wide, her face lit up. 'And why are you single?'

71

'I'm single because I'm in the habit of choosing unsuitable women.'

'There must be something wrong with you,' she added with a chuckle.

'Watch it, cheeky!'

'No, I'm serious, why is someone like you on dating apps?' she repeated.

'Because how am I meant to meet people? It's a little unethical to go chatting up my patients.'

'True. Can I take a look?'

'Oh why not,' replied Ben, thinking if he said no he would never hear the end of it anyway. Helly scrutinised the photo on the screen. 'But how on earth are you meant to match with the right people when half of your information is missing? You need to stand out from the crowd. You have so much to offer.'

'I just didn't know what to write. It's all a little daunting,' admitted Ben.

When Ben had hit thirty, he'd panicked slightly that he was never going to meet the love of his life. Signing himself up on the dating app had been his last attempt at meeting someone as he really was getting a little fed up with his own company. Of course, he'd had girlfriends in the past, and a couple of long-term relationships that spanned over twelve months, but things quickly fizzled out. Neither of those relationships had been perfect. Maybe Ben was looking for something that didn't exist, but he certainly wanted a partnership built on love and trust. He was beginning to get fed up with coming home to an empty flat and pinging microwave meals for one. Was it too much to ask to find your happy ever after? It seemed so, if dating apps were anything to go by.

'These photos are…not the best,' she finished diplomatically.

'I don't have many photos of myself.'

'Dur…' She waggled his iPhone in the air. 'Then take some.'

'That just seems a little pretentious. I mean, what man poses for selfies on a daily basis? Not me. I don't have time.'

'Really? You go to work and…you go to work. Then you sit in here all by yourself. You don't even have a fish,' she said as she took a quick look around the room.

'What's a fish got to do with anything? I'm not sure if I get myself a fish it's going to increase my chances of securing a date.'

'Or borrow a puppy. Women love men holding adorable puppies. Or a baby…actually, not a baby as they may think it's yours. What are you looking for in a woman?'

Ben wanted to meet a woman that made him feel like he was the only man in the world. He wanted those butterflies in his stomach, someone fun to be with. Of course, ideally, she would be stunning, loyal, trustworthy and have a good sense of humour, but real life wasn't like those romantic movies or books.

'Not someone with stupid bunny ears on their head,' he

answered, thinking every photo he had seen so far had been filtered.

'Mmm, that is proving a little difficult on here.'

'Why is it so hard to find someone down to earth and normal?'

'Depends on what normal is. Would you like me to fill this out for you? You can always delete it.'

Ben thought for a second. 'I've got nothing to lose. I'll put the kettle on.'

Helly kicked off her shoes and propped her feet up on the coffee table, then began tapping away.

Once the tea was made, Ben sat back down. He noticed that Helly was smiling.

'You look like you are up to mischief.' He eyed her carefully.

'I've gone and got you a date for Thursday night! I've gone for Thursday as it's too soon to be giving away your Friday nights. They have to earn that level of investment.'

'My Thursday and Friday nights are no different.'

'But they don't need to know that, do they?'

Even though technically he was Helly's boss, they really did have a good friendship. He trusted her judgement.

'Let me have a look.' He held out his hand. 'And don't forget I do have a level of professionalism to maintain.'

'But you do have a private life too. So, on Thursday night, make sure you have a clean shirt. Actually, not a shirt.' Helly tilted her head. 'I don't want to lie to you, but sometimes your shirts scream out old man shirts. And no wearing a tank top. They so look like those pictures on knitting patterns that my granny used to have back in the day.'

Ben pretended to look hurt. 'It's called fashion,' he replied, looking over the messages that Helly had typed. 'You have actually made me sound quite decent.'

'And funny. It's all about the humour – a little flirty but not crossing over the line to cringeworthy smut.'

'And where have you got these photos from?'

'I'm not revealing my sources, but what do you think of her picture?'

Ben was quite pleasantly surprised. 'Actually not bad.'

'There you go. Thursday night, 7pm at The Lake House.'

'That's a bit pricey for the first date.'

'Don't be a skinflint. This could be the love of your life. Don't mess it up.' Helly drank her tea and placed the empty mug on the table. 'And now I can see you haven't been traumatised by nearly drowning, I'll see you in the morning, boss. You don't need to thank me for setting you up with your future wife.'

Ben was shaking his head in jest as Helly stood up and disappeared through the front door. As soon as the door closed, Ben could hear voices outside in the hallway and recognised Katie's voice. He'd half expected her to have already knocked on the door with a huge grin on her face after yet another rowing blunder. He was up on his feet and tiptoed towards the peephole in the door. Being careful not to make a sound, he lowered his eye and watched.

Ben heard Helly's voice. 'No, he's not home.'

'But you've just come out of his apartment.'

The word 'apartment' made Ben smile – that's what posh people or people keeping up appearances called a bog standard flat. He was impressed that, as much as Helly pretended she didn't want to take any sort of side, it seemed her loyalty actually did lie with him. Ben listened, knowing that Helly couldn't deny that fact and had to think fast on her feet.

'I've just been in to feed the fish.'

Ben stifled his laughter behind the door. As much as Helly could be a wind-up merchant, she obviously realised the last thing he needed was Katie knocking on his door and basking in his disastrous attempt at kayaking on the river.

Katie gave her an odd look. 'You've been in to feed a fish.'

'That I have. Ben is very fond of…Swim Shady.'

Katie tilted her head. 'A very imaginative name.' Katie looked towards the door and Ben moved quickly to the side, even though she couldn't see him. 'Are you winding me up?'

'Would I?' replied Helly. 'I'll catch you tomorrow at work.'

Ben heard Helly's footsteps echo down the stairwell until they petered out. He dared to look out the peephole one last time and Katie was still standing there, looking puzzled, staring at his door and then at the stairs.

'Swim Shady,' she said out loud, then took her key out of her bag. Hearing her front door open and Katie's TV sounding out through the paper-thin walls, he heaved a sigh of relief.

With another drink in his hand, Ben had well and truly broken the drinking on his own rule and poured himself another drink. He flipped back on to the dating app and threw his head back and laughed after reading the bio Helly had concocted.

> ***** *One hell of a guy – New York Times*
> **** *Outstanding gentleman – Daily Mail*
> ***** *He's my screensaver – My mother*
> *** *Makes an average cup of tea – Receptionist*
> ***** *Always buys a round in the pub – Best mate*
> ** *Average kayaker!*
> * *Bellend – the ex*

Next, Ben looked over the profile of the woman Helly had set him up with and re-read the messages. Actually, there was nothing to lose by going on the date. She looked genuine enough and it meant he wouldn't be sitting at home alone. She lived in the next town, had a professional job and they had a couple of things in common. As he put his phone down on the table, he wondered about Katie's private life. Was she single? She hadn't spoken of anyone since she'd arrived and out of all the jobs in Scotland, he wondered again what had brought her to Heartcross.

Suddenly, he froze. He heard knocking on his living room wall. He knew it was Katie. Quickly, he turned the TV down and then he heard her laugh.

Damn, she knew he was home.

'There's no point pretending you aren't home. I can hear you, Mr Average.' She laughed again.

How had his life come to this? Ben didn't answer. God, she could still be so annoying.

Chapter Seven

Mornings came around far too quickly for Ben's liking, especially when he knew there was not a cat in hell's chance that Katie was going to let last night's TV news pass by without some sort of jeer. But he knew it was coming, so all he had to do was brush it off and make light of the situation. Hopefully, she'd get bored of ribbing him. After locking his front door, he stepped onto the landing and listened. There wasn't a sound coming out of Katie's flat, which either meant she'd overslept or she was already at work. He braced himself as he walked down the stairs to the office and noticed Helly arriving.

'Good morning to you!' sang Helly cheerfully, punching in the alarm code then swinging open the office door to let Ben walk in first.

'Are we the first ones in?' he asked, amazed that Katie wasn't already in the office.

79

'The only ones in until afternoon surgery.'

Ben stopped in his tracks. 'Why?'

'Because Katie has taken the morning off,' replied Helly, bounding over to the waiting area and placing a pile of new magazines on the tables. 'I can't abide old magazines that have been thumbed and re-read that many times,' she said, picking up the old ones and sliding them into the recycle bin.

'Can we just rewind? How do you know that Katie has the morning off and I don't?'

'Because it's on the chart.'

Ben was perplexed. 'What chart?' he asked, following Helly into the staff room. After hanging up their coats and placing their lunches in the fridge, Ben tossed a pound into the tea-fund caddy then switched on the kettle whilst Helly tapped the new annual leave chart that had been stuck to the kitchen wall with Blu Tack.

'It's all on here,' she said.

Ben walked toward the chart. It was the first he knew about an annual leave chart. 'Why do we need a chart? What's wrong with just writing it in our diary? After all, there are only three of us.'

Helly shrugged. 'I don't know. Katie's idea and the next time I walked into the kitchen, there it was.'

'It would just be nice to be informed...actually, consulted.'

'The last time you wanted to be informed, look what happened. You joined the WhatsApp group and were the talk of the village. My suggestion is it's best not to be informed and then you plead ignorance to everything that is going on around you.'

After making the first brew of the day, Ben walked into his office and fired up the computer. He sat back in his chair as Helly appeared in the doorway holding the files of the first few patients. She placed them on the edge of the desk.

'Any idea what Katie is up to this morning?' he asked, intrigued.

'None whatsoever, but on the plus side, by the time she gets in to do the evening surgery, your TV appearance should be old news.'

Before Ben could come back with a witty retort, they were distracted by the sound of a siren which was getting louder and louder. 'Sounds like a fire engine.' Putting his hands on his desk, Ben pushed his chair backwards and looked out the window in the waiting room. There was a fire engine with its blue flashing light whirling right outside Stuart and Alana's cottage. This wasn't the first time Ben had seen the fire engine outside their cottage. Not knowing whether Alana had called them due to her dementia or whether it was genuine, Ben and Helly abandoned the office and grabbed their coats as they hurried out onto the street where a crowd had already gathered. The sirens had stopped and the engine cut. The cab door swung open, and a burly fireman jumped down to the ground with a thud.

'Please can everyone move back,' the fireman ordered.

'I can't see any smoke,' observed Helly. 'Or flames, but

there's Alana up in the top window.' Helly pointed and Ben glanced in that direction.

Immediately Alana disappeared behind the curtain, but it kept moving slightly. The front door of the cottage swung open and a flustered-looking Stuart appeared, holding his hands up in the air. 'It's okay, there's no fire, just a false alarm,' he shouted towards the crowd that began to disperse when they realised there was nothing to see. Ben and Helly hung back whilst Stuart was in deep conversation with the fireman. Stuart was visibly upset, and when the conversation finished, he stood on the edge of the pavement and watched the fire engine drive off down the street.

'Is everything okay?' asked Ben, knowing it was far from okay.

Stuart exhaled.

'That sounds like a no to me,' continued Ben. 'Come on, let me put the kettle on.'

Stuart didn't object and he invited Ben and Helly inside. Once they were in the kitchen, Stuart sat at the table and Helly sat down next to him. Noticing a lonely tear run down Stuart's face, she squeezed his hand.

'I just don't know how much more I can take,' he said, his voice barely a whisper.

'I'm assuming Alana called the fire brigade?' questioned Ben tentatively.

Stuart managed a nod. 'It's not the first time. The bad days are now more frequent than the good days. I didn't want to say it or admit it, but I just can't go on.' Now the tears were free flowing down Stuart's cheeks. Helly passed him a tissue from the box in the middle of the table. 'Alana's hallucinations. I'm trying to reassure her they are not real, but...'

Ben passed him a hot mug of tea. 'Hallucinations are sensory experiences that seem real, but are created in the mind in the absence of an external source or event. Most are visual, but about half of people who see things that aren't there may also hear non-existent noises or voices. Seeing things that aren't there can be unsettling and even frightening. The best thing is to not to argue with someone who insists that what they are seeing or hearing is real.'

Stuart nodded. 'I'm trying my best but it's difficult. Alana is convinced that her own father is trying to burn down the house. The firemen were very understanding but she's called the emergency services for an incident that's not even happening...what if she puts someone else's life at risk?'

'I hear what you're saying,' sympathised Ben, seeing the stress that Stuart was under. 'Who is with Alana now?' Ben looked towards the door.

'Allie is up there with her while I take a breather.'

Ben sat down at the kitchen table opposite Stuart. 'I think we need to look at Alana's medication and also get you some help too. Maybe a little respite. Would that help you?'

Stuart nodded.

'We need to go and open up the surgery, but I'll look over Alana's medical file. Come and see me when morning surgery ends.' Ben's voice was warm and caring.

'Thank you,' replied Stuart.

Ben and Helly stood up and headed outside together. 'It's so sad. That disease is just cruel,' said Helly the second the door shut behind them.

'I know,' replied Ben, suddenly patting his back pocket. 'I've left my phone on the table. You go and open up the office, I'll catch you up.'

After retrieving his phone, Ben stepped back outside and crossed over the road. He noticed a car parked right outside the entrance to the flats with its engine running.

A notable-looking man climbed out of the driver's side and walked around the back of the car. Dressed in a suit that fitted him perfectly, he opened the passenger door and held out his hand. To Ben's surprise, Katie stepped out. She was wearing a lightweight dress in a boho print; the crinkle-cut fabric floated down towards her ankles, the belt around her tiny waist enhanced her figure and Ben couldn't help but think she looked beautiful. He didn't know why but he shielded himself in a doorway and watched. It reminded Ben of a scene out of a movie; they were looking into each other's eyes then they wrapped their arms around each other. The man rested his chin on top of her head and kissed her hair lightly. It didn't look like either of them wanted to let go. Ben's first thought was that maybe Katie was on a first date, but then it struck him they seemed too familiar in each other's company. Then Ben realised they must have spent the night together. Immediately, he felt his mood slump a little. A twinge of jealousy somersaulted in the pit of his stomach, which took him by surprise. He watched as she finally pulled away and the man returned to his car.

Katie stood on the edge of the pavement and waved until the car was out of sight. As she turned around, Ben noticed she had tears in her eyes. She dabbed them with a tissue and composed herself before heading through the side door that led to the flats. Ben was taken back: in all the years that he'd known Katie, he'd never seen her show any emotion. When she was around him, she was always upbeat, full of herself, or desperately annoying, but he'd never seen this side of her before. All sorts of feelings pogoed around inside him, and there was a stack of questions he wanted to ask. He was intrigued to find out who the man was and why was she crying, but he knew it was none of his business. What he did know is that he didn't like seeing her in the arms of another man – or being upset. Once she'd closed the door behind her, Ben gave a sideward glance. When he was sure she was gone, he hurried into the surgery, which was already packed to the rafters with patients.

As he passed the receptionist desk, he looked at Helly. 'Where did you say Katie had gone this morning?' he asked as she tapped away on the computer keyboard.

She glanced up from the screen. 'I didn't,' she replied,

knotting her eyebrows together. 'But hurry up, you're already behind with your appointments.'

Walking into his office, he shut the door and opened the first file. With Katie still very much on his mind, he picked up his phone and typed.

'It's all right for some to have a morning off.' He pressed send. He wasn't sure why he felt the need to send the text. It wasn't as though he'd asked her a direct question that needed a response, but, almost immediately, his phone vibrated on the desk. Katie's name flashed on the screen as he opened her message.

'It is, isn't it? I've only just woken up!'

Ben stared at the message. He knew that wasn't the truth. He'd just seen her step out of a car. It made Ben wonder: what exactly was Katie hiding and why did she feel the need to cover it up?

Chapter Eight

'What are you doing here?' Reluctantly, Ben opened his front door to find Helly standing there. 'I'm trying to get ready.'

'I know! Date night! That's why I'm here!' Helly said as she wandered into Ben's flat before he objected. 'Woah!' She stood and stared at the shirts thrown all over the settee.

'I'm not quite sure what to wear,' admitted Ben.

'It looks like a jumble sale. This one is too wishy-washy.' She held it up against Ben's chest. 'Looks like something your granddad would wear, and that one… I simply have no words.'

'Why don't you come round, boost my confidence and pull my wardrobe to bits?' Ben looked a little put out.

'That's what I am doing,' replied Helly, the sarcasm lost on her. 'I wish I had checked all these out before. We could have gone shopping.'

'Surely they aren't that bad?'

'Lighten up, I'm only kidding you,' she replied with a glint in her eye. 'But you are going to The Lake House, the most famous restaurant around these parts. You need to make an effort – look handsome and classy yet not too stuffy. I can do something about the classy and not too stuffy part.'

'I'll be chucking you out in a minute.' Ben grinned.

'Maybe your team T-shirt is the way to go,' she joked, pointing to the T-shirt on the table.

'I have my first team training session on Wednesday night. Have you seen the JustGiving page? The donations are already just under two thousand pounds.'

'Wow! That's amazing. I'm sure the TV news helped.'

'Mmm. The less said about that, the better.'

'How's Stuart?' asked Helly.

'He's doing okay. We've tweaked Alana's medication and Stuart is actually going to view some homes for Alana, so at least he can have a couple of week's respite.'

'It must be so difficult,' replied Helly, perching on the arm of the chair.

Ben held up a shirt. 'What about this one?'

'You know what? I think that's the one – it suits you and it brings out the sparkle in your eyes. In fact, you look pretty damn good for you.'

'You have such a way with words. I'll go and put it on.'

Within five minutes, Ben appeared in the doorway.

'What do you think?' He smoothed down his shirt and looked towards Helly, waiting for her opinion.

'That is the shirt that is going to change your life. I can feel it in my bones.' Helly waltzed towards the door. 'And on that note, my job here is done. I'll leave you to get ready.'

———————

Ben was filled with nerves when he set off. He hadn't been on a date in such a long time. He was meeting Poppy, a marketing manager from Glensheil, at 7pm, which gave him thirty minutes to walk to The Old Boat House and catch the water taxi across to the restaurant. After joining the queue on the wooden jetty, it seemed like everyone was heading to The Lake House this evening. He stood in line looking out across the water and jumped out of his skin when he felt an arm being linked through his. Katie was smiling up at him.

'Fancy seeing you here. What are you doing?'

He opened his mouth to speak but nothing came out.

She leant in towards him. 'Oooh, you smell nice… Creed aftershave. I know that gorgeous aroma anywhere.'

Ben was still staring at her as he took in her own delicious smell.

'Close your mouth. You're catching flies.' She nudged him playfully.

He was mesmerised; she looked stunning and he knew her aroma. 'Chanel Number Five,' he said.

'You remembered.' She gave him a playful wink.

It was the same perfume from the hallway, the same one she'd worn every day during university. It used to amuse Ben, knowing the perfume cost a fortune. But according to Katie, she deserved the simple pleasures in life.

'What are you doing here?' he asked, her arm still linked through his.

'Dinner at The Lake House. I haven't been yet so I thought instead of sitting in by myself, I'd treat myself and check it out. How about you?'

'With company?' Ben looked behind them.

'No, just me.' She tilted her head to the side, waiting for Ben to share his dinner plans.

'I'm having dinner…'

'With…' Katie wound her hand round in a slow circle to speed him up.

'Poppy.'

'Oooh, who is Poppy? Tell me more.'

Ben was quiet. He didn't know much about Poppy except her occupation and that she lived in the next town. He really didn't want to be getting into any conversation about his dinner plans but as Katie was going to be eating at the same restaurant, she was going to witness his dinner date for herself.

'Oh my God, it's a first date, isn't it?' Katie's eyes were wide.

How the hell would she even guess that? Ben blew out a breath and began to walk forward in the queue.

'Is she here?' Katie took a quick look over her shoulder and glanced at the line of people behind them.

'I'm meeting her at the restaurant,' replied Ben.

'That's good for me. Then at least we can share the boat ride together.' She leant in and whispered, 'She's a very lucky girl.'

'You can cut out your sarcasm.'

'Who said I'm being sarcastic?' Katie didn't unlink her arm as the queue began to move forward.

'You are the last two on the boat. We are now full,' declared Roman the boat driver, clipping the rope across to stop any more passengers from climbing aboard. 'The last two seats are over on the right.'

'Thank you. We can even sit together. It's your lucky night.' She beamed then turned to Roman. 'Do you have any spare life jackets?'

'They are hung up at the back of the boat, but the water is quite calm tonight. Would you like me to get you one?'

Katie's face broke into a grin. 'It's okay, Roman, I was thinking of my friend here. He has a hot date and every time he goes anywhere near water, he tends to end up in it.'

Ben rolled his eyes and shook his head. 'Please forgive her, Roman. She thinks she's a comedian.' Ben gave her a gentle push as he walked towards the seat. Katie squeezed next to him.

'This is very cosy, isn't it?' Katie bit down on her lip to supress her smile.

'Very.' Ben had to admit he felt confused by her most of the time. 'Do you know how annoying you are?'

A wide grin spread across her face. 'I wouldn't have it any other way.'

Ben got his second proper look at her as she held his gaze. She did have a very elegant look; her sterling-blue eyes matched the colour of her dress, her handbag and shoes fully colour coordinated.

Katie's eyes flashed instant warmth. 'I didn't mean to tease about the life jacket, you know.'

'Yes you did.'

'Okay, I did, but seriously I'm glad you got rescued. I was all for diving off the bridge and saving you.'

'Really? Were you?'

With a sarcastic look on her face, she said, 'No of course not. That river water would be no good for my highlights.'

'I walked into that one, didn't I?'

They watched Roman walk along the deck of the boat, welcoming the passengers as he made his way to the front. 'The water isn't too rocky today. The weather is being kind to us, but as we set off, there may be a little jolt, so please stay seated or hold onto the rails.' He sat behind the wheel and fired up the engine.

As soon as the boat moved, just as Roman predicted, the boat jolted a little and Katie immediately grabbed onto

Ben's knee. He put his hand on top of hers. She caught his eye and Ben's whole body tingled at her touch.

'If you wanted to hold my hand, all you had to do was ask.' She held his gaze.

Feeling his pulse quicken, he said, 'I think it was you who wanted to grab my knee.' He quickly removed his hand and noticed Katie still smiling.

'That's your story and you're sticking to it.'

'Sit back and enjoy the view.' Roman's voice came over the Tannoy.

'Oh, I am.' Katie nudged his elbow with hers.

Roman navigated the boat whilst Ben and Katie looked out across the water.

'Wow, look at the castle from here,' said Katie.

'Wait till you see the cliffs when we sail around this corner.'

Ben observed Katie as her eyes were fixed on the view; he watched how they widened as she stared at the sweeping bays and sand dunes. Her eyes darted upwards to the gulls that hovered over the white cliffs and Heartcross Mountain stretched towards the early evening sky.

'It's picture perfect, isn't it?' She looked in his direction.

'It is,' replied Ben, his gaze not leaving hers before he glanced back towards the water. 'Wait until you see'—the boat turned the corner and Ben pointed—'the secret coves.'

Katie tilted her face up towards the light breeze. 'It's just gorgeous, isn't it?'

The boat was beginning to slow down and sail towards the trees. 'We are going through there…that small opening. It will take your breath away.'

Roman steered the boat through the beautiful weeping willows that hung over the water's edge, then around a cluster of rocks.

'Look at that. I feel like I'm in the middle of a romantic novel,' said Katie.

The boat gently bumped the bank and Katie balanced herself by placing her hand back on Ben's knee, she didn't take her eyes off the water. They both gazed at the chalky-white rocks that hung over a tiny secluded beach of sparkling beige sand. Roman guided the boat towards the wooden jetty where it bobbed on the water. The Lake House restaurant with its old-fashioned shutters, purple wisteria and pink roses twisting all around the doorway was right in front of them.

'The hidden restaurant under the canopy of beautiful cliffs…' Katie murmured.

Ben hadn't seen this side of Katie before – she looked quite dreamy, relaxed, her guard down.

'What a fantastic location for a first date. One to tell the grandkids,' she added, looking at Ben.

Even though it had only been a short boat ride, it had completely slipped his mind that he was here for a date. It surprised Ben that he was actually enjoying Katie's company.

'And you're eating on your own?'

'I am. It's been a hell of a few days.'

Katie didn't elaborate, but for a second, Ben could have sworn she looked sad.

'Are you okay? You look kind of…' But Ben didn't finish his sentence.

'Of course I'm okay. I'm always okay,' she replied, standing up and smoothing down her dress. Katie didn't make eye contact with him. There was something he couldn't quite put his finger on, but he didn't want to pry further, especially if she was about to sit in the restaurant by herself.

'Here you are. The Lake House and all delivered safe and sound. And no need for life jackets,' joked Roman, looking at Ben before jumping onto the jetty and tying up the boat securely. He lowered the gangplank and saluted as the diners stepped off the boat and sauntered along towards the entrance of The Lake House.

Walking along the jetty side by side, Katie stopped in her tracks. 'We can't walk in there together. It may put your date on edge if she is already inside. The first flush of love is a wonderful thing. I hope you both enjoy your night.'

She took Ben by surprise with her words. 'It's not like you to be so…' Ben was searching for the right way to say it.

'Thoughtful? I can be nice sometimes, you know.'

'It appears so, but can you please bring sarcastic Katie back? I know where I am then.'

She looked him straight in the eyes. 'Do I make you nervous?'

Even though she was pretending to jest, Ben could tell she was asking a serious question.

'You wish,' he replied, giving her a lopsided grin. Then Katie walked on ahead towards the restaurant.

He turned the question over in his mind. Did she make him nervous? Of course she made him nervous. Every time he was in her company, there was a nervous fluttering in the pit of his stomach. He wiped his sweaty palms on his trousers, then raked his hands through his curls. He felt nervy as hell knowing that he was about to meet his date and that Katie was there to witness the whole thing. The timing couldn't be any worse.

For a moment, he waited outside the restaurant and wondered if Katie ever thought about the night they spent together. He felt himself slightly blush as the vivid memories came flooding back. That night, the attraction had been off the scale and their kisses were electrifying, the passion so raw. They devoured each other all night, finally falling asleep in each other's arms.

But the next day, everything had gone back to the way it was. Katie was back to her competitive self in the lecture room, and she never spoke about it. Soon after, the video of the boat race had appeared on YouTube, leaving Ben confused by their whole relationship and wondering who the hell had uploaded it. Even though Katie made him no promises, it had devasted Ben. He tried to put the whole thing behind him. But he still thought about that night – often.

As he opened the restaurant door, the question very much on Ben's mind was: out of all the doctor's surgeries in all the world, what had brought Katie O'Neil to Heartcross?

The inside of the building was just as breath-taking as the outside, with the central dining bar and signature large windows overlooking the bay. There was beautiful oak panelling and striking wall art hanging on the walls to give it a luxurious feel. In the corner of the dining area stood an ebony baby grand piano. There had been numerous famous people sitting at that piano, including world-famous Dolores Henderson's *Trip Down Memory Lane* TV appearance, which had been televised from that very spot last year, pulling in viewing figures of over five million. It had put The Lake House well and truly on the map. Ever since, business had been booming.

Ben was greeted by Callie. 'Welcome to The Lake House,' she trilled. 'It's lovely to see you. Have you got a booking with us this evening?'

'I have,' replied Ben, taking a quick glance around the restaurant. 'I'm dining with Poppy…'

'Poppy…?' asked Callie.

It was at that second Ben realised he didn't actually know her surname. 'Just Poppy.'

'Poppy hasn't arrived yet. If you would like to take a seat at the bar, when she arrives, I'll show you to your table.'

Katie was sitting at the bar. Ben pulled out the stool next to her, then perused the bottles of alcohol lined up on the shelves.

'You just couldn't stay away from me, could you?'

'It just so happens it's the only free stool,' replied Ben with a smile. 'Would you like a drink?'

'I've just ordered one, but thank you.'

After ordering himself a drink, Ben looked towards the door. There was still no sign of Poppy and it crossed his mind he might actually get stood up.

'This place is fabulous, isn't it? A really chilled-out atmosphere. I believe the chef is top-notch… Giavani?' said Katie.

'Apparently he's dating Callie.' Ben nodded towards Callie.

'You are very much up on village gossip, aren't you?'

'Ever since I joined the WhatsApp group. Cheers.' He held his glass up and clinked it against hers.

'Cheers,' replied Katie, taking a sip of her drink.

They looked up to see Callie standing behind them. 'Your table is ready, Katie, when you are?'

'I'll just finish this drink if that's okay?'

Callie nodded and returned to the front desk.

'I can't have you waiting all nervously by yourself, now can I?'

Ben's phone pinged. He looked at the screen and saw it was a message from Poppy. Ben exhaled. She wasn't coming; a family emergency. Why had she'd left it until the last minute to message?

'Don't tell me she's stood you up?' asked Katie.

'It appears that way,' replied Ben, bracing himself for Katie's teasing. But he was pleasantly shocked when she stood up and hovered at his side.

'Aw, it looks like you'll just have to go on a date with me instead. Care to join me?'

'What's the catch?' he asked.

'No catch. I can't have you eating on your own.' Katie looked at Callie. 'I'm ready for my table, and if it's okay, Ben will be joining me.'

Callie looked surprised for a second. Ben was booked in at a different table with a guest, but in her professional capacity, she didn't ask questions.

'I've been stood up,' explained Ben.

'And I've rescued him,' added Katie, slipping her arm through his.

Callie smiled at them both. 'If you'd like to follow me, I'll show you to your table. You'll be on the rooftop. The view is romantic and spectacular up there.'

Katie leant in towards Ben. 'Romantic and spectacular,' she repeated in a whisper.

Callie led them up the stairs and onto the rooftop. Their table was laid with a crisp white cotton cloth and a tealight candle in a silver holder, flickering away. Ben did the gentlemanly thing and pulled the chair out for Katie before sitting down opposite her.

After they were handed the menus, Callie told them a waiter would be with them very soon to take their order. As soon as Callie disappeared down the stairs, Katie walked over to the balcony to take in the view.

'Just look at that. Who would ever think this place is tucked away in the middle of nowhere?'

Ben watched Katie as she stared out at the white chalky cliffs towering over the water and the spectacular waterfall trickling down into the bay. The summer sun made the water sparkle. It looked so pretty.

'This is the perfect backdrop for a first date. Poppy's loss is my gain,' she quipped, taking a sip of her drink.

'And the wisecracks just keep coming.'

'It's not a wisecrack.' Katie pretended to look hurt as she sat back down. 'Relax. You look so on edge. Shall I look at you all dreamy-eyed over the table and hold your hand?' She reached across the table and took Ben's hand. 'Are you wearing blusher?'

'I am not,' he replied, quickly removing his hand. It was the touch of Katie's hand sending the instant blush to his cheeks.

'What do you fancy?' asked Katie.

Ben swallowed.

'To eat,' she added, lightly shaking her head.

Trying to relax, Ben took the menu from her. 'Thank you.'

'And how lucky are we to be sat here together?' Katie's eyes sparkled as she caught his eye.

'It's like winning the lottery,' he said as a witty retort, but, deep down, there was a part of him that actually meant it. As much as they had previously had a love-hate relationship, Ben was still intrigued by her and knew the air was charged between them. Before the conversation could continue, the waiter appeared at their table.

'Shall we share a bottle of champagne?' suggested Katie.

'Champagne? Are we celebrating?'

'Of course we are! My welcome to Heartcross and the fact that we've been reunited after all these years.'

'Champagne it is then,' agreed Ben.

The waiter soon reappeared with the bottle of champagne standing in an ice bucket, which he positioned halfway between Ben and Katie before placing down two crystal flutes on the table.

'We'll open it, thank you,' said Katie. The waiter nodded his acknowledgement, then jotted down their food orders.

'Isn't this perfect?' asked Katie with the most gorgeous smile. She picked up the bottle and twisted the cork, which popped, then poured the fizzy liquid into Ben's flute. 'Perfect setting and perfect company.'

She held out his glass towards him and there it was again, that instant shiver as his fingers brushed against hers. He wondered if she felt it too. He could feel the air charged between them, the chemistry fizzing over just like the bubbles in the champagne. Her smile was warm and Ben felt nervous. He knew he was watching her closely, and he'd noticed how much more relaxed she seemed, which made him wonder about her life in the past few years.

'So, tell me about Swim Shady.'

Ben was puzzled. 'Swim Shady?'

'Your fish,' Katie prompted.

'My fish…that's right, my fish.' He quickly attempted to steer the conversation into another direction with a question that was burning inside him. 'I have to ask: what brought you to Heartcross?'

She bit down on her lip, amusement written all over her face. 'Nice swerve. You haven't got a fish, have you?' She waggled her glass at him. 'Which leads me to the question, what was Helly covering up when she was sneaking out of your apartment?'

Ben shifted in his seat. 'She wasn't sneaking.'

'Oh my God.' Katie's mouth dropped open. 'You and she are—'

'Of course not. That wouldn't be ethical, I'm her boss.'

'Okay, I believe you,' she said, keeping one eye on him and one on the waiter who'd appeared at their table with food. Katie wasn't letting Ben off the hook. 'Shall we go back to the fish then?'

'Let's not...let's go back to how you ended up here.' It was Ben's turn to keep one eye on Katie as he thanked the waiter and picked up his knife and fork.

Katie was playing him at his own game as she avoided the direct question and instead gestured to the food in front of her. 'This looks amazing!'

'Why Heartcross?'

'Why not Heartcross?'

'Did you know I was here? And to arrive on my birthday...'

Katie looked up and for a second pressed her lips together. 'Maybe...okay...yes.'

Ben gave her an incredulous stare. Taken by surprise at that revelation, he was secretly pleased and felt his heart beat a little faster.

'How?' he asked, intrigued.

Katie sat back in her chair. 'The national medical magazine. There was an article about Dr Taylor and his career, how he'd dedicated his whole life to working in this place and how he was going to miss the community. The way Heartcross was described was like something out of a fairy tale. Dr Taylor was in awe of this place – the scenery, the people, and after the last few years, I just wanted to be transported to a place like that. It's just what the doctor ordered.'

She looked sad, but before he could ask any more questions, Katie continued.

'And that's when I saw your name – his successor, Dr

Ben Sanders. I Googled the village and your photograph came up. It was strange to see you after all these years. I did think about you from time to time.'

Ben mirrored her actions, putting down his knife and fork and picking up his drink as she did so. They exchanged glances. Ben was mystified. Had Katie O'Neil just said she thought about him? He really wasn't expecting that. He'd done everything in his power to try and not think about her over the years, even though she had a habit of creeping back into his thoughts when he least expected it.

Ben swallowed, then bit the bullet. 'You've taken me completely by surprise,' he admitted. 'Our university days were spent battling with each other, pushing each other to the max... I didn't think you even liked me that much.'

Now it was Katie's turn to look a little bewildered. 'Of course I liked you. I wanted to be like you. How could anyone not like you?'

'You wanted to be like me? But you had everything, the brains and the beauty. You were the captain of most clubs and came from one of the most affluent families at the university.'

Katie slowly placed her glass on the table. 'No, you had everything. You were intelligent, handsome and it was you who had the perfect family... I have to say, though, your clothes were a little hit and miss. I often thought you'd be arrested by the fashion police. I admit I was jealous of who you were and what you had.'

Ben was amazed by what Katie was saying. Apart from

his outrageous fashion sense during his university days, he'd struggled with his family situation for as long as he could remember, though he hadn't confided in anyone about it. At school, Ben had been the shy type. In the early years, his curly hair had attracted unwanted attention from the other boys and as he grew older, he learnt that he was adopted and didn't look like his parents. He towered above his father, who was a small man and lost his hair at an early age. His mother was of a slim build and had carrot-coloured hair, which complemented her green eyes.

He was an only child and, with older parents who were very protective of him, Ben found it difficult to make friendships with the other children. He was never allowed to go to the park or hang out after dark and he moved further and further away from his peers at school. Their protective ways stifled Ben. He spent a lot of playtimes finding jobs to help the teachers and taking himself away from playground mockery. High school hadn't been much different, either. He'd spent a lot of time in the library and biology labs, which confirmed his interest in becoming a doctor.

Ben wanted to say something but didn't. He swallowed as he became emotional.

'What is it?' she asked tentatively, reaching across for his hand. 'A problem shared.'

This was the first time these words had ever left his mouth, but for some reason, the moment seemed right.

'Katie, I've struggled with who I am for most of my life.'

Finally, the words were out in the open. Even though he felt a twinge of disloyalty to his adoptive parents, Ben felt a huge weight had been lifted off his shoulders.

For a moment, Katie was speechless. 'I wasn't expecting that. Have you ever spoken about this before?'

Ben shook his head. 'So you see, I find it difficult when you say you were jealous of me. You were the one with everything.'

They were staring at each other as Katie moved her hand from the top of his to entwine their fingers together.

'What exactly are you struggling with?'

'Not knowing where I belong,' he admitted. 'Or who exactly I am. I know I'm adopted, but my parents would never talk about it. I didn't have any siblings and found it difficult to form relationships, make friends. But since arriving here, I've put everything into my new life at Heartcross. I fitted in straight away. The whole community welcomed me. I've never felt anything like it before and it's giving me renewed strength...'

'Renewed strength?'

'To take the plunge. Helly's birthday present...the DNA test. I've thought about it for years. I've been torn. Could I cope with being rejected again? I know that sounds daft at my age. I'm petrified yet excited to see what it brings up.'

Katie listened. 'It doesn't sound daft. There's nothing to say you were rejected in the first place if you don't know the circumstances of your adoption. Whatever that test brings up, we can get through it.'

Ben noticed the word 'we', which made him feel a little better about the situation and Katie was right: Ben didn't know. He had no clue why he'd been given up for adoption as a baby. All he knew was that his adoptive parents shied away from telling him the truth, so he could only assume that they didn't want him to be hurt anymore.

'Sometimes when people seem to have the perfect family, they don't.'

Ben thought it sounded like Katie was talking from experience.

'People are rejected by their real families and that hurts just as much,' she added with a tear in her eye. 'We all have ways of masking our own insecurities and sometimes all we want is the perfect family relationships that are portrayed in the movies. Most of us learn those relationships are far and few between.'

'Your insecurities?' questioned Ben, releasing her hand and filling up both glasses with more champagne.

He would never in a million years have thought that that anything would ever faze Katie. She was confident, beautiful and intelligent to boot. In all the time he'd known her, there seemed to be nothing insecure about her.

She sat back in her chair and glanced over to the balcony at the beautiful scenery before looking back at Ben. 'I threw myself into medical school and, believe me, my family life wasn't much fun for me either. I know I need to apologise to you. I know we were super competitive and pushing each other to achieve. Things did get out of hand on many occasions and I'm sorry. Please will you accept my apology?'

This was a night of firsts. He'd opened up and now Katie was doing the same with an apology. Ben was taken aback but of course he was going to accept it. Katie was mellow and sincere. He wondered what she meant about her family life. He wanted to ask more.

'Of course I accept your apology. Anything for an easy life. After all, we still have to work together.' He gave her a lopsided smile.

Even though Katie shook her head and laughed, Ben knew there was more. He could see a sadness in her eyes.

'Tell me about your family life,' he said softly.

'I've learnt their opinion of me doesn't matter.'

'Are you talking about anyone in particular?'

Katie's body language had changed; she'd bristled. 'My parents.'

Ben wasn't expecting that. He knew Katie's family was affluent. He could remember her turning up at university in a brand-new Audi convertible, which must have cost an arm and a leg, whilst he owned a battered old blue Ford Fiesta that he had picked up from a car auction for next to nothing. It was a car he'd nicknamed Baby Spice back in the day and a car he still proudly owned. She always had the latest technology, phone and laptop and her wardrobe reminded him of a fashion icon. It was rare to see Katie in the same outfit twice.

'I was always the black sheep of the family, the

underachiever – the one who was frowned upon if I didn't get top marks on essays at school.'

Ben was amazed to hear this. 'How were you ever an underachiever?'

'I have a confession to make.' She took a breath. 'You think I aced every paper, every exam with no help. You thought I had natural intelligence and that I didn't have to put in any effort.'

'And didn't you?'

Katie shook her head. 'I was the youngest of my siblings. They were the ones who aced everything. I was always told I must try harder, asked why couldn't I grasp simple concepts. When you thought I was out at glamorous parties or being the It-girl about town, I was working in the city taxi rank at all hours of the night.'

Ben's jaw fell open. 'You are kidding me, aren't you? Why would you need to do that?'

Katie was shaking her head. 'I needed the money to pay for tutors to help me pass my exams. My parents were doctors, my brothers and my upbringing were strict, and it was expected that we all flourish in our careers. When I expressed an interest, when I wanted to take art, can you imagine the look of horror on their faces? There was a family outcry. It was just easier to go along with what they wanted. I couldn't admit to them I was struggling or finding the work difficult. I wanted them to be proud of me, but I always felt they favoured my brothers. So, you see, it didn't come easy to me. Maybe because I felt bad about myself, I teased you and pushed you harder to make myself feel better.'

Ben was astounded to hear this. 'I don't know what to say.'

'It wasn't an option for me to not get the grades.'

'How is your relationship with your parents now?'

'Non-existent, but that's a story for another day. All my hard work in wanting them to be proud of me, to like me for me, was wasted. It takes a certain situation to make you realise the only person you can ever rely on in life is yourself.'

Her voice faltered and she didn't elaborate. His gut feeling was there was more to this story, but he didn't want to push Katie any further. This was the first time she'd ever let down her guard in his presence and he was starting to see a side to her he quite liked – a vulnerable side. She was leaving herself wide open, but it made Ben wonder how her parents had let her down. Even though he didn't feel particularly close to his adoptive parents, they'd loved him and encouraged him to do his best and to be whatever he wanted. If anything, the way they were a little overprotective of him was probably just down to him being an only child.

Katie extended a hand over the table. 'Truce?'

'Truce, but with one condition,' replied Ben.

'You aren't having your old office back,' she quickly fired back with a glint in her eye.

Ben laughed. 'You can have the office, but how about,

even though we both know the boat race is going to be a little competitive, let's not push each other to the max or go sabotaging anyone's boat.'

'I didn't sabotage anyone's boat; you were just unlucky.' Katie was quick to object.

'Mmm, and how did that video get uploaded, I wonder?'

'Honestly, it wasn't me, but I'll shake to all is fair in love and rowing for the next race.'

Ben shook her hand and caught her eye. Once again, there was that tingly feeling. His pulse quickened and goose bumps rose to the surface of his skin.

'So, you thought about me from time to time, did you?' Ben wondered if she meant the night that they had spent together. He wanted to ask why she'd given him the cold shoulder afterwards and he knew he had a silly grin on his face when he asked the question.

The eye contact between them was strong. He stretched out his leg, which brushed against hers. The connection between them was strong and Ben liked it.

'I may have,' she said, beaming, not giving anymore away.

'Let's have a toast – to a blossoming new friendship.'

Katie grinned and tilted her head to one side, 'Friendship,' she repeated, holding her glass towards his then taking a sip of her champagne. 'But just so you know…'

Ben wondered what she was about to say next as her eyes twinkled.

'There is no way on earth that you are going to win the boat race.'

'There she is, the real Katie is back,' he said, leaning forward in his chair and folding his arms on the table. 'And I'll tell you now – there is no way I'm going to lose.'

She gave him the tenderest of smiles. 'Whatever!'

Ben was breaking down her barriers. He was secretly pleased that his date had stood him up. Feeling a presence at their side, he looked up to see an elderly couple hovering at their table.

'Please forgive me for interrupting your dinner, but can I just say what a lovely couple you make. You two look adorable together,' the woman said.

'Aww thank you,' replied Katie, giving Ben a gentle kick under the table.

'It was our golden anniversary last week,' continued the woman, 'and you just reminded me of me and my Bert all those years ago. I used to look at him in that way too. The first flush of love is so special. Hold onto it. Always make time for each other no matter how busy your lives become – that is the secret – and, of course, laughter.'

'Congratulations and if we are half as happy as you two look after all this time, then we will be so lucky, won't we, darling?' Katie looked over at Ben, then reached across the table and gave his hand a squeeze.

'Absolutely,' Ben replied, noticing the mischievous glint in Katie's eye.

Katie turned back towards the couple. 'You've made our day. The perfect end to our perfect date.'

The woman gave a little chuckle as she linked her arm through her husband's and they walked to the steps, taking them down to the main restaurant.

As soon as they were out of sight, Katie put her hands on her heart. 'Aww they think we are together, how adorable was that?'

'Adorable,' replied Ben, wondering what it would be like to date Katie. 'Shall we get the bill?' He waved the waiter over. 'I'll get this. Thank you for rescuing me, otherwise I would have been sitting here eating all by myself.'

'We couldn't have had that now, could we?'

Once the bill was paid, they ambled down to the water taxi and stepped on board. Ben followed Katie towards the open viewing area at the back of the boat and stood beside her. It was only a matter of minutes before the engines started and Roman steered the boat out of the jetty. They watched the beautiful bay disappear behind them as the boat joined the main river.

With the wind in her hair, Katie leant on the rail and took in her surroundings. Her eyes were fixed firmly on the water, but then she looked sideward and smiled at Ben. 'And just for the record, I never did think you were Mr Average.' She bumped her shoulder playfully against his.

They looked out across the river and, as the boat hit a choppy part of the water, Katie jumped. 'Eek, my stomach literally flipped!' She steadied herself and held onto the rail. 'I'm actually feeling a little queasy.' She swayed again and Ben noticed her face had paled.

'Try not to focus on the water. Tilt your face up towards the breeze.' He stood behind her and stretched out his arms, holding the rail on either side of her.

Katie looked over her shoulder and leant back into him. 'Thank you.'

He knew his heart was beating fast and hoped she couldn't hear it. Feeling her so close to him, Ben's whole body was trembling. Katie stayed snuggled into his chest until the boat sailed into the jetty.

'Are you feeling any better now?' he asked, stepping back.

'I will be once I'm back on land. You'd think I'd be used to boats,' she joked.

'I think it's a little different when you aren't in control of them.'

They thanked Roman as they stepped onto dry land and followed the line of diners who ambled down the river path back towards the village. Ben had to admit Katie had taken him by surprise tonight, and he'd enjoyed every second of her company. He had a feeling life was going to become a little more interesting with Katie around. He stole a furtive glance in her direction as they walked down the high street. She was grinning back at him.

'Why are you smiling at me?' he asked.

'Just because,' she replied.

Reaching the end of the high street, Ben sniffed the air. He noticed a strong smell of burning, then pointed towards Stuart's cottage. 'Stuart must be burning some rubbish in the garden.' But then something caught his eye and he stopped dead in his tracks. There was a flash of light. It was flames. 'Christ! The cottage is actually on fire.'

Katie gave Ben a grief-stricken look. 'There's smoke coming out of the bedroom window.'

They took off and sprinted down the road with Ben dialling the emergency services from his phone. Running up the garden path, Ben was calling out Stuart and Alana's names at the top of his voice. There was no sign of anyone. He raced towards the front door, but it was locked. Then they both ran around the back of the cottage to try and find an open window, but no luck.

'Are they in there? What if they're trapped? We need to get in.' Katie was frantically rattling the back door, but it was firmly shut.

'The fire engine is on the way,' said Ben, hearing voices shouting from the street. He ran back round to the front of the cottage where people had begun to gather. He turned back towards Katie, but she was no longer behind him.

'Katie!' he bellowed but there was no answer. He ran to the back door but she was nowhere to be seen. The window next to the door had been smashed and the door was wide open.

It was at that second that Ben knew Katie had entered the burning building.

'Katie!' he screamed at the top of his voice. 'KATIE!' but there was no answer.

'Ben!' He swung round to see Helly, who started to pull at his arm. 'Do not go inside. The fire engine will be here soon.'

'I can't leave her in there.' Ben tried to pull away from Helly's grip.

'Don't be stupid,' she exclaimed. 'Ben!'

A plume of fire exploded into the sky from the already-shattered upstairs window. Ben was praying with all his might that somehow, just somehow, everyone inside was okay. Pain and uncertainty gripped his stomach as Helly tugged at his arm. 'Come on, it's safer round the front.'

Ben was rooted to the spot.

'Ben! Now!' ordered Helly with authority.

The heat was immense; an inferno fuelled by the furniture inside. The glowing embers swirled in the air, the sky illuminated and ash floated to the ground like dirty flakes of snow.

Ben's eyes were glued to the windows, frantically switching from one to the other, hoping for any signs of life. His face crumpled, the colour draining as Helly successfully guided him back to the street.

'Where the hell is the fire engine?' Ben shouted.

Standing helpless, the villagers watched in horror as the fire continued to rage. Ben began to pace up and down, raking his hand through his hair. Another explosion punched a fist of orange flames, causing the other upstairs window to blow out. The eerie gasps and cries of the villagers were drowned out by the sound of the fire engine's siren, which was thankfully heading towards them at top speed.

To Ben, it felt like Katie had been gone hours, but it had only been a matter of minutes. The sirens stopped as the fire engine came to a halt right outside the cottage. The firefighters jumped out of the cab, their boots thudding on the ground as they quickly guided the spectators to the far side of the road.

'Is there anyone in the property?' asked the fireman.

'Yes, Katie.'

'Wife?' asked the fireman.

'No, work colleague, Dr Katie O'Neil, but we have no idea if Stuart and Alana are in there too. They live here.'

The fireman nodded. 'We've been called out to this property a few times recently.'

'Alana has dementia,' replied Ben, his eyes firmly fixed on the cottage. 'Just be okay, please be okay,' he mumbled under his breath. He prayed with all his heart she'd be okay, in that moment Ben knew he still very much cared about her.

'Get back,' ordered the firefighter as more spectators spilled out from the pub onto the street. The cottage continued to crackle and spit flames. Ben and Helly watched, helpless, as the firefighters entered the property.

'Where are Stuart and Alana? Has anyone tried to contact Rory?' Meredith dialled her daughter, but Allie didn't pick up. She dialled Rory's phone next.

'Rory, thank God, it's Meredith. Are Stuart and Alana with you?' Meredith was flapping her hand frantically in front of her face with relief. 'Stuart and Alana are not inside! They're with Rory on the Clover Cottage estate!' bellowed Meredith.

'Which means Katie entered the building for no reason,' said Ben, turning towards Helly, who held onto his arm tightly.

'They're bringing someone out,' shouted a voice from the back of the crowd.

'Katie!' shouted Ben.

She was over the fireman's shoulder. He carefully manoeuvred her away from the burning cottage to the back of the waiting ambulance. Ben was quick to follow. He felt sick to his stomach and helpless, but thankful she was out of the cottage. He was shaking and one of the paramedics checked if he was okay before asking him about Katie.

'Do you know her name?' asked the paramedic.

'Katie,' replied Ben. 'Katie O'Neil.'

'Are you a relative?'

Ben shook his head. 'A work colleague over at Peony Practice.' His stomach was twisting in knots as he watched them place an oxygen mask over her face.

'We need to take her to hospital.'

'Can I come with you?' asked Ben.

The paramedic nodded. 'Of course.'

Ben climbed into the ambulance.

'She's in the best possible hands. Don't worry,' Helly said.

As the ambulance prepared to leave, Ben spotted Allie and Rory running down the road. Stuart was hurrying behind, holding onto Alana's hand. This was going to be pure devastation for them. Ben had no idea what had started the fire, but he knew their whole life had just gone up in smoke.

Ben shouted to Helly. 'Open up the surgery in case people need a place to gather. Make tea.'

Helly nodded her understanding.

Katie was still unconscious as Ben reached for her hand. The ambulance door slammed shut and they sped off towards the hospital, sirens blaring.

Chapter Nine

As soon as the ambulance reached the hospital, Ben was left in the waiting room whilst Katie was whisked off down the corridor and out of sight. Ben knew that Katie had inhaled a lot of smoke; the stench of it was potent. He seated himself on a red plastic chair and flicked open the WhatsApp group, which was manic with messages, but he noticed that Helly had taken control and opened the surgery waiting room. Ben cupped his hands around a warm polystyrene cup of tea and waited for Katie to reappear.

Katie had looked lifeless. He couldn't believe one minute they'd been sharing a meal at The Lake House and the next, she'd disappeared inside a burning building without a thought for her own life. He would do anything to swap places with her at this moment in time. The waiting seemed to take ages, but it also felt like time had stood still. His stomach churned as the waiting room door opened and he met the eyes of the doctor who smiled warmly.

'Katie's awake if you would like to see her?'

Ben didn't need asking twice. He was instantly up on his feet and walking down the corridor by the doctor's side.

'Katie has suffered a nasty blow to the head. She's had a couple of stitches and suffered burns to her hand, but nothing serious. She's also inhaled a lot of smoke, but she's going to be just fine.'

Ben was relieved. 'She'll do anything to get out of work,' he quipped, trying to make light of the situation.

'Running into a burning cottage is one way to try and get out of morning surgery. As you already know, we need to keep her in for twenty-four hours as a precautionary measure. Katie's through there.'

Ben walked into the room; his face broke into a beam when he saw Katie smiling back at him.

'What are you trying to do to me? You nearly gave me a heart attack. One minute you were behind me and the next, you were gone.'

Katie's eyes glistened with tears. Ben noticed that, despite the streaks of black soot across her face, she looked pale. There was a bandage wrapped around her head and she was hooked up to a heart monitoring machine. He sat on the chair at the side of the bed.

'I'm sorry,' she said in a hoarse whisper. 'I can't stop crying.'

'It's the shock,' replied Ben, resting his hand on top of hers.

'Did they find Stuart and Alana?' Katie's eyes were wide as she waited for Ben's answer.

'They weren't in the house. They were over at the Clover Cottage estate with Rory and Allie. The house was empty.'

Katie exhaled. 'Thank God,' she replied, then began to cough.

Ben poured her a drink of water from the jug on the bedside table and handed it to her. 'I thought there must have been someone in there. I shouted but no one answered. I figured they must be trapped upstairs but couldn't hear me.'

'You could have been killed, and, for what it's worth, I don't like that thought.'

Katie smiled at him. 'Well that is nice to hear, but I'm sure it's just because it would double your workload.'

'Funnily enough, even though you are a complete pain in the backside, I've kind of already got used to having you around. How did you hurt your head? Can you remember anything?'

'I was convinced Alana must be trapped upstairs. I checked all the downstairs rooms, but there was no one there. The smoke was beginning to make me feel light-headed, so I grabbed a jumper that was hanging on a hook and held it over my mouth as I ran to the bottom of the stairs. I shouted and shouted but I couldn't hear anyone. I assumed Alana had passed out from the smoke inhalation. The fire must have started upstairs – the flames were getting worse and the heat immense. I could see the bedroom door was shut and the sirens were blaring in the distance. Then there was a loud creak and a shower of sparks as the bannister became engulfed in flames. Then something hit me on the head, but I've no idea what it was.' Katie gave a fragile smile. 'But thank God Stuart and Alana weren't home.' Katie held her throat as she spoke.

A nurse entered the room. 'How's the sickness?'

'I still feel nauseous,' Katie replied, taking a small plastic cup from her with a tablet in it.

'As you know, this will help. Take the tablet with water,' said the nurse. 'How's your head?'

'Sore. I feel exhausted.'

'I'll be back in a second to take your observations and then you must rest.'

Katie nodded, swallowing the tablet, her eyes began to droop.

'I'll let you sleep. I'll go check on Stuart and Alana, then pop back later or after surgery in the morning.'

But there was no answer from Katie. Her eyes were closed and she'd already fallen asleep.

Ben stood up and watched her for a second. She looked so fragile laying in the bed with her charred face. Without thinking, Ben planted a soft kiss on the top of her head. He knew that Stuart and Alana had most probably lost everything, but he couldn't help thinking he could have lost

Katie. He knew she'd only just come back into his life, but he didn't like the thought of that at all.

With Katie sleeping it gave him chance to go home and see what the damage was to Stuart and Alana's cottage. This would be a devastating blow and even though he knew that they would move in with Allie and Rory, a change in routine for Alana might confuse her more.

Making his way quietly to the door, he stopped by the chart that was hanging on the end of her bed. It was a natural instinct to pick it up. Her name was written on the front with her date of birth and address. The next piece of information caught him off-guard, though, his chest heaving at the words staring back at him.

Next of Kin – Oliver Green – Husband.

Ben stared at the file as he placed it back on the bed. Husband? Since when had Katie got a husband and why hadn't she mentioned it? His eyes flicked towards her; she was still asleep. His heart slumped – Katie was married. Ben was momentarily thrown and looked at the sheet of paper again. He felt like he was riding the weirdest roller coaster today; his emotions were all over the place.

He honestly thought they'd connected during the meal at The Lake House and had felt a closeness to her on the boat trip home. It didn't make sense. He had so many questions he wanted to ask her. Ben knew he couldn't let it lie. They'd flirted over dinner, she made his stomach flip when he was close to her and his heart kept racing. But according to this, Katie had a husband.

Maybe there was a simple explanation – they'd separated, perhaps, but surely she would still have mentioned it. As he walked out the door, he looked back at her. His thoughts turned back to the morning when he'd seen her get out of the car with a man outside the surgery. Katie hadn't been truthful with him, claiming she'd only just woken up, so what was it she was hiding? Where was her husband now? It was possible he was on his way to her. Ben knew he shouldn't have gone snooping in her file, but he had, which had him wondering all about Katie's personal life.

Chapter Ten

Ben walked sullenly towards the taxi rank and, five minutes later, he was travelling over the bridge from Glensheil Hospital back into Heartcross. Lost in thought, Katie and his discovery of her husband was very much on his mind as the taxi travelled along the high street. Ben asked the taxi driver to pull up and after he paid for his fare, he stepped onto the pavement and noticed the smell of burning still lingered. The cottage looked like it had been in the wars, and he noticed Drew and Fergus busily boarding up the blown-out windows.

'How's Katie?' shouted Fergus across the street, noticing Ben walking towards them.

'A few cuts and bruises and smoke inhalation. They are keeping her in for observation.'

'And how are you?' asked Drew, climbing down the ladder and walking towards him.

'Me? I'm fine.' Ben managed a fragile smile. He wouldn't admit that when he realised Katie had disappeared inside a burning building, he was terrified. 'This is a mess, isn't it? Do we know what caused the fire?'

Drew shook his head. 'There will be an investigation, but from what the firemen said, it's possible the fire started in the bedroom. Thankfully Stuart and Alana were out. We are going to wait until tomorrow to take a proper look but in the meantime, we'll get these windows boarded up.'

'Helly was fantastic. She opened up the surgery and provided everyone with tea and coffee to help with the initial shock,' added Fergus. 'Stuart and Alana are staying with Rory and Allie.'

Ben looked at his watch. 'I'll pop in and see them tomorrow. All I want to do now is grab a drink, get out of these clothes and get some sleep.'

Drew patted Ben on the back. 'Sounds like a plan.'

Once inside, Ben threw his keys onto the table. It was strange to hear the silence in the flat next door. Even though Katie hadn't been there long, he'd got used to hearing the TV or songs from the radio playing out during the last week. After making a cup of tea, he opened up his laptop and the first thing he did was google Katie O'Neil. Immediately, it threw up that she was an ambassador for the dementia charity. It was commendable the amount of fund-raising she did for them. But Ben couldn't find any social media for Katie – absolutely nothing.

Closing his laptop, Ben lay down on the sofa. It had

been a hell of a night, but all that was whirling around in his mind was that Katie had a husband. He knew he shouldn't have been snooping, but since reading that name, his thoughts had been consumed by it and had caused a slump in his mood. He cared for her and felt a strong connection to her, but Ben was fully aware he couldn't let those feelings escalate. If that happened, there was a possibility he was the one that was going to end up hurt.

The next day, Ben was awake early. He'd tossed and turned all night with Katie very much on his mind. Feeling tired, he climbed out of bed and, after making a strong coffee, he got himself ready for work. Then he phoned the hospital to check if Katie had had a comfortable night.

'Katie's checked herself out?' Ben was perplexed. Why would she do that? He hung up the phone and pressed his ear against the wall. He could hear the sound coming from the TV in her flat.

Within seconds, he was knocking on her door and a tired-looking Katie opened it.

'What are you doing here? You should be resting.'

'I'm okay. I just couldn't lie there any longer and I need to get ready for work.'

Ben gave a strangled laugh. 'Work? There is no way you are coming into work today. You've just been rescued from a fire. What are you thinking?'

'I'm thinking I need to keep busy. I need to come to work.' Katie sounded adamant.

Ben blew out a breath. 'Katie, as much as you wanting to come into work is commendable, you are staying here. I mean it. You need to rest. You look exhausted and there are bandages on your head and your hands. Whatever were you thinking checking yourself out of the hospital?'

'I couldn't lie there anymore… I could just do some admin work. I just need to keep busy…'

'Rest is what you need, not keeping busy and that's an order.'

She looked up at him, eyes brimming with tears, but she didn't say anymore.

'Are you still feeling emotional after what's happened? It's understandable.'

'It's not that,' she replied.

'A problem shared.' He touched her arm, but she still wasn't forthcoming. 'Whatever it is, I'm always here.'

She nodded. 'Thanks, Ben. That means a lot.'

'But you are still not coming into work today.'

'Okay,' she said, giving in. 'But I've not got any food in.'

'I'll grab you some lunch and will send Helly on a breakfast run, but you have to promise me you will rest. Have you got anyone to stay with you?'

Ben looked over her shoulder. He knew exactly why he'd asked that question. Katie had just been through a traumatic experience, so where was her husband in all this?

'No one,' replied Katie, her voice faltering.

'Okay, I'll check in with you at lunchtime.'

After Katie shut the door, he made his way down the stairs to the office. Helly was already sitting behind her desk, beavering away.

'How's the patient?' asked Helly, looking up from the computer.

'Stubborn. She discharged herself from hospital and thinks she's coming into work.'

Helly raised an eyebrow. 'Katie discharged herself? Why would she do that?'

Ben shrugged, then pulled ten pounds out of his wallet and held it up in the air. 'I've no idea, but the breakfast run is on me. Can you get Katie her usual?'

'The boss buying breakfast. Are you sure it's not you that's had a bash over the head?' teased Helly, standing up and slipping her arms into her jacket.

Before Ben could say anything, Helly had whipped the tenner from his hand and was already through the door as the office phone began to ring out. It was a rule to let the answerphone pick up any calls before nine o'clock, but, without thinking, Ben reached across the desk and answered.

'Could I speak to Dr Ben Sanders or Dr Katie O'Neil, please?' asked the voice on the other end of the line.

'Dr Ben Sanders speaking.'

The woman explained she was from the radio station and had just heard about the up-and-coming boat race. She wanted to invite Ben and Katie onto the show to chat about it. Without hesitation, Ben accepted. The date of the show was the morning of the medical school reunion, which would fit in perfectly. He could share the details with Katie at lunchtime.

By the time lunchtime had arrived, Ben had been run off his feet. He'd already got used to Katie being around to share the load. As the last patient left the surgery, Ben was up and out of the office, taking full advantage of his lunch hour. After grabbing food from Bonnie's teashop, he knocked on Katie's front door and waited.

It only took a moment before she answered, looking glum. 'I want to know how is it people stay at home and watch daytime TV and think it's the best thing in the world? It would drive me out of the house to go and get a job. It's driving me insane. I'm so bored.'

Ben gave a chuckle and held up her lunch in a carrier bag. 'Quiche, salad and a slice of Rona's chocolate flapjack.'

'And flowers? You've bought me flowers. I can't remember the last time someone bought me flowers.' Katie gratefully took them from Ben.

'Don't get too excited. They didn't break the bank...it was a grand total of four pounds, but that's all that Hamish had left outside the village shop.'

'You're a keeper, aren't you?' She chuckled.

It was the first time Ben had been inside Katie's flat and it was a burst of colour with its pink floral plush cushions that matched her curtains. It was very homely with pictures on the wall and trailing plants from the bookshelves. Ben immediately noticed the spines of the books were colour co-ordinated.

'This is definitely a girly flat,' he observed. 'Lots of flowery colourful things.'

'Funny that – being a girl,' came Katie's sarcastic reply.

He swung a glance towards the pristine kitchen, which didn't resemble his kitchen at all. He suddenly felt ashamed of last night's dishes left in the sink; he'd been too lazy to stack them in the dishwasher. Katie's kitchen was clutter-free and her appliances colour coordinated with the window blind. Not to mention the floral canisters that were similar to the ones Helly had put in the surgery kitchen.

'Unlike yours, which is grey...grey and oh let's colour coordinate even more grey.'

'Oi, cheeky, how would you know that? I like grey,' replied Ben, pretending to look offended. He had to admit his flat was sterile and clinical compared to Katie's, though.

'Just a good guess.' Katie was grinning as she retrieved a couple of plates, knives and forks from the kitchen.

When she returned, Ben was sitting on the settee and holding up a knitting needle.

'Thank God I spotted this before I sat down.' Ben hadn't seen a knitting needle in years, but it was something his granny from Ireland often did. He remembered the multi-coloured jumper she'd once knitted him for Christmas with a huge hole under his arm. The sleeves were different lengths and he had struggled to get his head through the neck hole. But of course, he wore it all Christmas day just to please her.

'What are you making?' he asked, opening the carrier bag and passing Katie a white polystyrene box. They transferred their lunch to the plates.

'Blankets for the care home. When the elderly are watching TV, they can throw a blanket over their knees to keep themselves warm. Shawls too.' Katie pointed to the pile over in the corner. 'I always make sure I have a good pile before I send them off. It doesn't hurt to give back but today's attempt proved a little difficult with these bandages on my hands.'

Ben looked at Katie with such admiration. She was surprising him more and more.

'It was something I learnt to do...' She stopped in her tracks. 'A little while back.'

'Well, I'm impressed,' he said. 'Talking of giving back, we've been invited to talk about the boat race on the radio. It happens to be the morning of the university reunion, so I was thinking, like you suggested, we could travel together. We'd take part in the radio interview then continue to the reunion. I need to book the hotel as no doubt it'll be busy and I won't be driving back. Would you like me to book you a room too?'

'Sounds perfect,' said Katie, tucking straight into the chocolate flapjack first.

'Do you know you're eating your lunch the wrong way round?' Ben pointed at the quiche and the salad.

'Funnily enough, it's the joys of being an adult. I can do what I want! This is good.' She waved the rest of the flapjack in the air before popping it into her mouth.

'Double bed or single bed?' asked Ben, flicking onto his phone.

'Double would be great.'

'Will you be going on your own?' he asked.

'I thought we were travelling together?' She looked over to him.

'No, I mean is the room just for you?'

'Yes, just me.' She narrowed her eyes at him.

'I just thought you might be sharing a room.' Of course he was thinking about the name he'd seen on the notes at the hospital – where was Oliver Green?

'That's the thing about you. It's better if you don't think. But I do need to talk to you. I just want to come back to work.'

'Katie! You are not coming back until next week. Make the most of it.'

'But I feel okay,' she spluttered, beginning to cough.

'And that's your body telling you not to argue with me as I know best.' He wagged his finger at her. 'And don't you dare say you know better than me on this occasion.'

'Okay.' She held her hands up. 'But I'm back to work on Monday and if I can't come into the office before then, I'll work on my rowing strategy.'

'Rest. The boat race is meant to be a leisurely sail down

the river,' Ben replied, hoping he could convince Katie to loosen up on the competition. No such luck.

She scoffed. 'I may have inhaled a fair bit of smoke, but I don't have brain damage. I'm going to give it my all and cross that line before you and your team.' She nodded towards the bedroom.

'Are you offering to take me to bed? Because I've already said you need to rest,' he joked.

'Don't be so bloody daft,' she replied, grinning.

'I'm not sure if I'm offended now!'

Katie rolled her eyes. 'Go and take a look.'

Sceptically, Ben stood up and walked to the bedroom door, which was ajar. He took a look inside the room and then turned back towards Katie. 'Wow, you really are serious, aren't you?'

'I don't like losing at anything.'

'But that's some extreme just to win a charity boat race.'

In the middle of the room was a high-tech rowing machine that was hooked up to a TV.

'That machine lets you navigate any river in the UK.'

'You are absolutely bonkers,' he replied, totally flabbergasted. 'Your hands are bandaged.'

'And you think that's going to stop me? This week when you are working your socks off, I'm going to be rowing in the safety of my own home.'

'It may be worth letting you back into work.'

Playfully, she threw a cushion at him. 'You can't go changing your mind now.'

'I'm not. You row all you like but you are still not coming back to work until next week.'

After finishing his lunch, Ben placed the empty plates on the table. 'Is it okay to use your bathroom?'

'Just through there. It's the same layout as your apartment.'

Ben disappeared off towards the bathroom. He assumed Katie's bedroom must be the one before the bathroom if she'd set up the spare room as a tribute to Steve Redgrave. He thought about what Katie had told him over dinner about her parents; maybe she was still trying to be liked by going to extreme lengths to win. Her door to her bedroom was open and as he walked past, Ben didn't mean to stop and stare, but of course he did. The bed was made up with a ditsy pink ruffled bedspread and matching curtains. With plush pillows on the bed and a vibrant rug, there didn't seem to be any sign of a husband.

As he shut the bathroom door, Ben observed numerous creams and lotions scattered around the bathroom and only one toothbrush. Maybe Katie was separated from her husband, or maybe he was away on business, but then his thoughts turned to the man he'd seen her with on her day off. Maybe that was him. It wasn't unusual for high-flying career people to be living in different towns. Anything was possible in this modern world. He thought about asking her outright, but then he would have to admit to looking at her notes whilst she was in hospital. He didn't know how Katie would react to that. He decided it was best not to considering the ordeal she had just been through.

Back in the living room, Katie had her feet up on the coffee table and the TV was switched on. She was flicking through the channels and blew out a breath, then tapped her watch.

'You need to go back to work. No rest for the wicked.'

Ben smiled. 'And your plans for this afternoon?'

'Absolutely nothing, but I do need a shower.'

She sniffed at her T-shirt. 'I can still smell smoke. Can you smell smoke?' she asked, pulling her T-shirt out towards him.

'It smells like you need a shower,' he said, wrinkling up his nose. 'Right, I best go. Shout if you need anything.'

'That I will and thank you for my lunch.'

Ben shut the front door behind him and as he walked down the stairs, he was greeted by a luxurious bouquet expertly handcrafted with the finest flowers and a large pink ribbon which put his four-pound flowers to shame. He stepped to one side to let the man carrying them walk past. Ben recognised him. He was the same man he'd seen with Katie.

'Wow! Someone is a lucky lady,' remarked Ben, catching the man's attention.

'She's definitely worth it.' The man gave a smile and went to carry on walking.

There were only two apartments at the top of the stairs

and one was his, so Ben knew exactly where the man was heading.

'Can I help you?' asked Ben, giving a smile.

'No, it's okay. I know where I'm going, thank you.'

The waft of expensive aftershave didn't go unnoticed either and now he was standing outside Katie's door. There was no denying Ben felt a little wave of jealousy. He watched the man knock on the door and within seconds, it swung open.

'Oh my gosh, look at these. They are stunning!' Katie's voice rose an octave, then she gasped. 'I love them. Absolutely love them! They smell gorgeous.' The excitement in her voice echoed down the stairwell.

'I leave you alone for a couple of days and it's another fine mess you've gone and got yourself into,' said the man.

They hooted with laughter and their voices petered out as the front door shut behind them. Ben knew he had no right to feel jealous, but he did – he couldn't help himself. Katie was creeping into his thoughts more and more and he knew his feelings were becoming stronger because he couldn't stop thinking about her. She was the first thing he thought of when he woke up in the morning and the last thing on his mind when he went to bed. If he wasn't careful, his heart was going to be in a mess. Feeling miserable, he questioned why life couldn't be straightforward.

'What's up with you? You look kind of deflated. Katie's okay, isn't she? Did she like the flowers?' Helly's fingers were poised on the keyboard as she waited for Ben to answer.

'I'm fine. Yes, Katie is fine. More than fine.'

Helly gave him a doubtful look. 'So everyone is fine… glad we've established that. More than fine? She just ran into a burning building with the intention to rescue whoever was trapped inside. I'm not sure anyone would be more than fine.'

'She'll be back to work next week.' Ben swallowed hard. 'Has she ever mentioned much about her private life to you?'

Helly shook her head. 'No, not really. Why do you ask?'

'No reason. So she doesn't have a…'

Helly scrunched up her features. 'Doesn't have a what?'

'Nothing, honestly, it doesn't matter.' As much as Ben looked at Helly as a friend as well as a damn good receptionist, it wouldn't be right to go discussing Katie's private life with her. They needed to maintain some professionalism.

Helly must have sensed that she shouldn't push the conversation further. She slid back her chair. 'I'll make you a cup of coffee. A caffeine boost should help cheer up your mood.'

'I am cheery,' objected Ben.

'Well, if this is cheery…and I forgot to ask, how did your date go?'

'Date?' The first thing that popped into his mind was his dinner with Katie.

'Yes, Poppy, the girl from the dating app,' replied Helly, jogging his memory.

Being stood up was less than twenty-four hours ago and already seemed like a distant memory. 'She was a no-show, but you know what? I think going out more is just what I need.'

'If I were you, I'd drop her a message. You have nothing to lose.'

'You're right, I haven't.' And if it helped Ben stop thinking about Katie, it could be a welcome distraction.

Ben shut the office door behind him and pulled out his phone as he stared at Poppy's message. It seemed she had a legit reason for cancelling at the last minute. Ben pondered for a moment and was about to click on the message, but stopped himself. Would it be fair of him to instigate a date knowing his heart wasn't in it at the moment? He'd begun to realise what he was looking for and, unfortunately, it seemed it was out of reach.

He was just about to toss his phone in the drawer when a notification flashed on the screen. He'd been invited to join a new group on Facebook – Medical School Reunion. The group had been set up over a week ago and there were already hundreds of posts and numerous photographs. Ben began to scroll through them. Some of the memories made him smile; there were photos from toga parties, tennis competitions and murder mystery nights. Then he stumbled across a photo of himself and Katie. The photo was labelled 'the power couple' with numerous comments underneath.

He smiled as he read them. Ben thought about Katie's university life. It still surprised him how she worked every hour to pay for tutors to obtain her marks just to make her parents proud.

According to the group, Katie had been asked to kick off the reunion with a speech around 7pm, followed by a buffet and disco. Plus ones would be welcome.

With the words 'plus one' on his mind, Ben thought about Katie. She didn't seem to be taking a plus one as she'd agreed to Ben booking her hotel room. He forwarded her the confirmation.

'I've just emailed your hotel details for the reunion.'

Almost immediately a text pinged back. 'I'll send you the over the money now. Thanks for booking!'

Ben thought about asking how her afternoon was going, but what was the point in that? He already knew Katie had company. He checked back on the dating app and re-read Poppy's message. Once more, he thought about setting up a new date and hovered over the keys, but he couldn't. Switching off his phone, he placed it in the drawer of his desk. All he knew was that she just wasn't Katie.

Chapter Eleven

With the boat race only three weeks away, Ben had called a Sunday morning meeting with his team to put them through their paces. The second he'd opened his curtains, he just knew the weather was not going to be kind. The sky was dark and, within seconds, the heavens had opened. He was in two minds about whether to cancel, but after checking the team's WhatsApp group, they were surprisingly up for the practice session that morning.

An hour later, with the rain bouncing off the pavements, people were racing along the high street with their lightweight summer jackets pulled over their heads, trying to keep the drenching to a minimum, unlike Ben, who was embracing the raindrops. For a brief moment, his head was tilted up towards the sky as he walked quickly along the coastal path towards The Old Boat House. Thankfully, there was a brighter sky trying to break through the clouds. He was looking forward to releasing some stress. He'd spent the last week running the surgery whilst Katie was recuperating and he could categorically state that he'd missed her sharing the workload.

Of the team members, Ben was the last one to arrive. Everyone else was shielding from the rain inside The Old Boat House. They were sitting on the benches and looked up towards Ben as he stepped inside.

'Team… I'm glad to see you are all here, but it does look like you are deciding to make a run for it.'

Allie, Drew, Rona, Flynn and Meredith were sitting with their coats on, all looking like drowned rats. Ben took a swift glance over his shoulder. 'The rain is due to stop anytime now. So shall we get our wetsuits on and head out to the river?'

'Yes, Captain,' they chorused back in unison, causing Ben to smile.

As they stood up and hung up their coats on the peg, all eyes looked towards the door as it opened. Ben was amazed to see Katie standing there.

'What are you doing here?' he asked.

She waggled her hands. 'Ta-dah! No bandages on my hands so I thought I'd come down and have a quick paddle.'

'What…now? Are you spying on my team tactics?' Ben narrowed his eyes. 'Did you know we would be here?'

'Why would I need to spy on your team tactics?' She shook her head. 'No offence, guys, but my team will "Seas

144

the Day". Did you see what I did there...used my team's name...'

'Yes, very clever. But I don't think it's fair that you are here the same time as us. I know it's a light-hearted race...'

'But you still think you can beat me and my team.' Katie jokingly patted him on the back. 'Delusional Sanders! But all is fair in love and rowing. Okay, you have your little team talk and I'll just hover outside until you're done.'

As the door shut behind Katie, the team was looking at Ben with amusement. 'Why are you looking at me like that?'

Rona raised an eyebrow. 'I spy with my little eye more than a little friendly rivalry between you two.'

'What do you mean?'

'I saw the way you looked at each other.' Rona gave him a knowing look.

Ben rolled his eyes. 'Now it's you lot that are delusional. Let's concentrate on the rowing and winning.'

'What is the plan for today?' questioned Allie, kicking off her shoes and placing them under the bench. 'Surely we aren't going to kayak too far up the river?'

'I think it's best we ease in gently as some of us have never been in a kayak before. Don't forget it's only a little over two kilometres that each of you will be rowing on the day.'

'Only!' Allie raised her eyebrows.

'And don't forget we have no clue what the weather will be like on the day. We can't expect to only practice when it's sunny. This is how the race is going to work: we will all travel by speedboat to the start line, which is over near The Lake House, and we need to decide what order you'll be racing in. I will be up last against Katie as we battle it out to the finish line. There will only be one kayak. We'll all use the same one. After the race has started, the rest of the team will travel by speedboat alongside the kayak. The buoys dotted along the river will be markers to indicate when the team member will be changed. We swap with the existing rower, slipping into the water on the far side of the kayak whilst the next person climbs in. The previous rower will then join the team on the speedboat. This way, we will all be at the finish line together when we are crowned winners!'

The team gave out a cheer.

'Then we will head straight for the drinks tent. Obviously, after we have all taken part in the winners' interview! But don't be complacent. Katie's team is just as strong as ours, so we need to make sure we give it our all – we aren't called Making Waves for nothing!'

'Are we taking the speedboat out today?' asked Rona.

'Not today. We are going to start with the basics.'

'Do you mean climbing in the boat and managing to stay in it?' asked Meredith with a serious look on her face.

'Exactly that!' replied Ben with a grin. 'We have six kayaks today and as it's our first training session, we are going to stay close to The Old Boat House and learn how to row and navigate the kayak to the right and left. More importantly, learn how to manoeuvre the kayak to go straight on.'

Everyone nodded.

'Let's get changed and get these boats on the river!'

They grabbed their wetsuits from the rail before disappearing behind the curtains of the changing cubicles.

'Oh my gosh, I can't get it past my chest. Breathe in,' Rona said out loud as she struggled. 'This is worse than those leather trousers in the sixties, and it doesn't leave a lot to the imagination.' Rona pulled back the curtain and waggled her backside. 'Does my bum look big in this?' she joked, standing back and staring at her reflection in the mirror. 'It really isn't good to have this place filled with mirrors. These legs remind me of the black puddings that are hanging up in the butcher's window.'

Meredith was chuckling. 'I second that, these suits are really not attractive.'

'They aren't meant to be attractive or a fashion accessory – the purpose is to provide insulation,' chipped in Ben. 'On the day, we will be wearing our team T-shirt over the top.'

'How wet do we actually get?' asked Rona.

'It depends on if you fall in,' joked Drew. 'But your bum gets wet and your feet.

All heads turned as Flynn stepped out of the changing room and put his hands on his hips. He began to strut around the room.

'And how come Flynn looks like a male model in his wetsuit?' Drew looked down at his own and patted his stomach. 'I suppose I need to stop sampling all the produce up at Foxglove Farm. The cheese is a killer.'

'You've either got it or you haven't,' replied Flynn.

'Well, I've definitely not got it,' chipped in Allie, looking down at her wetsuit as the door opened and Katie stepped back inside.

'Someone's got it.' Katie looked Ben up and down.

There was something about the intensity of her gaze that made Ben blush.

'Have you finished with your team talk now?'

Ben nodded, hoping Katie hadn't noticed the crimson flush to his cheeks.

'Have you any objections if I go out on the water?' Katie was clutching her wetsuit and was already walking towards the changing rooms. She looked over her shoulder, waiting for Ben's answer.

'Of course not,' he replied, even though he would have preferred for her to be anywhere else other than out on the water.

As Katie disappeared into the changing room, Ben's team stood in the doorway, looking out at the abysmal weather. Each one was reluctant to step outside.

'Pub?' suggested Rona. 'Sunday roasts all round.'

'No! Not until afterwards. Think how exhilarated you'll feel when we finish the training session. Don't forget it's all for a good cause.' Ben handed each of them a life jacket.

'That it is,' replied Allie. 'It's a difficult time for Stuart and Alana and if we can raise awareness and funds to make people's lives a little easier, then I'm all for that.'

'Hear, hear,' replied Ben. 'Are we ready?'

Leading the troops out of The Old Boat House, Ben took them down towards the shallow edge of the water. The rain had finally eased off even though there were still a fair few dark clouds looming in the distance. All the kayaks were lined up in front of them, with one end of each boat still lodged on the shale whilst the other end was in the water. The oars were lying on top of each boat.

'Flynn, Drew, if you can help pull the kayaks into the water, then we can help Rona and Meredith inside. How are you feeling, Rona?' asked Ben, noticing she'd suddenly gone quiet.

'Apprehensive, but I'm pushing myself out of my comfort zone.'

With the water lapping around Ben's ankles, there was no denying it was cold, and as the women lowered themselves into the boat, each gave a little squeal as the water seeped through their wetsuits and swirled around their feet. Ben passed an oar to each of them and showed them how to paddle. Before they knew it, Ben had pushed them out onto the water.

'Eek!' shrieked Meredith. 'I can't believe I'm saying this, but I'm actually quite enjoying it.'

Rona had relaxed and taken control of her kayak, with Allie bringing up the rear. Flynn and Drew were out in front whilst Ben positioned himself in the middle of everyone.

'Stay close and just get yourself feeling comfortable in your kayak,' shouted Ben.

Meredith was going around in circles. 'I can't get it to go straight.'

'Left, right, left, right,' Ben shouted from his kayak. 'Don't grip the paddle too tightly or your arms will tire quickly and it will make kayaking difficult.'

'When you keep your legs together, you have better torso rotation and your paddling will be less difficult,' shared Katie, wading into the water and pulling her kayak behind her.

'Are you helping my team?' asked Ben.

'Of course I am. It's all for charity.' Katie splashed Ben. He ducked, failing to avoid the cold droplets of river water. He powered away and Katie climbed into her boat and began chasing him.

'Children!' shouted Drew. They both turned around and began to paddle back towards the group.

'I can't seem to balance.' Looking petrified, Rona was rocking from side to side. 'I'm going to fall in.'

'Don't do that, otherwise you'll be up the creek without a paddle,' joked Ben as he quickly paddled towards Rona. Katie followed him. They sandwiched her kayak between the two of them.

'If you need extra balance, you can spread your legs slightly so that they press against the inside of the kayak,' advised Katie.

'I dare not move,' replied Rona, looking petrified. 'The water has already frozen my backside.'

'You aren't going anywhere,' reassured Katie, but Rona panicked as the water rocked the boat. She let out a squeal and Ben quickly leant forward to steady the kayak, but as Rona jolted, her oar flew upwards and connected with Ben's cheek at full force. The impact startled him and his boat overturned, leaving Ben floundering in the cold river water. The water swirled around his stomach and splashed up against his chest, but he bobbed in the water thanks to his life jacket.

'Flynn!' Katie shouted. 'Help Rona back to the bank.'

Ben's kayak had already gone up the river and Katie was paddling furiously to catch it. Drew was suddenly at her side and between them, they managed to flip over the abandoned kayak and drive it back upstream towards Ben whilst Allie retrieved the oar before it drifted further up the river. Still bobbing in the river, Ben squeezed his eyes shut for a moment as he felt the trickle of blood running down his cheek. Katie and Drew pushed the kayak towards Ben and he clawed his way back into it.

'Don't touch your face. You have a deep cut and you don't want to get river water in that.' Katie was now at Ben's side and handed over his oar.

'Woah! That does look nasty,' exclaimed Allie.

'It bloody hurts. I have to admit I've gone a little light-headed,' said Ben with a grimace.

Katie got as close as she could. 'I don't want to be the

bearer of bad news, but I think you are going to need a couple of stitches.'

'It's throbbing.'

'Let's get you out of the water.'

'I just can't believe this. The proper first team meeting and there's a casualty: me.' Ben blew out a breath.

'You need to get out of that wetsuit into warm clothes. It may be a summer's day,'– she looked up to the sky – 'granted not the best summer's day, but it's still cold. Do you feel dizzy?'

The cut on his face was smarting and was making Ben feel a little nauseous. 'A little. I could definitely do with some painkillers. I'm beginning to think boats and me are just not a good combination.'

'And you've only just realised that?' Katie gave him a friendly smirk. 'It's a good job you know a doctor. Let's get you back to the surgery and I can take a proper look.'

A mortified Rona was back on dry land and as she helped Ben pull his kayak onto the shale, she couldn't apologise enough. 'I don't know what happened. I just panicked, I'm so sorry.'

'It's okay, it's just one of those things.' Ben could see how upset Rona was and touched her arm. 'Honestly, it's fine. Accidents happen.'

'It doesn't look fine.'

'It will be after I've stitched it. Good job I'm handy with a needle and thread,' said Katie, disappearing inside The

Old Boat House with Ben whilst the others carried on pulling the kayaks out of the water.

Katie rummaged in her bag and pulled out a packet of tissues. 'Here, you need to put some direct pressure on that cut. Do you need help peeling off your wetsuit?'

For a second, Ben couldn't work out if Katie was winding him up but when her face broke into a grin, he rolled his eyes. 'Actually, if you could just unzip me.'

'Turn around,' she ordered. After Katie pulled down the zip on Ben's wetsuit, she gently pushed the suit off his shoulders. For a second Ben forgot the throb of pain in his cheek as his whole body trembled at her touch. She was standing so close he could feel her breath on the back of his neck.

He looked over his shoulder, their faces centimetres apart. Did he just imagine it or did her gaze just drop to his lips? Neither of them faltered; they held each other's eyes until the door of The Old Boat House flung open and Allie, Rona and Meredith walked in.

'Drew and Flynn are upping their stamina and have gone for a paddle down the river,' announced Allie. 'I think now they've seen how strong Katie is in the water, they aren't leaving anything to chance.'

'Still keeping the boys on their toes, I see,' teased Ben, noticing Katie was still looking in his direction.

Allie took a step closer to Ben and scrutinised his cut. 'That does look bad. You are going to need stitches in that.'

'And that's exactly what's going to happen when he's got out of his wetsuit,' said Katie.

Everyone disappeared into the changing cubicles and, five minutes later, Ben and Katie stepped out at the same time.

'Back to mine then. I bet you never thought you'd hear those words,' she joked.

'I hoped I'd never hear those words.' He was shaking his head in jest. 'But as all the medical stuff is in the surgery, your office or mine?'

'Now there's an offer,' replied Katie.

Ten minutes later, they were back at Peony Practice and Ben was standing in his office looking at his reflection in the mirror.

'Mirror, mirror on the wall,' joked Katie, walking into the room. 'Who is the fairest of them all?'

'Obviously the answer would be me, every time,' replied Ben, giving her a convincing look.

'I'm not sure with that gash on your face, but if it scars, it's going to look kind of sexy. A very manly scar,' Katie said, sitting on the edge of the desk and gesturing towards the office chair. Once Ben sat down, Katie tilted his face upwards to hers. He watched the concentration on her face.

'Let's get you cleaned and stitched up; hopefully I won't hurt you too much.'

As Katie began to clean the wound, Ben's brows sloped down in a serious expression and he bit down on his lip.

'Is it stinging?' she asked softly.

'A little.'

Even though Ben was trying not to look in her eyes, it was difficult – they looked exactly the same as the night they'd spent together, with a glint of adventure and mischief. He closed his eyes, briefly wondering what it would be like to kiss her again. He gave himself a little shake; it wasn't going to do him any good thinking thoughts like that.

'Keep still. You're shaking,' she ordered softly. 'Otherwise your stitches are going to be wonky.'

Ben looked at her nervously, hoping she couldn't read his mind. He closed his eyes again and inhaled her gorgeous perfume. He realised he'd made a tiny gasp. His eyes pinged open to discover Katie had stopped what she was doing and was looking at him intently, yet with amusement.

'What are you thinking about?'

'Absolutely nothing,' Ben replied.

'Would you ever think after all these years I'd be attempting to stitch up your cheek? It's funny how the world works.'

'I hope there's no attempting about it. You did actually qualify as a doctor, didn't you?' Ben watched as Katie sterilised the equipment, then laid it all out on a piece of kitchen towel on the desk.

'I can neither confirm nor deny...' She threw her head back and laughed. 'Obviously,' she added, lining up the edges of the wound to be stitched.

'So where were you before you decided to come to Heartcross?' Ben watched Katie. 'I never did ask.'

For a moment, a heavy silence settled over them, taking Ben by surprise. The atmosphere changed from light-hearted banter to what seemed uneasy tension.

'Is everything okay?' asked Ben. He could see by the look on Katie's face that something was weighing heavily on her mind. Why was she reluctant to answer?

'I've had some time off recently.' Katie shifted uncomfortably on the desk, but she kept her eyes firmly on the wound.

'Off work?'

'It's nothing and will you stop talking.'

Ben couldn't help thinking that it was definitely something. He wondered if Katie had encountered a problem at work. It wasn't unusual for complaints to be made against doctors. It was difficult being challenged by patients on a daily basis and sometimes one small complaint could escalate, leaving you totally exasperated.

Whatever was going on for Katie, she apparently found it difficult to talk about or just didn't want to. Her eyes gleamed for a moment with unshed tears whilst she made an excuse to open the window, claiming it was hot in the office. By the time she sat back down, she'd composed herself. Ben didn't like to see anyone struggling. It was one of the reasons he had become a doctor – he had a caring nature and he knew that having a friend to talk things through with and support you was worth its weight in gold. Soon after arriving in Heartcross, even though his job was to support the community, they supported him too. He knew he'd already made friends for life in the village.

'Well, whatever it is, I'm always here,' he said tentatively.

Katie didn't answer as she carried on stitching the wound. After tying a knot in the end of the thread, she snipped off the excess with a pair of surgical scissors before leaning back and admiring her own handiwork.

'That's good to know,' she acknowledged, but swiftly changed the subject. 'And I have to say, not a bad job – in fact, very tidy. Take a look. A job well done.'

Ben stood up and walked over towards the mirror hanging on the wall. 'A very good job indeed. It actually looks like it's been done by a professional.'

Katie swiped his arm playfully.

Ben was still studying his face. 'That doesn't look too bad at all. Thank you.'

'You are very welcome. And I've been thinking about this boat race. Each time you've taken to the water, it's been a disaster, so I'm thinking we need to alert the river rescue team and have the paramedics trailing the route on the water taxis. I've already had a chat with Roman and he's up for sailing the route just to keep you alive.'

Ben laughed. 'Normally, I'd object and say that is way

over the top and I know you are trying to wind me up, but actually that sounds like a good plan to me.'

'I'll get that arranged,' she said with a grin as she continued to sterilise the equipment once more before putting everything away in the surgery cupboard. 'Right, that's us done here.' She swiped her hands.

Ben's stomach let out a growl. 'I think I need to be fed with one of the pub's roast dinners.' He looked at his watch. 'Do you care to join me? No doubt the rest of the team will already be propping up the bar.'

Ben did love a good roast dinner with all the trimmings. It was the perfect ending to his week and when he discovered how good Meredith's roasts were at the pub, he knew exactly where he would be most Sundays. He didn't think he had missed a Sunday yet. 'Meredith's Yorkshire puddings are the best in the Scottish Highlands. Believe me, I know a good Yorkshire pudding when I taste one.'

Katie looked tempted, but reluctantly shook her head as her phone rang out. She picked up and confirmed she was on her way before hanging up.

'Anything special planned?' asked Ben.

Once more, Katie looked like she was going to share something with Ben. 'I just need to be somewhere this afternoon, but you enjoy that roast dinner.'

Her voice waned and once more a wave of sadness seemed to wash over her, but Katie didn't look in his direction as she made her way to the door. 'And stay away from the river, especially when I'm not around. That's an order.'

'I'll do my best,' he shouted, but the surgery door had already shut behind her.

Ben appreciated Katie had opened up to him about the expectations of her family during their meal at The Lake House, but he couldn't help but think there was a part of her that was still guarded. He watched her from the window and as Katie stepped out onto the pavement, she was greeted by the same man who had delivered the flowers to her door. He hugged her tight, kissed her cheek and held the passenger door of the car open for her. The car soon sped off towards the high street. Ben could only assume that the man was Oliver Green.

Chapter Twelve

Bashing the top of his boiled egg with a spoon, Ben thought about how Katie hadn't come home last night. He hadn't been intentionally spying on the flat next door, but no sound had filtered through the paper-thin walls by the time he fell asleep just after midnight. He'd already texted Helly to see whether Katie had booked a day off, but the immediate reply was that to Helly's knowledge, she hadn't. It left Ben wondering where she'd spent the night and if she was okay.

He gave himself a shake. He was overthinking things. Why wouldn't she be okay? She was a grown adult and could stay out all night if she wanted to. After finishing his breakfast, Ben knew he was snooping as he once again put his ear to the wall, but curiosity was getting the better of him and there was still no sign of life next door. Katie was cutting it fine if she was going to make it to work on time. The surgery doors opened in twenty minutes.

Ben placed his empty coffee cup in the sink and after a quick brush of his teeth and a pat of cologne on his face, he declared himself ready and walked back into the living room and picked up his briefcase. At that very moment, he heard a loud crash coming from Katie's flat. He stopped dead in his tracks and listened.

Deadly silence.

For a second, he wondered if he'd imagined it, but now he wondered if something wasn't quite right. Before he could think about it anymore, he found himself knocking on the door of her apartment whilst shouting her name. But there was no reply. He flicked open the letter box and peered inside, but the door to the living and bedrooms were closed. All he could see was the small hallway and the coats hanging on the hooks alongside an umbrella.

'Katie!' he shouted again, but still no reply.

For a nanosecond, Ben thought about banging down the front door like he'd seen at the movies, but then decided that was ridiculous. All he'd do was put his shoulder out. He bounded down the stairs two at a time and flung open the door to the surgery. Helly looked up.

'Where's the fire? Yikes! I don't suppose I should be saying that after recent events.' Helly's eyes were wide as she waited for Ben to answer.

'Have you seen Katie this morning?'

'Not yet, but she'll be here any minute for morning surgery.'

'She's not been home all night,' declared Ben.

'Are you keeping tabs on her? Please tell me you aren't stalking her every move because that will end in disaster. I know I'm thinking about myself here, but I'm all for an easy life, especially at work.'

'It's a long shot, I know, but you don't have a key to her flat, do you?'

Helly stopped what she was doing and gave Ben her full attention. 'A key? You're not thinking of breaking into her flat, are you?'

'It's not breaking in if I have a key. Katie hasn't been home all night and I've just heard a massive crash coming from her apartment and then nothing.'

'It could be anything. Maybe she's left the window open and the door has slammed in the wind.'

'Or maybe she's hurt or something?'

'That seems a little far-fetched, but there's never a dull moment in this village. Have you tried her desk? You keep a spare key in yours. Maybe she does the same. Do you think we need to call the emergency services?'

'Let me just take a quick look in her drawer first.' Ben hot-footed it to Katie's office whilst Helly picked up the ringing telephone.

Katie's drawer was a clutter of pens, paperclips, a lipstick, and Post-it Notes, but Ben struck lucky. Attached to a large fluffy pompom pink pig keyring was a key similar to his apartment. He grabbed it and waggled it at Helly. She was still on the telephone and covered the mouthpiece as she shouted something after Ben, but he never heard as he quickly disappeared through the door.

Bounding back up the stairs, Ben was standing outside Katie's apartment in no time at all. He banged on the door one last time and called her name through the letter box but still there was silence. Taking the plunge, he tried the key in the lock and it turned easily. The door swung open. He was in.

'What the hell do you think you are doing?'

Ben spun round; the sound of Katie's voice made him jump out of his skin. She was looking confused as she glanced between the two front doors and placed an overnight bag on the ground.

A puce colour crept up her neck to her cheeks. His mouth opened the closed as Katie folded her arms and had the look of a toddler who was about to have a tantrum. 'Well?' she demanded, the tone indicating she was far from pleased.

She looked livid and was still in yesterday's clothes. He braced himself.

'Are you just coming out of my apartment or going into my apartment? Have you been snooping?' Her eyes were fixed in a stare that showed she couldn't quite believe what she was seeing. 'And where the hell have you got those keys from? You've been snooping in my office drawer too? This is unbelievable.'

Helly had arrived at the top of stairs and realised there was tension in the air, and from where she was standing this was going to be more explosive than the Heartcross Castle firework display on bonfire night. Helly raised her eyebrows at Ben as she leant against the wall. Ben was going to get it with both barrels.

'Don't you need to go and man the desk? The surgery will be opening soon.' Ben gave Helly a stare.

'Nah, there's five minutes yet and there will be no surgery if the two doctors end up killing each other. I need to be witness to whatever goes on here.'

'I'll ask again, Ben: why do you feel the need to rifle through my drawers and break into my flat?'

'It's not exactly breaking in. I have a key.' Ben held up the fluffy pig pompom keyring and for a second thought it had snorted, but that was the anger beginning to escape from Katie.

'Okay, I hadn't heard a sound from you all night.'

'You've been listening through the wall?' Both of her eyebrows rose.

'No…yes…no…'

'Make your mind up.'

'Now you're living next door, I'm more aware of the noise coming from your apartment and yesterday it was obvious that you'd not returned to your flat. But then this morning, only a few minutes ago, I heard a huge crash coming from in there, then there was silence again.'

'And you didn't think to ring my phone or text me?'

That thought hadn't crossed Ben's mind. 'I thought you were hurt and I was more concerned about getting to you. I asked Helly if she knew of a spare key and she suggested I try the top drawer of your desk.'

Katie looked towards Helly, who threw her arms up in the air. 'Don't bring me into this. You are your own man; make your own decisions.'

'I literally put the key in the lock and opened the door when you appeared behind me, but I can see you aren't hurt or collapsed.' Ben quickly looked her up and down. Usually Katie's appearance was immaculate. 'And still in the same clothes from yesterday.'

Ben's observation left him feeling a little downhearted. Katie had definitely spent the night somewhere else – no doubt with the man who'd picked her up in the car yesterday. She was entitled to do what she pleased, but the feeling in the pit of his stomach told him that he didn't like it.

'Oooh, did you have a good night? Is there gossip to be had?' chipped in Helly with an amused look on her face.

'No gossip whatsoever.' Katie stepped forward and took the key from Ben's hand. 'And how long ago was the crashing sound?' Katie was quick to steer the conversation back on track.

'Enough time for me to find the key and get back here.'

'So literally in the last five to ten minutes?'

'Yes,' replied Ben.

'That will be Romeo,' declared Katie.

Ben looked towards the door; the name had taken him by surprise. 'Romeo? You have a man in your flat?'

'Apartment, and yes I do.'

Helly was loving every second of this.

How many men was Katie fraternising with? If anything, Ben was expecting to hear the name Oliver, but it seemed he was about to rush in and rescue someone called Romeo. He might have known the handsome guy in the suit, driving the expensive car and bringing huge bouquets of flowers had the same suave and sophisticated name as a Shakespearean character. Why couldn't he just have a dull name like Dave?

'I let him into the flat whilst I went and got my bag from the car.'

A slight smile hitched onto Ben's face. He might be handsome and drive a posh car, but what gentleman lets a lady carry her bags up a flight of stairs whilst they swan about inside?

Katie glanced at her watch. 'You might as well meet him now that you're here. You'll be seeing a lot of him. He's a keeper.'

Once more, Ben's heart plummeted to an all-time low. Those words cut to the core and he knew exactly why. He'd begun to carry a torch for Katie O'Neil and even though that pang in his heart was growing bigger, Ben was thankful that the surgery was opening in less than a minute. At least he wouldn't have to hang around and make small talk with Katie's new man. Yet he was still curious.

It seemed Helly, too, was curious about the type of man that Katie went for and she was right behind Ben as he stepped into Katie's hallway. Apparently, she couldn't wait to set eyes on Romeo and wasn't going to miss this introduction for the world. Opening the door to the living room, they all stopped and stared.

'Shit,' was the word that left Katie's mouth.

Ben was expecting Romeo to be sitting on the settee but there was no one there. Instead, they were greeted by carnage. Ben saw where the crashing sound had come from –the vase of flowers had been knocked off the window sill and had bounced off the coffee table. The water was spilt all over the carpet and the flowers had been dragged all around the room, which was strange.

'Is he in the bathroom?' asked Helly.

Immediately, Ben was thinking it was going to be awkward for anyone to walk out of the bathroom and be greeted by strangers.

Katie gave her a strange look. 'I hope not, because it would just be my luck that he would have got stuck down the toilet. He likes to get up to mischief at the best of times.'

Perplexed, Ben and Helly watched as Katie got down on her knees and reached behind the TV. She pulled out a small furry body and deposited it in Ben's arms.

'Meet Romeo,' announced Katie, formally introducing them all. 'Romeo, this is Ben, your new neighbour and Helly.'

'Oh, my days!' exclaimed Helly.

'It's a kitten?'

'Great observation. What were you expecting? Or should I say *who* were you expecting?' Katie narrowed her eyes at Ben.

The kitten's eyes opened wide and Ben held Romeo at arm's length. 'My god those claws are sharp.'

Helly reached out to take the kitten from Ben's hands. 'He is absolutely gorgeous.'

'I brought him home this morning. It seems as soon as I dropped him in the apartment and returned to the car to get my bags, he explored his new playground.' She turned towards Ben. 'He's very cute, isn't he?'

The kitten looked straight at Ben, his eyes full of energy but with a huge dollop of nervousness, his mew as soft as his fur.

'I think he quite likes you,' said Katie, picking up the knocked over vase and scooping the flowers off the floor. 'And as much as it's lovely for you all to meet the newest member of my family, we really need to get to the surgery.'

'Yikes, there will be a queue of disgruntled patients.' Helly handed the kitten over to Ben, who immediately handed it to Katie. He followed Helly to the door.

'I'll hold the fort until you get there but you might want to think about changing your clothes and at least pull a brush through your hair,' Ben said. Romeo might not have been who he was expecting to meet, but Katie was still in yesterday's clothes and hadn't been home all night.

'And you might want to think about not letting yourself into my apartment without asking.'

Leaving Katie to take care of the kitten, Ben and Helly hurried down the stairs towards the surgery. But ten minutes later, when Katie rushed through the door, Helly was sitting in the chair behind the reception desk whilst Ben was leaning against the desk with his arms folded.

They both looked at her and Katie surveyed the waiting room, but row after row of plastic chairs were empty. There wasn't a patient in sight. The surgery waiting room was completely empty except for the happy spider weaving its web in the corner of the room. After thinking they were running late, it appeared the rest of the world was running even later.

'What's going on? Where is everyone? We have got the right time, haven't we?' Katie fired out the questions whilst looking up at the clock in the middle of the wall behind the desk.

'Maybe no one in the village is ill this morning?' suggested Helly, putting both hands in the air.

'I can't believe that for a minute. Never in my career as a doctor has that ever happened before,' said Ben.

'Well, it seems to be happening now?' replied Helly, picking up the office telephone. 'Yep, it's working.'

'Okay, granted, this is very weird. Check the village WhatsApp group?' suggested Katie.

'Why? Do you want me to send a message asking if

there's anyone out there who is ill this morning just so we have a job to do?' replied Ben.

'No, don't be stupid. Just to make sure we haven't missed something.'

Ben checked the group and stood up. 'Helly, you need to stay here and keep the surgery open. Katie, we need to get over to the pub.'

'It's too early to be going on a bender,' joked Katie, but became serious as she looked at Ben's face. 'What's going on?'

'It seems Alana is missing. Everyone's gathered at the pub to start searching.'

'Oh no,' said Katie, her mind flashing back to her past. For a moment, she closed her eyes tightly, knowing exactly how Alana's family would be feeling. The anxious feeling swirling around in the pit of their stomach would only ease once Alana had been found. This was a feeling Katie had experienced in exactly the same circumstance, many times.

'Are you okay?' asked Ben, noticing Katie was suddenly silent.

She gave herself a little shake and quickly rallied herself together. 'Yes, I'll grab the doctor's bag and supplies. You never know if we may need it.'

'Good idea,' replied Ben.

'I'll catch you up. You go ahead,' suggested Katie as she rushed towards her office and Ben disappeared through the door.

Katie only arrived a couple of minutes after Ben. The atmosphere was unsettling as she walked into the Grouse and Haggis pub. With a blanket wrapped around his shoulders, Stuart looked visibly upset, sitting at the bar with a whisky in his hand. Ben was sitting next to him and Katie pulled up a stool on the other side. She placed a supportive hand on his back.

'Stuart, what's been happening?' she asked tentatively.

'It's been a terrible twenty-four hours,' admitted Stuart. The tears were welling up in his eyes and Ben passed him a tissue. 'Since the fire, things have escalated. It's affected Alana so much not being in her actual home. She can't settle and keeps saying they want her dead.'

'Who's they?' asked Ben.

Katie cut in softly and held Ben's gaze. 'They…may not even be a real thing. Unfortunately, the disease seems to be completely taking over Alana.'

Stuart nodded. 'I knew this time would come and I'm trying to be positive…for better or worse,' he said, quoting his wedding vows. 'But this isn't my Alana.'

Katie grabbed onto his hand. 'It's hard. I can feel your pain, and what we have to do is be there for each other no matter what.'

For a second, Ben watched them. Katie's words weren't just comforting words. The way she expressed them suggested that maybe she had first-hand experience of this, which took him completely by surprise.

'Each person is unique in the way this terrible disease affects them,' said Katie.

'She woke up in the night and began screaming. She wanted to know what I was doing in her bed. She thought I was trying to kidnap her. I explained I was Stuart, the man she married and loved. I wasn't a stranger and I had been by her side for a lifetime. I told her I'd make her a cup of tea just the way she likes it, with a little dash of milk and half a teaspoon of sugar. It was only then she began to settle. I tucked her back into bed and returned with a drink. I only make her half a cup so she doesn't spill it and scold herself. She smiled at me when I placed the cup of tea next to her. She recognised her favourite mug and then I gave her a hand massage, and I know it sounds daft, but I sprayed her favourite perfume in the room.'

'It doesn't sound daft at all,' reassured Katie. 'Stimulating their senses helps so much. You are doing all the right things.'

Stuart nodded. 'I'm trying my best, but I don't think my best is good enough now.'

Katie squeezed his hand. 'We can help to get Alana settled in a home with around-the-clock care. I know it's difficult to even think about, but we have a duty to look after your well-being too. Don't we, Ben?'

'Absolutely we do,' replied Ben, impressed by Katie's caring nature.

'We need to find Alana,' replied Stuart. 'But yes, I think that time is fast approaching. I feel like I've failed.'

'You have far from failed,' said Katie. 'You have loved and cared every step of the way. Don't ever think that.'

'I don't even know when she went missing. I woke up just after eight o'clock and she wasn't there. I don't even know what she's wearing. I usually have to dress her because sometimes she can't manage those fiddly blouse buttons, so I've tried to make things easier with just T-shirt type tops in this heat.'

'You are doing everything right, believe me,' Katie encouraged him. 'So, we don't know what she is wearing?'

Stuart shook his head. 'Afraid not. And today is our wedding anniversary. I'm sure Alana won't remember.'

'At least the weather is being good to us today. We'll find her,' comforted Ben.

They turned around as Rory banged on the table. 'Thank you all for coming. I can't thank you enough for helping us look for Mum. As all our supportive friends know, Mum's dementia has worsened in the past twelve months. Please, please if you spot her, ring myself, Allie—'

Katie and Ben put up their hands. 'Or us. Has anyone called the police?' Katie asked Rory, who nodded. 'They are on their way and are going to co-ordinate with the coast guard and search the mountain, but it's okay for us to search the immediate area.'

Rory began to hand out a photocopied picture of his

mum. 'This might be useful to show tourists and ask if they've seen her. The village is so busy this time of year.'

After Rory had allocated each table a different area to search, the villagers were on their way.

'We'll take the riverbank,' suggested Katie. 'And when we get back and Alana is found safe and well, we can sit down and make a few decisions about the best way forward for you both.'

Stuart nodded his appreciation.

Outside, Ben and Katie set off towards the river, strolling quickly along the high street in silence. Ben kept taking a sideward glance at Katie. When she'd appeared at his birthday party, Ben thought he was living in a nightmare, but now he admired her caring nature – the way she'd spoken to Stuart and the reassurance she'd given him. It was like the old Katie had disappeared.

'Why are you looking at me?' she asked, not turning her face towards his.

'How do you know I'm looking at you?'

'Because I can feel it.'

'I have to say I was impressed by the way you handled that situation.'

They glanced at each other, but Katie didn't say anything.

They began to trawl the banks of the river. The tourists were out in full force, walking, fishing and boating on the river. They scanned the area quickly, but Alana was nowhere to be seen. They began to stop the passers-by and show them the photo of Alana, hoping that someone might recognise her. But every person they stopped shook their head.

Katie tied up her hair in a ponytail, the anxiety written all over her face.

And that's when Ben asked the question that was burning inside of him.

'Don't bite my head off…'

'But…'

'You've had first-hand experience, haven't you? Of dementia?' he asked with unease. He wanted to know everything about Katie.

Katie shifted her gaze towards him for a split second, her chin trembling, but then she focussed on the path in front of her.

'Yes,' she replied, still not catching Ben's eye. 'My brother Ellis.' Katie was on the verge of tears.

Ben sucked in a breath. That wasn't what he had been expecting. He'd assumed it was an elderly relative. 'Your brother?' He remembered Katie talking about her brothers briefly over dinner at The Lake House. 'But your brother was young.'

'Yes, Ellis and Luke are five years older than me. They're twins.'

It suddenly dawned on Ben that the man who'd passed him on the stairs with the beautiful bouquet of flowers must have been her brother Luke. Now he came to think about it, the family resemblance between them was obvious.

'Dementia in the young is a terrible disease. How did you all manage?'

'I juggled my career and put it on hold near the end of his life. I also became his carer. The day I discharged myself from the hospital was the anniversary of his death – it was too difficult to just lie there and think of the past.'

Ben stopped in his tracks; this was another side of Katie that he never knew existed. Ben was full of admiration. He'd had no idea that Katie was going through this and was sad that she'd had to cope with losing her brother at such a young age. He wanted to hold her and hug her tight. Choosing his words with care, he said, 'I'm so sorry to hear this. I just can't imagine how you've coped. It must have been a difficult time for you; for everyone. Your parents must be proud.'

Katie stopped walking and met Ben's gaze. 'We don't speak anymore.'

Ben wasn't expecting that, even though he knew there had been difficulties. 'You, Katie O'Neil, are a very special person.'

'Please don't be nice to me. You'll make me cry. It's been a difficult time and there's a little more to the story. I will talk to you about it, but I still get very emotional, and this isn't the right time. We have to find Alana.'

Ben understood. They carried on walking in silence for a while. 'Is that why you became an ambassador for the charity?'

Katie nodded as she mustered up a wobbly smile. 'Yes.

With what I've been through and how difficult it is…if I can use my experience to help anyone…'

Ben exhaled and felt a pang of sadness. He couldn't believe that Katie had juggled her career as a doctor while being a carer for her brother. It was such a selfless thing to do. They carried on walking towards The Old Boat House, which was a hive of activity with tourists. 'Do you know what? You amaze me every day.'

'You amaze me and not always for the right reasons.' She bumped her shoulder against his, trying to lighten the mood.

'You should take a compliment when you are given one. It's only polite. You are one hell of a woman and a doctor.'

'Thank you,' she replied, staring up at the cliff.

Katie pointed and Ben looked up. There, sitting on the edge of the cliff, swinging her legs and seemingly oblivious to the steep drop onto the rocky terrain beneath her, was Alana.

Chapter Thirteen

Ben narrowed his eyes and focussed. 'I'll ring Rory and follow you up.' But before Ben could finish his sentence, Katie was already making her way up the narrow path towards the cliff top.

Careful not to frighten Alana, Katie spoke softly and introduced herself. 'Hi, Alana, I'm Katie.'

Alana narrowed her eyes. 'Do I know you? Are you a wedding guest?'

'Wedding guest?' asked Katie, edging her way slowly towards Alana.

'There are so many guests. That's my mother's doing. Always has to take over. She never listens to what I want.' Alana rolled her eyes. 'She had to invite so many people and most of them I don't even know. Keeping up appearances, that's all it is, because Aggie had a big wedding you know at the bowls club – but she likes being the centre of attention. Today is my special day and I should be able to spend it how I want.'

'I agree,' replied Katie. 'Today is all about you, and whatever you want goes.'

Alana looked at Katie accusingly, but Katie knew facial expressions were a sign of how a person was feeling in the late stages of dementia.

'Can I come and sit with you?' asked Katie warmly. 'I'd love to hear all about your wedding day.' Katie's main priority was to coax Alana away from the edge of the cliff and out of danger.

Alana looked down at the white dress she was wearing. 'Marriage is just a nice word for adopting a fully grown man who can't take care of himself.' Alana gave a little chuckle. 'And it's my wedding day, but he seems to have disappeared altogether. I'm not sure where he's gone.'

Katie looked up to see Ben cautiously walking towards them.

Alana looked over her shoulder. 'Here he is now. Did you bring me a glass of champagne? I'll know if it's cheap wine.' She patted the ground next to her and Ben looked towards Katie, who nodded.

Slowly Ben positioned himself on the other side of Alana and looked over the cliff edge. He wasn't a fan of heights and took a deep breath. He could already feel his heart pounding nineteen to the dozen as he diverted his eyes from the steep drop in front of him.

'Alana, this is Ben. He's the local doctor,' said Katie.

'Ben? Who's Ben? You look just like my—'

'Stuart,' chipped in Katie.

Alana was scrutinising Ben. 'Doctor. Is that what you want to be when you grow up?'

Katie had a slight smile on her face. 'Ben is a doctor. He works here in Heartcross – at Peony Practice.'

Alana didn't question what Katie was saying, but she still didn't look convinced. 'It's my wedding day today. I don't know where he's gone…'

'Stuart.' Katie filled in the blanks again.

Alana seemed to be getting a little agitated. She shifted on the rock, causing Ben to panic and grab hold of her arm.

'What do you think you are doing?' exclaimed Alana, scrunching up her face. 'I could have fallen all the way down there. Are you after my money? Well, I don't have any. And where is my drink? What future do we have if you can't even bring me a drink? It's today though, isn't it? Our wedding day. Where is my drink? You need to go and get me a drink.'

Alana was getting muddled and beginning to ramble. Her voice began to rise and Katie spoke softly to try and calm her down. Looking towards Ben, Katie noticed all the colour had drained from his face and her educated guess was that he wasn't very fond of heights.

'Shall we move over to that grassy spot just over there?' Katie pointed to a flat area where it would be perfect to sit and talk.

'I'm not going anywhere with you. I don't even know

you. Who are you?' Once more, the tone in Alana's voice changed. Restless now, she started to swing her legs, but Katie didn't panic. She knew first-hand how to cope in these situations, which was to carry on talking in a calming voice.

'I'm Katie, the other local doctor.'

'No, you aren't a doctor. Dr Taylor is the doctor. Are you an imposter?' Her accusing look towards Katie was intense.

'That's right, but Dr Taylor is now enjoying retirement.'

'Retirement? He's too young to retire. He's at my wedding, you know. It's today, my wedding, and I have to say I don't think much of your suit.' Alana gave Ben a look of disdain, then flapped her hand. 'Is this what it's going to be like now, zero effort made now you've got that ring on my finger? Don't think I'm going to be a pushover.'

'This isn't Stuart, this is Ben, the local doctor,' Katie repeated.

'Too young to be a doctor,' Alana said, still looking at Ben. Alana's mood seemed to shift slightly. 'And what have you done with the boat? It's not in the bay.'

'Boat?' asked Katie. 'Tell me about the boat.'

Alana's face lit up. 'We have our little boat. We tie it up down there.' She pointed towards the jetty. 'And see that little bay? He takes me for picnics just over there. And that rock was where—'

'I proposed,' replied Stuart. 'For better or worse.'

Katie looked up to see a relieved but exhausted Stuart standing behind them.

Alana cupped her hands around her mouth. 'Alana

Reid, will you marry me?' she shouted up towards the sky. She was grinning and looked over her shoulder towards Stuart, who was tearful staring at her wedding dress.

'She's remembered the date and still looks as beautiful as the day I married her.' Stuart's words carried in the light breeze as he gazed adoringly at Alana. He held out his hand and gently helped her to her feet.

'Have all those guests gone home now? I hope so. I could murder a glass of champagne.'

'Me too. Your wish is my command,' replied Stuart. With tears in his eyes, they began to slowly walk away from the cliff edge. Stuart looked back over his shoulder towards Katie and Ben.

'It's time,' he mouthed and Katie nodded.

Watching them walk slowly away, Katie brushed a lone tear from her cheek with the back of her hand. She'd lived through many moments like this with her brother and it was heartbreaking to watch someone you love deteriorating before your very eyes.

'You're shaking.' Ben slipped his arm around Katie's shoulder. For a moment, she snuggled into the warmth of his chest as she calmed her beating heart. 'You were amazing; so calm.' Ben pulled her in tighter and rested his head on top of hers as they watched Rory and Allie running towards Stuart and Alana and wrapping their arms around their parents in a group hug.

Katie slowly pulled away and looked up at Ben. 'It's a brave decision knowing it's time to hand over the care of your loved one, the person that's been by your side for a lifetime. It's going to be so different for them both.'

'It will,' agreed Ben. 'I'll set the wheels in motion today, but can I ask one thing?'

'You can,' replied Katie.

'Please can we get off this cliff? I'm absolutely petrified.'

They began to walk back along the river path, both lost in their own thoughts until Katie broke the silence. 'Life is just so cruel. Their love is undeniable and there's such care and adoration between them. The life they've had together is special and you can just feel that love. That's exactly what I hope for, that unconditional bond that just happens between two people, no matter what the obstacles are.' Katie linked her arm through Ben's.

'Are you going all mushy on me here?' Ben teased, looking into Katie's eyes.

'Maybe a little, but you have to promise to keep that to yourself. I don't want my hard reputation being ruined.'

'Of course. I won't say a word.' Ben smiled at her. He was still curious about Oliver Green and how the man fitted into her life, but he was going to let Katie tell him in her own time. 'You have certainly begun to mellow in your old age. I quite like it.'

'Less of the old,' Katie replied, swiping his arm playfully. 'This place is special, isn't it?'

They reached the high street. All the villagers that had helped in the search for Alana were dispersing in different directions.

'It's one hell of a community. Rumour has it that once you arrive in Heartcross, you never leave.'

'In that case, it looks like you are stuck with me, Ben Sanders.' She smiled warmly at him then bumped her head against his shoulder as they reached the door of the surgery. They hovered outside.

He looked at her. 'I was just wondering if you'd like to join me for dinner tonight?'

'Dinner? That would be lovely.' She accepted without hesitation.

As they walked towards the office, Ben knew he wanted to know more about Katie and the changes in her life since they left medical school. He wanted her to open up. He was beginning to like her more and more and, although he knew that she might be off limits, he was still hoping Katie would tell him about Oliver Green – her husband.

Chapter Fourteen

Ben was flustered. He couldn't remember the last time he'd cooked a meal for anyone. Usually, when it was just for himself, it was a ready meal for one, and you really couldn't boast that as Michelin star cuisine. So now the pressure was on. He wanted to impress Katie and after trawling the internet for recipes, he finally settled on a dish that looked simple yet tasty – pie. Now the decision he faced was whether he should cheat and just buy a shop-bought pie or go the full hog and make it from scratch. Looking over the recipe, it looked straight forward enough, and with a nice bottle of red to wash it down, he was sure it would be a hit.

Picking up his keys, he made a note of what he needed and headed out to the corner shop to pick up the ingredients. Hamish's village shop stocked everything and anything, even if the place looked a little chaotic at times.

There were spices on the shelves that Ben wasn't too familiar with, but he soon had a basket full of ingredients and pointed to an expensive bottle of red that was on display on the shelf behind the counter.

'Aren't you racing tonight?' asked Hamish, ringing up the items on an old-fashioned till that looked like it had been through the war. Hamish still hadn't come to terms with technology and, after struggling to operate the card machine, Ben handed over the cash.

'Racing?' queried Ben, picking up his carrier bag.

'Team talks down by the river,' said Hamish.

'Ah, that will be the opposition! Apparently, all this healthy competition is good for you,' remarked Ben, not sounding convinced.

'Apparently so,' said Hamish. 'And that is a lovely bottle of wine you've purchased there – for a special someone?'

'For the opposition.' Ben winked, leaving Hamish to make of that what he wished.

As he made his way back home, Ben took a quick stroll towards the river. He told himself it was for the fresh air, but of course it was to check up on what Katie was up to. He paused on the bridge and looked up the river until he spotted Katie. He had to smile to himself; she really was taking this very seriously. Standing in the middle of a speedboat, she was wearing a wetsuit with a colour coordinated baseball cap with the pink letter K on the front. She bellowed instructions at the crew through a megaphone. Her team was lined up in their kayaks in front of her.

Ben watched as she sounded a horn and the kayaks went racing off down the river competing against each other. Ben was impressed; Katie's team was slick, their paddles gliding through the water at top speed. Katie sounded a high-pitched whistle and the team stopped rowing and turned back towards her. She was punching her arm enthusiastically whilst looking at a stopwatch. *They must be upping their game and increasing their speed*, thought Ben as he headed back along the high street towards his flat. He had just over an hour and a half to make the pie and now he was wishing he'd bought a bag of frozen chips instead of making his own.

Twenty minutes later, Ben was flustered again. All the ingredients were laid out on the kitchen table and he was rifling through his cupboards.

'Damn and blast,' he muttered to himself as he stood up, banging his head on the cupboard door. Why had he ever uttered the words 'I'll cook' when there was a perfectly good pub up the road? He could have cheated and bought two delicious pies from there. 'But that defeats the object, it's all about the love of home-cooked meals.' He was still muttering away to himself when he realised that he lacked the key utensils to make a pie from scratch – namely, a rolling pin and a pie dish.

'Don't give up,' he said, still talking to himself as he took the premade pastry out of the wrapper. At least he wasn't making that from scratch, but if it tasted good, he was up for telling a little white lie and passing it off as his own. He was all out to impress Katie, but as plans went, this wasn't one of his better ones. He set to work, pulling out the pastry and using the handle of the wooden spoon to try and roll it out, but it was proving way too difficult. It was continuously sticking around the handle and breaking as he tried to peel it off.

'Flour, I need flour,' he mumbled, opening all the cupboard doors, but of course his cupboards weren't full of condiments or baking ingredients.

With the beef and mushrooms sizzling in the pan, Ben looked at the pastry with despair. It would have to do, but it now had so many holes in it that it resembled a pair of fishnet tights. He was beginning to feel under pressure, which was daft compared to some of the intense medical situations he'd been in. The kitchen had gone from an average temperature to boiling and Ben threw open the kitchen window. Thankful for the blast of cool air, Ben had a brain wave: all he had to do was cut the pastry into quarters, wrap up the beef and mushroom inside and brush them with an egg, and they would pass as homemade pasties. Brilliant.

He was thinking he was an absolute genius until smoke from the sizzling beef activated the smoke alarm. Waving the tea towel frantically to try and shut up the high-pitched din, Ben wished he'd kept a closer eye on the beef. With the beef now cremated and the mushrooms shrunk to half their size, he scooped them out of the frying pan and folded the burnt mixture inside the holey pastry. A bit of gravy poured on top would bring it back to life, he thought, hoping the burnt bits of beef weren't too chewy. He scooped out four heaped teaspoons from the Bisto gravy granule jar into a jug, then filled the kettle up with water.

'Okay, they don't actually look that bad.' He admired his culinary skills and bunged the pasties into the oven and whacked the temperature up to 180 degrees. 'Now how difficult can it be to make mashed potatoes?'

With the potatoes cut into bite-size chunks and boiling away on top of the stove, Ben was starting to feel a little more relaxed. He'd picked up a small bouquet of flowers from Hamish's shop and they were now in a vase in the middle of the dining table, but he wasn't sure about two things. First, could he actually see Katie over the top of the flowers? And secondly, did the table look like it was set up for a date?

Ben took the vase on and off the table umpteen times before deciding to leave it where it was. Remembering the potatoes, he stuck a knife straight through a piece bobbing about in the boiling water and it seemed soft enough, so he switched off the hob and looked around. The kitchen looked like a bombsite.

But with the food in the oven and thirty minutes to spare, he had time to have a quick shower then tidy up the kitchen. Pondering what to wear, Ben headed for the shower. After the day he'd had, there were many thoughts running through his mind as the water ran over his body. He admired Katie and how calm and caring she'd been whilst talking to Alana on the cliff edge. Ben hadn't felt calm; in fact, he'd felt scared out of his wits and not just because he was scared of heights but because Alana was swinging her legs over the edge of a high cliff and the drop below was mainly rocks and boulders. He shuddered just thinking about it.

Tomorrow was a big day for Alana and Stuart. Ben and Katie had organised for Alana to take full-time residency in a nearby private care home. It was a home that Stuart and Alana had fully researched in the past and were waiting until the time was right – which was now. It was going to be a huge change for each of them. But as Alana's memories and communication were deteriorating quickly, Ben knew that Stuart had come to the right decision, no matter how hard that decision was.

Just as Ben soaped up his mass of curly hair, he thought he heard banging. Poking his head around the shower screen, he listened. Yes, there it was again. Absolutely typical – why do people always knock on the door at inconvenient times? Quickly pulling a towel around his waist, he left sodden footprints on the wooden floor as he walked towards the door.

Katie stood on the doorstep with a bag slung over her shoulder and a bottle of wine in her hand. Her face broke into a grin. 'Well, this wasn't the welcome I'd anticipated, but I don't mind it one little bit.' She ran her eyes over Ben's glistening wet toned torso and stopped at the towel that clung around his waist.

She leant forward playfully and Ben panicked. He thought she was about to whip the towel from him.

'Don't you dare!' He didn't like the playful look in Katie's eye. 'You go and pour yourself a drink. There's beer and wine in the fridge.' He pointed towards the kitchen. 'I'm just going to get some clothes on.'

'You don't have to on my account,' she joked, 'but I'd probably wash that shampoo out of your hair. You look kind of strange.'

Ben took a quick glance in the mirror. His midnight black curls had flattened to his head. It wasn't how he'd imagined opening the door to Katie.

'Woah! What the hell has gone on here? Has World War Three begun and I've been oblivious?' she shouted as she placed her bag on the coffee table and wandered through to the kitchen. She picked up the pan and stared at the burnt beef stuck to the bottom of it.

'You're early. I was going to get all this cleaned up before you came. I'll do it in a minute…just need to get changed.' Ben's voice petered out as he disappeared back inside the bathroom, locking the door firmly behind him.

Ten minutes later, dressed in jeans and a casual shirt, Ben returned to find Katie lounging on the settee with her feet propped up on the coffee table and a beer in her hand. 'There's one there for you.'

'Thank you, I'll just clean up the mess in the…' Ben

stood in the doorway of the kitchen and stared. The kitchen was spotless, gleaming in fact. Katie had even watered the green leafed potted plant fighting for survival on the window sill. He turned around, amazed. 'Thank you.'

'You are very welcome. Now come and have a look at this.'

On the coffee table was a large sheet of paper. 'What have you there?' asked Ben, sitting on the settee and looking at the map drawn out on the page alongside numerous coloured Post-it Notes.

'This is a map of the boat race and these are all the refreshments tents and stalls that have signed up to take part.'

'This is very impressive.' Ben examined the map.

Katie pointed to a spot. 'The majority of the stalls are in the vicinity of The Old Boat House and at the end of the race, with more dotted along this stretch of the riverbank.'

'I'm particularly liking the beer tent right at the end of the race.' Ben tapped the map.

'If I've not drunk it dry by the time you arrive.' Katie nudged his arm playfully.

'Yeah, yeah, whatever.' Ben rolled his eyes as he took a swig of his beer. 'We'll see, but can I just go back to today? Katie, you were amazing the way you handled the situation.'

'I've just had an awful lot of experience.'

'What was it like looking after your brother?' Ben asked cautiously.

Katie took a deep breath in, as though she knew talking about this issue was going to be hard. 'With my brothers being five years older than me, I think I was more than likely a mistake for my parents. Ellis had always been my parents' blue-eyed boy, but when things started to change with him, my parents struggled. Dementia in the young isn't expected and they…disowned him.'

'They disowned him? Why would they do such a thing?'

Katie took another breath and got herself comfy on the settee. 'The twins were successful at everything they touched. Ellis in particular had a certain charm and wit; he was so charismatic.'

'That must run in the family,' chipped in Ben, causing Katie to smile.

'But then his behaviour started to change. It wasn't as though he was an unruly teenager. He was in his mid-thirties, but my parents thought Ellis was into drugs or that he'd got in with a bad crowd, which was just ridiculous at his age, but at the time, no one understood what was going on.' Katie took a sip of her beer. 'Things slowly began to escalate over a couple of years. He even got himself arrested a couple of times. There were numerous incidents, including shoplifting and driving away from petrol stations without paying. Ellis was given community service. The local press went to town on it; you can imagine the headlines. The arguments between him and my parents became explosive, and it just got worse and worse until they wiped their hands of him.'

'But they didn't know he had dementia?'

Katie shook her head. 'I had a suspicion that something wasn't quite right. Ellis had never put a foot wrong in his life and after talking at great lengths with Luke, we began to research what might be wrong with him. And that's when we stumbled on dementia in the young. Ellis's facial expressions started to alter and he'd begun lying to us about what he'd been up to. He'd also developed a bad temper, especially towards Mum. He was awful physically and emotionally. They couldn't do anything to calm him down or reason with him and that's why they just gave up on him. I had to make a choice – stay united with my parents or support Ellis. I was stuck in the middle and so everything was left to me. I wanted to get to the bottom of it and although it was difficult when my own career was so demanding, I knew it was the right thing to do. So my parents fell out with me too, but it wasn't just because of Ellis…'

'What could you have possibly done that could cause your parents to stop speaking to you?' asked Ben, noticing that Katie suddenly paled.

She swallowed, obviously unsure whether to share. 'I got married.'

Even though Ben was aware of this information, it still took him by surprise when the words left Katie's mouth. Her words hung in the air.

'I married a man called Oliver Green and it's safe to say my parents didn't approve.'

Ben wasn't sure how he felt that Katie had been married, but he was relieved that she felt comfortable enough to open up to him about it.

'Why didn't your parents approve?'

'Because Oliver was so different to them. In their words, not the right class. He had no real career prospects and didn't have a job. He sofa surfed then rented a room on a notorious housing estate. According to them, I could do better. Oliver had gotten himself into trouble with the police – not ideal. He was involved in petty crime but he had a heart of gold, and I know that's difficult to understand but he was good to me. He listened to me and was there for me. However, according to my parents, I'd brought shame on my family by even talking to this class of person.' Katie rolled her eyes. 'I shouldn't smile but my parents infuriate me with their judgemental ways. They always have an opinion when no one has asked for it, but Oliver got me through one of the hardest times of my life while I was caring for Ellis.'

'How did you meet?'

'Ellis introduced us. They met on community service and, as you can imagine, my parents were not impressed. Doctor's daughter shacks up with a petty criminal.'

Ben was speechless but listened. He wanted to know everything.

'We married on a whim. Maybe I was making a point to my parents that they no longer had control over me. I never felt good enough for them and it seemed the right thing to do at the time, but it was short-lived. Looking back, we weren't in love – we were just thrown together because of our love for Ellis and broke up amicably a few months later. We are still the best of friends, despite what my parents think. Ellis and Oliver built an instant bond the moment they met, but Oliver was by my side during the conflict with my parents and he helped out with Ellis right up to the end. He's a kind and decent man to me, and if it wasn't for his help with Ellis, I would have been completely on my own. For most of the time, Luke was out of the country with work, but he tried his best to get back as often as he could.'

'It sounds like Oliver was just what you and Ellis both needed.'

Katie's eyes brimmed with tears. Ben held his arms out to her and she shuffled across the settee towards him. He wrapped his arms around her.

'Thank you, I needed that,' she said, snuggling into his chest. 'With Ellis, I began to speak with lots of families going through the same thing and we decided to ask for help, get tests done, et cetera, and my suspicions were right. I gave up work for a few months so I could concentrate solely on him.'

'I'm so sorry to hear all this, Katie. You really have been through the mill.'

'Not as much as Ellis. His plans for his own future were taken completely out of his own hands. I loved him with all my heart, and it seemed it was only me who could reason with him. Luke was devastated, of course. I think because they were twins, he began to blame himself. Why Ellis? Why not him? He would have swapped places with him in a heartbeat. In the end, Ellis deteriorated fast; he didn't recognise any of us anymore. We became complete strangers to him.'

Ben pulled Katie in closer and lightly kissed the top of her head.

'I wasn't coming around here for a therapy session, but I actually feel better for talking about it.'

'And that's why you got involved with the charity.'

'Ellis and Luke were the first ones to take me kayaking out on the river all those years ago, and when Stuart wanted to do something to raise awareness, the boat race seemed perfect, especially with the River Heart right on our doorstep. It would have been something Ellis would have loved to get involved in. Hopefully Luke will be proud of me.'

'And Oliver?' The question had left Ben's mouth before he could think about it.

Katie looked up at him and smiled. 'Oliver became a father a few weeks back. Our divorce is just going through, but he's back on the straight and narrow with a decent job. Would you believe he was involved in a rehabilitation programme and he's actually working in a care home? That's the reason I knit the shawls and scarves – to donate to the home. I like to give something back to his residents after he helped me.'

The only word that Ben could muster up was, 'Amazing.'

'And Oliver is happy. He's found his one true love and I couldn't be happier for them all. He's already made a donation to the fund-raising page.'

'Was Luke the man I saw bringing you flowers the other day? And the man who dropped you off early in the morning on your day off?'

Katie sat up and narrowed her eyes. 'Nothing gets past you, does it?'

She took a breath. 'That day was the twins' birthday. I'd been with Luke to visit the grave and we'd spent the evening looking through lots of old photographs whilst drinking copious amounts of red wine. It's Luke's cat that's had kittens, hence why I've taken Romeo off his hands.'

'I often wished I had a sibling,' shared Ben, finishing the beer while thinking about the DNA test. He'd checked his emails religiously every day, waiting for the results, but there was still nothing from the ancestry test. 'It just wasn't meant to be. I often thought it would have been nice to have a partner in crime. But as I was adopted, I'm assuming they couldn't have children. Having no one can be lonely at times,' admitted Ben. 'But is that better than the unknown, the truth? Knowing I was rejected by someone.'

Katie took his hand. 'You don't know that yet. How are you feeling about the DNA test? When we took that test, I didn't realise that the results could have such a major impact on your life.'

'The wait is terrible, but there's no point in me worrying or second guessing. The test might throw up the answers about why I was adopted or it may not. I'll just have to deal with it when the time comes. But in, the meantime, I'm trying my very hardest not to think about it. However, I'm feeling settled in my life and I am ready to deal with whatever it throws up for me.'

'Whatever happens, I'm here. We can face it together.'

'Thank you. That means so much to me.' Ben knew that Katie was being genuine and she was ready to support him. He had no clue what the test was going to uncover and he was grateful she was there. He could see she had been through a traumatic time with the death of her brother; he'd been so young and it was such an extreme circumstance. It had significantly changed her as a person and he admired her strength and courage.

'And having no one at all, does that mean there is no one else on the scene? No special someone?' probed Katie.

Ben shook his head. 'And these dating apps are hard going.'

'Dating apps? Come on, let me take a look at your profile.' Katie was holding out her hand with a slight smirk on her face.

'You may as well have more ammunition to take the mick out of me.' He swiped on his phone and passed it to Katie.

'Nice photos, except that one. You look a bit stuffy.'

'What's wrong with that one? It's my favourite shirt.'

'Really?' She grinned before howling with laughter. 'That's a very humorous bio.' She handed the phone back.

'I can't quite take the credit for that – the bio is the wit of Helly.'

Katie laughed. 'I'm sure you don't need dating apps. Just let the universe take control. You never know who will cross your path. But in the meantime, I'm hoping that there is more beer in the fridge.' She held up her empty beer bottle. 'And I have to say, you are a terrible host. You've made me cry, my beer has run dry and what the hell are you cooking in there? I don't mean to sound rude, but there's a funny smell coming from your kitchen.'

Panic engulfed Ben as he shot up from the sofa and rushed into the kitchen. Quickly grabbing the oven gloves, he flung open the oven door to be greeted by a waft of heat. He reached inside and flung a hot tray of blackness onto the top of the hob, then stared at it in despair.

'What the hell is that?' Katie was peering over his shoulder at the cremated pasties.

Ben sighed. 'Homemade beef and mushroom pasties with cold lumpy mashed potatoes.'

'Sounds delicious! You really do know how to show a girl a good time, don't you? You need to add that to your bio…useless cook!' She grinned.

Ben flung the oven gloves onto the worktop then switched off the oven. Then he opened the drawer and handed Katie numerous menus. 'Takeaway it is!'

'Curry, always curry for me. Chicken balti, pilau rice and let's go all out…a keema naan,' she suggested.

'Good job we have the best curry house on the other side of the bridge.'

Within twenty minutes, the curry had been delivered and Ben placed the foil trays onto the table. Katie grabbed the bottle of red from the kitchen. 'This is the good stuff; it would have washed the burnt pasties down a treat.'

Ben did the gentlemanly thing and pulled the chair out for Katie as she sat down.

'You even have flowers.' Katie admired the pink carnations in the vase in the middle of the table whilst Ben switched on some background music.

'Picked by my own fair hands. Those are just for you.'

'Really?' asked Katie. 'Is that why I saw the cellophane in the bin whilst I was scraping off burnt beef from the bottom of the pan?'

'Okay, busted. I picked them up from Hamish's.'

'Well, they are a lovely touch,' replied Katie, breaking off a bit of poppadom and scooping up the sauce. She watched as Ben piled everything onto his plate in one go, then leant in towards Katie's curry. She quickly put her hand over the foil tray.

'No, you don't. I never share my curry! If you want to try some, buy your own.' She swiped his hand away.

'You are being serious, aren't you?'

'Absolutely I am. Growing up in a house of boys, it was survival of the fittest. So don't even think about it.'

'You can be a feisty one at times.'

'Not all is fair in love and curry,' she quipped, now spooning all her own curry onto her plate before Ben could attempt to pinch more. 'This is cooked to perfection unlike those pasties.'

'How do you know, though? You never even tried them. But I am sorry, I wanted it to be perfect.'

'You don't need to apologise, this is perfect.' Katie met his gaze. 'And actually, I'm having a wonderful time.'

'I'm really enjoying your company too. I hope we can do more of this…without the burnt pasties, of course.'

Twenty minutes later, neither of them could eat another morsel. With the plates in the dishwasher, they made themselves comfortable on the settee by propping up their feet on the coffee table.

'I'm absolutely stuffed,' declared Ben.

'Me too. I'll have to row harder to burn off these calories tomorrow.'

'You really do intend to win, don't you?' Ben looked sideward and gave her a mischievous grin.

'Absolutely. Losing is not an option.' Katie looked straight into his eyes; his gaze was fixed on hers as he peered up under his dark lashes. 'Do you mind that I've been married?'

Ben was taken aback by the question. Katie had put him on the spot. At first, Ben did mind. He didn't like the thought of Katie being married at all and he knew that feeling like that only meant one thing – he cared for her. But after hearing the circumstances and her explanation, he understood. With everything she had coped with, she needed that constant support in her life during her most difficult time. He was glad that she had had a shoulder to lean on.

'The past is past, and you needed to do whatever you needed to do to get through it.'

'Thank you,' she said. 'And for not judging me.'

They were staring into each other's eyes, and neither of them faltered until Katie lowered her eyes towards his lips. He could feel his heart hammering against his chest. Katie was so easy to be around, not to mention drop-dead gorgeous.

'You're very welcome,' he murmured. Their eyes stayed fixed on each other for a second longer before Ben turned back towards the map. 'What I want to know is, have you actually studied the route we will be rowing down the river?'

Katie leant forward and tapped the drawn-out plan. 'I don't want to worry you, but I've studied every fallen tree, every boulder, and the bends of the river.'

Ben was finding it hard to concentrate as Katie's leg brushed against his, but he forced himself to look over the map as he took another sip of wine. 'I haven't but if you leave this map with me, I'll soon memorise it all.'

'Haha, not a chance.' She took a breath and suddenly looked pensive. 'Ben...when Ellis died, my whole world stood still for a while. Since arriving in Heartcross, it's felt as though I'm beginning to get a little bit of me back. I knew you'd be the best tonic for me. And I know over the years I may have wound you up a little…'

'Only a little?' he replied light-heartedly.

'But the second I saw your photograph and knew you were in Heartcross, my gut feeling was telling me to apply for the job. I knew it would be good to see you and this is the first time in a long time that I feel like I've got a career and a future to look forward to again. It's good to be part of the community. I know it must have been a little bit of a shock when I turned up on your birthday, and there was a part of me that still wanted to make an entrance…'

'I knew there was still some of the old Katie in there somewhere.' Ben was smiling.

'But you have helped me without even knowing it.'

'It was a shock seeing you, I have to admit. My initial thoughts were what the hell had I done to deserve such a thing.'

Katie swiped his arm.

'But you have definitely mellowed in your old age and I can understand the reasons why.'

Katie nodded. 'Life and experience changes you,' she admitted, smiling a sad smile.

Ben instinctively leant forward and tucked a stray strand of hair behind her ear like it was the most natural thing in the world to do. He could see she was thinking of Ellis and fighting back the tears. He stretched out his arm and pulled

Katie in close; the pair of them sat in a contemplative silence.

'I'm glad you chose Heartcross to get your life back on track. You really are an amazing woman. I mean –' He leant forward and jokingly tapped the map. ' – who else draws up plans of the river and marks out fallen tree trunks and boulders just in an attempt to win a race?'

Katie slightly slapped his chest with her hand, and the look she gave him caused his stomach to give a tiny flip – something he had only ever felt when he was with her. The intensity of her gaze made him shiver in anticipation and a warm feeling that had been missing for far too long flooded through his body. His head and heart were fighting each other.

This was the perfect moment to kiss her, but, the reality was, they worked together. Did he really want to complicate things further? But he didn't have to think about it as Katie sat up and cast her eyes up towards him.

'I have to go; no doubt Romeo will be treating my living room like his very own playground and I really shouldn't leave him unoccupied for a long period of time.'

Ben nodded, took her hand and pulled her to her feet. 'We've got a couple of options now,' he said, still holding her hand as he walked her towards the front door.

'Options?' repeated Katie, not quite understanding.

'I can either grab my coat and walk you home or call you a taxi.'

Katie pretended to think about it then laughed. 'Walk,'

she answered as she hovered on the doorstep. 'You could come into mine for a glass of wine?'

Ben of course wanted to say yes. It felt so good being in her company and the night had been perfect…except for his cooking. Katie had opened up to him, he'd listened, and he had a better understanding about the past few years of her life. And even though he didn't want the night to come to an end, he knew it was probably best on this occasion to say no.

'Next time; you go and spend time with Romeo and I'll see you at work in the morning.'

She nodded and put her key in the lock of her front door. As the door shut behind her, Ben knew he had a soppy grin on his face, which didn't go unnoticed by Katie as her front door swung back open.

'Have you forgotten something?' he asked, smiling, hoping there was a small chance she was going to lean across and kiss him.

'Absolutely, I have,' she replied, taking a step closer to him. 'I've forgotten my map. I can't have you studying all those fallen tree trunks.'

'I wouldn't dream of it.'

After handing over the map, her front door closed firmly behind her.

Ben reminded himself to breathe normally as he shut his door behind him and leant against it. Katie O'Neil was back in his life and he didn't want her going anywhere. Ben Sanders was falling for her hook, line and sinker.

Chapter Fifteen

The day of the medical school reunion arrived. Ben smoothed down his shirt as he knocked on Katie's front door and waited. Within seconds, the door swung open, and Katie looked him up and down.

'Are you going to the radio station dressed like that?'

'What's wrong with what I'm wearing?' asked Ben, casting an eye over his clothes.

Katie screwed up her face. 'It doesn't scream hip and trendy, it screams doctorish and stuffy.'

'But I am a doctor and I quite like this suit. In fact, it's my favourite suit.'

Katie turned him around and put her hands on his back, gently pushing him back inside. 'Jeans and a polo shirt. Anything but a suit.'

Ben blew out a breath. 'You are so bossy,' he exclaimed, reluctantly returning to his flat. He rifled through his wardrobe and picked out a casual polo shirt and jeans and slipped his feet into a pair of shoes. With his suit carrier in one hand and his overnight bag in the other, he was ready for tonight's reunion. He joined Katie, who was chatting to Helly on the landing outside her apartment.

'Tonight Helly has a date with Romeo.' Katie grinned, handing over the key. 'He's in your safe, capable hands.'

'Oh God!' replied Helly. 'The pressure! I'm sure we will be just fine, and I'll be listening into the radio show this morning.' Just then, all three of them turned towards the window. The sunshine from the past few days had completely disappeared, and the heavens had opened. 'Just drive safely. This rain isn't giving up anytime soon.'

'I'll go and open up the car, then you can jump straight in. Leave your bag here—' Ben stopped in his tracks. 'How many bags? It's only one night away, you know.'

'Believe me, this is packing lightly,' she replied with a smile.

'Jeez! How is that packing lightly? I'll come back up for it all in a minute.'

Helly gave Katie a cheeky wink. 'Such a gentleman; you've got him well trained already.'

'It seems that way,' replied Katie, following Ben down the stairs and shouting a thank you back up at Helly for looking after Romeo.

Downstairs, they both sheltered under the porchway of the door. The rain had worsened and was bouncing off the pavements. People were racing along the streets, clutching their umbrellas and trying to keep the drenching to a minimum. Ben stood hedging his bets about whether to wait a moment longer or make a dash towards the car.

'And which one is your car?' asked Katie, taking a sweeping glance up and down the road.

Ben pointed straight in from of him. 'There she is… Baby Spice.'

The look of horror all over Katie's face said it all. 'For a second, I thought you were implying you've named your car after Baby Spice.'

'I have,' replied Ben proudly. 'The Spice Girls are the best girl group ever.'

'It's more like Scary Spice,' muttered Katie, staring at the garish turquoise-blue Ford Fiesta which had seen better days. 'And you think that contraption is going to get us to St Andrew's?' Her eyes widened as the penny dropped. 'Oh my God, that was the car you had at university?'

'It certainly is and she is still going strong.'

'And you've never thought to update her because…'

'Because we have come this far in life, she's loyal and has never let me down yet!'

Katie raised an eyebrow at his exuberance. 'That's good to hear because I don't want to be stranded anywhere in this rain if good old Baby Spice breaks down.'

'Have faith. She won't, she will sing and dance all the way there, and it'll be good to get out of the rat race for at least forty-eight hours and let our hair down.' Ben smiled.

'And you don't know how lucky you are, spending your weekend with us – me and Baby Spice.'

She did, actually, Katie thought with a secret smile. She been looking forward to spending time with Ben away from work, but of course she wasn't going to admit that to him. Katie found him humorous, charismatic and, of course, he was intelligent. She found it so easy and natural to be in his company. With the rain not looking like it was going to give up any day soon, she watched Ben make a run towards the car. He unlocked it and grabbed an umbrella from the glove compartment. He was drenched, the rain soaked through to his polo shirt that was now clinging to his chest. Katie knew she was staring at him; she couldn't help it. His body was perfect.

'Here.' Ben put up the umbrella then extended his arm around Katie's shoulder. They ran the short distance and once Katie was sitting in the passenger seat with the door shut, Ben returned to fetch all the bags from upstairs. Within five minutes, the luggage was safely stored in the boot and Ben was sitting behind the wheel.

'First stop, the radio station and then St Andrew's here we come,' he trilled. 'It's like a mini adventure.'

'Let's put the radio on. They might give us a mention before we go on air,' suggested Katie, looking at the hole in the dashboard where there's usually a radio in a car. 'Has someone stolen your radio?'

'No, there's no radio.'

'There's no radio,' Katie repeated. 'Why don't you have a radio?'

'Not had one since uni days, when Eddison decided it would be fun to use the tape deck part as an ashtray and dispose of his lit cigarette in it. The whole thing burnt out, but don't despair, you don't have to listen to my dulcet tones for the whole journey because we have a plug-in CD player that runs off the cigarette lighter.'

'You are all about the mod cons,' replied Katie, with a hint of sarcasm as she watched Ben rummaging in the side pocket of the car.

'Ta-da!'

'Just look at that and the choice of music…'

'Only one CD and it's already in there… If you can just balance it on your lap as sometimes, when there's a bump in the road, the CD jumps.'

Katie looked horrified. 'Dare I ask what the CD inside is?'

'The Spice Girls.' He grinned, turning the key and attempting to start the engine. Which failed.

Katie rolled her eyes. 'I feel like I'm in some sort of weird dream.'

Ben turned the key in the ignition a second time. 'Don't panic, she never starts the first time.'

'I'm not panicking. Half of me is hoping she doesn't start and we can travel First Class on the train in luxury.'

Ben pretended to look hurt. 'She will hear you, you know. Baby Spice has got feelings.' He coughed lightly whilst turning the key for the third time. The engine started. 'Told you. She may be temperamental at times, but she never lets me down.'

Katie rolled her eyes again. 'Bang goes First Class on the train.'

Ben adjusted the mirror and raked his hand through his unruly hair.

'You need to put your seatbelt on, but make sure you give it an extra hard tug.' He switched on the wipers before checking over his shoulder to make sure the road was clear. Then Baby Spice kangarooed up the road and Katie immediately grabbed the sides of her seat just as the CD player kicked in.

At the top of his voice, Ben began singing out the lyrics, whilst Katie was muttering under her breath. 'I'll tell you exactly what I want – to get out of this contraption! Can this journey actually get any worse? I suppose heated seats is a no or just a little bit of heat would be welcoming.'

Ben gave her a sideward glance. 'No to either, I'm afraid, but there's a blanket on the back seat.'

Katie looked towards the flea-bitten blanket that had seen better days, then put her hands up to her ears as Ben crunched the gears. 'You know what, I think I'll be okay.'

Driving along the high street towards the bridge, the wind had picked up and the river looked angry as it raced along. An enormous clap of thunder broke overhead and the sky was leaden with an angry-looking storm and not a chink of sunlight could be seen. With the windscreen wipers thrashing to and fro, the sky was split in two by a crack of lightning that cast a momentary flash of light over Heartcross Mountain.

'Goodness, did you see that?' exclaimed Katie.

'Yes, let's hope the weather calms down soon,' replied Ben, who'd stopped singing and was concentrating on the road ahead. A second burst of thunder, even louder than the first, boomed across the sky. The wipers were struggling to compete against the rain as it hammered against the windscreen. The storm continued to shake the trees and there wasn't a soul in sight for the next thirty minutes as Ben drove carefully along the twisting winding lanes leading out of Glensheil.

'It doesn't look like it's going to give up soon.' Katie pointed to a fallen tree that was blocking half of the road. The traffic in front began to slow down and blue flashing lights could be seen up ahead. 'It looks like there has been an accident.'

'I'm not surprised in this weather.' He took a quick glance at his watch. 'Let's hope we make it on time for the radio show.'

'Is that your phone ringing?' asked Katie, looking towards Ben's jacket pocket. 'It sounds like it.'

'Yes, can you grab it and answer it for me?'

'What, no hands free?' Her face broke into a smile as she grabbed the jacket off the back seat and rummaged through his pocket. She glanced at the screen and looked surprised.

'It's Eddison, your old flat-mate. I didn't realise you were still in touch with him.'

'I'm not really. I've not spoken to him for years. Truth be told, we never really got on that well at university. We just shared a flat together. He was way more of a party animal than me and apart from being the untidiest student I'd ever shared a house with, I found him very loud and annoying. Always attracting the wrong type of attention.'

'I'm glad it wasn't just me then,' she replied. 'I found him a little creepy and spent most of my university days dodging his advances.'

'He could be a little full-on, but you never know, he might have changed over time. You best answer his call before it kicks into the answerphone.'

'Too late!' exclaimed Katie. 'Do you want to ring back?'

Ben shook his head. 'No, we'll see him in a few hours anyway.'

The traffic began moving past the accident. It appeared a fallen branch had smashed through the windscreen of a truck, which may have caused it to swerve and hit the oncoming traffic.

'I noticed on the reunion forum that you are kicking off the night with a speech.'

'Followed by a trip down memory lane. I've been putting together old photos from the university days that I'll project onto the screen. All in all, it should be a good night. I thought the visuals would help break up my speech,' replied Katie, turning off the CD and switching on the radio app on her phone. 'Jeez! They are playing the blooming Spice Girls on air, can you believe that?'

'Of course I can believe it!' answered Ben. 'Turn it up.'

As the song came to an end, they both fell silent as the presenter of the show Kim Smith began talking about the up-and-coming boat race to raise funds for the dementia charity. 'Dr Ben Sanders and Dr Katie O'Neil will be joining us in the studio very soon. Please stay tuned and in the meantime, please do look up the Heartcross Boat Race Facebook page. There's so much going on throughout the whole day. Get involved. It's going to be the best family day out, and the race begins at The Lake House at 11am. I believe the funds raised so far for the charity is a whopping ten thousand pounds. That is amazing!'

Kim's voice led into the weather, followed by an advert break whilst Ben and Katie were whooping with delight.

'Already ten thousand pounds! Stuart is going to be over the moon.'

'It is just amazing. And here we are.' Ben took a right turn into the car park of the radio station and manoeuvred the car into a space before cutting the engine. 'Let's go and raise some more money!'

Neither of them moved as they stared through the windscreen. The rain was still lashing it down and the trees in front of the radio station were trying hard to keep hold of their branches as the gusts of wind were still extremely strong.

Katie checked her watch. 'We are due on air in five

minutes, and we are cutting it fine thanks to the traffic and the weather.' She jumped as the rain pelted against the window. 'We need to make a run for it. It's brutal out there. Are you ready?' she asked, grabbing her coat and flinging open the door. With her bag grasped in her hand, she pulled her coat above her head to shield herself from the rain. Katie made a run for it and was blown towards the magnificent revolving glass door entrance. Ben was soon by her side and drenched from head to toe.

The receptionist looked up with a warm smile. 'You are brave venturing out in this. Can I help you?'

'Dr Ben Sanders and Dr Katie O'Neil. We're guests on Kim's morning show today,' announced Ben.

'Hi, I'm Genie. We were just wondering whether you'd make it in this weather. Let me get you a coffee and as soon as Kim has finished the weather forecast, even though it's quite self-explanatory today, she'll go into an ad break and I'll let her know you are here.'

'I'd love a coffee,' replied Katie, sitting down on one of the oversized plush red chairs in the foyer.

'Double that. Thank you,' added Ben, slipping into the chair next to Katie. As soon as Genie disappeared through the double doors, Ben looked all around. 'I've never been on the radio before. It's quite exciting.'

At that very moment, the heaven's drum roll caused them to jump out of their skin. The huge clap of thunder boomed across the sky.

'Woah!' exclaimed Katie, glancing up towards the ceiling. 'That felt like it was right above our heads.'

Ben noticed the bright red 'on air' sign that was flashing above the door to the studio suddenly stopped, followed by a loud click. The reception computer switched off and the room darkened as Genie came back through the double doors holding two mugs of steaming hot coffee.

'You were just in luck,' said Genie, placing the coffee down on the table in front of Ben and Katie. 'There's a power cut.'

'Unlike me.' Kim appeared at the door of the studio. 'That's the show over until the electricity is back on. Is everyone out?' she asked, walking across to the window and looking out towards the street.

Kim was just what Ben expected a radio presenter to look like. There was a quirkiness about her as she stood in the doorway with her short blonde spiky hair with a streak of pink that matched her lipstick. Her vintage David Bowie tour T-shirt was on show underneath a black loose-fitting jacket, which Ben was completely envious of.

'This is British summertime at its best.' Kim turned back around and raised her eyebrows then smiled towards Ben and Katie. She extended her hand. 'Ben and Katie?'

'Yes,' they chorused.

After they'd shaken hands, Kim pointed out the obvious. 'We can't go back on air until the power comes back on. Now it's just a waiting game.'

Ben felt a little disappointed; he was looking forward to

getting in the studio and talking to the nation. He was hoping the power would be on soon.

'And my show wraps up in thirty minutes. It's unlikely we are going to get to talk much if the power doesn't come back on soon, but do tell me all about the boat race. This is very exciting. What is your connection with the dementia charity?'

As soon as the question was asked, Katie became emotional and her eyes welled up with tears. Without hesitation, Ben placed a supportive hand on her knee. 'Katie's brother developed the disease at a very young age, but we also have a close friend who lives in our village that is suffering too.' Ben went on to explain the idea behind the boat race and how they would like to make it an annual event in Heartcross, involving the whole community as well as the tourists.

Kim was impressed and began to jot down all the details. She excused herself for a moment and they watched as she checked the diary behind the reception. Looking over with a big smile on her face, she said, 'Why doesn't the radio station get involved too? We can help increase awareness about the day, but we can also commentate on the event live from the banks of the river. What do you think?'

Katie and Ben beamed as they exchanged glances.

'What do we think? We think that would be incredible, wouldn't it?'

'Absolutely awesome,' Ben agreed. 'In fact, brilliant.'

'The power might be off,' pointed out Kim, 'but that doesn't stop us. I can't wait. I love a good boat race and you pair are competing against each other?'

'Damn right we are! But we already know who the winning team is.' Katie patted Ben's knee, who was once again rolling his eyes.

'Yeah, yeah, let's just see, eh!' Ben replied jokingly.

'I sense a little competition between the pair of you. I've written it down in the diary, which means it's the law! The radio show will be there.' Kim looked up at the clock. 'However, it looks like my show will be over before the power comes back on, but I'll plug the event more tomorrow and I'll be in touch.'

After finishing their coffee, Ben and Katie made a run for it back to the car. The rain seemed heavier than before and it didn't look like it was giving up any time soon.

'I'm a little disappointed we didn't make it on air, but what a gesture! How fantastic. Everything is coming together.' Katie pulled down the sun visor to take a quick glimpse at her reflection in the tiny mirror. 'Jeez, look at the state of my hair.' Her hair was wet and limp and stuck to the side of her face. She pushed it to one side. 'I might have had a face for radio, but now I'll never know,' she said, laughing.

Ben was looking straight at her. He was thinking that, even in a downpour, she still managed to look beautiful. 'You look mighty fine to me,' he replied, catching her eye.

'Whereas I…' Ben looked in the mirror, then they both burst out laughing.

His curls were tighter than usual with the dampness of the rain. Uncontrollable was the only word to describe them – he shook his head and the coiled curls sprung in every direction.

'I look like a clown who's had an electric shock!' He grinned, continuing to shake his head.

'Woah!' Katie exclaimed, bringing her hand up to shield herself from the flying droplets of water.

Ben was still grinning as he put the key in the ignition. Once again, Baby Spice didn't start until the third attempt. After checking the travel information on his phone, Ben turned towards Katie. 'Inverness to St Andrew's…three hours' drive. It could be more in this weather.'

'We have plenty of time,' replied Katie, checking her watch. 'Even taking it slow, we should arrive by mid-afternoon, which still gives us plenty of time to relax and get ready for tonight. After a few scoops in the bar, of course.'

Ben put the car in gear and went to turn on the CD player, but like an overzealous traffic warden, Katie put her hand up.

'Stop!'

Ben burst into one of his favourite Spice Girls songs. 'Stop right there, thank you very much.'

Jokingly, Katie put her fingers in her ears. 'I don't know what is worse: your singing or that CD.'

'Me and you will not get on if you are dissing the Spice Girls.' He pretended to look hurt.

'Me and you will not get on if I have to listen to one CD on loop. And we are getting on, aren't we?' Katie had a spark in her eye when she asked that question.

'Is that a serious question?'

'Might be,' she replied, not giving away any more.

'I think we are.'

Even though he was dampened by the rain, he felt a rush of warmth inside and glowed with happiness. He smiled broadly. Ben felt like they had come full circle. From the rivalry in the past to a mutual understanding of respect, tinged with a little flirtatious behaviour, their relationship was blossoming and he liked it.

'You do know you have dimples to die for,' said Katie, giving him a cheeky sideward glance.

'So my mother told me,' he replied, crunching the gears again and causing Katie to laugh.

'On your wage, you could afford to get rid of this contraption, you know. Have something a little more luxurious.'

'Shh, she'll hear you,' he joked, concentrating on the road ahead. 'And as the commute to work is only a flight of stairs...'

They followed the slow-moving traffic through the quaint villages towards the mountainous terrain. Even in the haze of the rain, the craggy hillside looked stunning. Ben drove past stones and boulders that dotted the landscape, tree lines demarcating the edge of the forest and the low hanging rain clouds covering the mountain tops in mist. Ben pointed towards Katie's window. She looked up to see the most spectacular waterfall gently running down the rock face.

'It's breath-taking,' she murmured. 'Such beauty.'

After a moment of silence, Ben replied, catching her eye. 'I agree.' There was a warmth about the way she stared at him with her soft blue eyes. Electricity sparked between them. He looked back towards her meaningfully.

'Why are you looking at me in that strange way?' Her voice was soft, her eyes wide.

Ben pressed his lips together; he knew his feelings towards Katie were growing and it was at that very moment he wondered if there could be something more between them. If they crossed that line, could things get tricky at work?

Katie was still gazing at him intensely and he could feel her eyes on him. He had already accepted a permanent job at Peony Practice, but Katie's position was currently a six-month temporary contract with a view to be made permanent for the right candidate. If she wanted to stay, Ben would have some influence over the medical board in the making of their decision.

'Just because,' came his reply.

'I liked how you took over this morning when Kim asked us why we were supporting the dementia charity. Thank you.'

'You don't have to thank me; I can see how difficult it is for you to talk about. I understand. I know it's not the same thing, but I still get choked up when I think about my biological parents. Especially at Christmas and birthdays.'

'I get that. I miss Ellis every day. I feel like my family has been torn apart and my relationship with my parents is non-existent.' Katie took a breath. 'In my view, a parent's job is to support their child no matter what. I'm not sure whether it's a generation thing, but all they did was wipe their hands of him. I used to have a really good relationship with my father, but even he didn't stick up for his own son. He didn't even challenge my mother or visit Ellis until we got his diagnosis, but, by then, it was too late anyway. Ellis didn't recognise anyone. It's caused a lot of damage to the whole family. They couldn't even say sorry for their actions – how they treated him, how they treated me. That's all it would have taken.'

'The world can be a very difficult place to live. There's one thing I've learnt: the only person you can truly count on is yourself.'

'Agreed.'

'It's a funny old world. You're estranged from your family and I have no clue about my real family.' Ben was thinking out loud.

'Maybe we can be our own little medical family. And what I've learnt is it's impossible to feel low around you. You make everything okay.' She smiled across at Ben.

'That's what friends are for,' Ben replied, returning her

smile and wishing those words hadn't just left his mouth. His feelings towards Katie were blossoming fast and he wasn't quite sure what to do about them. He concentrated on the road ahead.

The rain was still falling heavily and even with the wipers swishing back and forth, it was still difficult at times to see through the windscreen. They fell silent as Ben kept his eyes on the road, but his mind was still firmly fixed on Katie. He admired her bravery and even though he'd always felt like he hadn't somehow fitted into his own family life, he could never imagine ever falling out with his adoptive parents. He had the upmost respect for them and they'd supported him through good and bad times. That's the way it should be. He had no clue how he'd feel if they abandoned him or said such cruel things about him when he was at an all-time low.

Since his parents had passed away, arriving in Heartcross had given him a new purpose. His life at the moment was fresh and exciting and he felt the happiest he had in a long time. He knew the potential reason for that was sitting right next to him. He took the moment to look across towards Katie, whose eyes were closed. He did a double-take.

'Are you sleeping?' he whispered.

There was no answer.

'You are sleeping, aren't you?'

Still silence.

Ben watched Katie for a second. She looked beautiful

and restful and he felt a tiny flutter in the pit of his stomach, but his gaze was torn back towards the road. For the next two hours he drove towards St Andrew's whilst Katie slept.

Much to Ben's relief, time passed quickly and, despite the weather, the journey was stress free. Ben had already spotted the ruins of St Andrews Castle situated on the cliff top and, as he drove, he saw the home of golf; West Sands Beach. He was instantly transported back to his university days. He reminisced as he spotted the delightful cafes and independent family-run businesses that had once been a huge part of his life. With the hotel literally at the end of the road, he noticed Katie beginning to stir.

'Wake up, sleepyhead,' he said softly.

Katie sat up, startled. Her eyes widened like a rabbit caught in headlights. 'Oh my gosh, have I been sleeping?'

'Just for the whole of the journey. The hotel is just up here and Baby Spice was a dream as usual. She's got us here safe and sound.' He patted the steering wheel with pride. 'I knew she wouldn't let us down.'

'Got to love Baby Spice,' replied Katie, the sarcasm not going unnoticed by Ben.

'Here we are.' The car bounced through the large puddles on the uneven ground and Ben gripped the steering wheel a little tighter.

'Jeez, you didn't tell me you'd booked us into this place.' Katie was staring at the picture postcard view in front of her.

'It seemed the sensible thing if this is where the reunion

is being held… Scotland's most luxurious and spectacular venue situated on the seventeenth road hole of the renowned old course. To be honest, I've pounded this golf course and have always wanted to stay here, so why not? We work hard. We have the luxurious spa, the award-winning whisky bar and not to mention the outstanding cuisine.'

'Wow! You sound like an advert for the place,' teased Katie. 'I wonder who else will be staying here?'

'We'll soon find out.' Ben was looking at Katie as the car dipped into a large pothole.

Bang!

Ben hit the brakes and the car stopped. 'What the hell was that?' He raised an eyebrow, knowing full well he'd just hit a pothole, but it didn't sound good. He wound down the window. It was just Ben's luck the car was stopped in the largest puddle of water he'd ever seen.

'Well, she nearly got us there. Thank God we can see the hotel entrance.'

'Every cloud,' replied Ben, knowing full well he hadn't got a spare tyre in the boot. Only six months earlier, Baby Spice had a puncture and he hadn't replaced the spare tyre. After switching off the engine, he opened the car door. Thankfully the rain had eased a little and there was sunlight breaking through the clouds, but at this very moment, Ben was going to get wet no matter what. There was no way out of the car except by stepping into the large puddle.

'Typical, isn't it? Of all the places she could get a flat

tyre, it's right in the middle of the biggest puddle known to man,' Ben murmured, not impressed as he moved his seat backwards. He thought it would be a good idea to take off his shoes and socks. That puddle looked deep.

Amused, Katie watched him roll up his jeans and take off his shoes and socks. 'I know we aren't far from the beach, but this really isn't the time to go for a paddle.'

'Haha, very funny.' Ben looked at the ground again. 'Maybe I do need to keep my shoes on. The ground underneath will be gritty, but they are going to get soaked.'

'Just change into dry shoes later.'

Ben looked at her and remained silent.

'Let me guess, they're the only ones you've brought, aren't they?' Katie narrowed her eyes. 'Typical man. Always packing light.'

'I have my suit, essentials and a clean T-shirt for tomorrow. These shoes were the only ones I needed. How many pairs have you brought with you? It's only one night away.'

'It's probably best not to answer that. I'm a woman,' replied Katie, grinning, knowing at least four pairs of shoes suitable for all occasions was stuffed into one of her overnight bags. 'But in my defence, I was in the Brownies – be prepared.'

Ben gave her a look. 'I'm not sure I could see you as a Brownie. You'd be too bossy.'

Katie brought her hands up to her chest. 'You take that back. I was very well behaved.'

'Actually, why doesn't that surprise me?'

With his socks on the dashboard, but his shoes back on his feet, Ben slowly submerged his right foot under the water. 'This puddle should make the Guinness Book of Records. I could probably swim ten metres in this,' exclaimed Ben as the cold murky water quickly covered his shoes.

'You do exaggerate,' quipped Katie, leaning over towards the driver's side and taking a look.

'Urghh.' Ben's feet squelched as he lowered the other foot into the water.

Katie was trying to stifle her laugher but was failing miserably.

'Well, I'm wet now,' he said, stating the obvious as the rain carried on falling.

He took a step back and steadied himself. The driver's side tyre was as flat as a pancake, and there was no way he could push the car into a vacant car park space. After surveying the damage, he slid back into the driver's seat and closed the door. Pushing his curls out of his eyes, he turned towards Katie. 'We are going to have to make a run for it. The entrance isn't far and I'll bring the bags.'

'There's no way I'm lowering my trainers into that water.' She looked horrified. 'I think the best thing to do is call a taxi.'

Ben burst out laughing. 'Don't be ridiculous. The entrance to the hotel is right there.'

'I'm telling you now, these are new and there's no way I'm plunging them into that muddy puddle.'

Ben could tell by Katie's face she was deadly serious. 'You are such a diva!'

'I'm not!' she protested.

For a second, they stared at each other. It was ludicrous to order a cab and if Ben explained their journey was no more than a few hundred yards, they were sure to think it was a hoax anyway.

'Right.' He exhaled. 'There's only one thing for it. I'm going to have to carry you.'

Katie's eyebrows shot up but before she could protest, Ben was sploshing in the puddle towards the passenger side. As the door opened, he could hear Katie protesting.

'You are soaking wet.'

'It's either me that's wet or your feet. Take your pick but I really want to get out of this rain, grab a warm shower, change out of my wet clothes and sink a beer. So, you better hurry up and make your mind up otherwise I'm leaving you here.' He was deliberately keeping his tone light as he pretended to walk off.

'No wait. Don't leave me here!' Katie called after him.

Ben spun round and leant across Katie to unclip her seatbelt before he lifted her clean off her seat.

'Ben!' gasped Katie, but she didn't give much of a fight. 'I do love it when you're forceful,' she said cheekily, pinching his arm and giving him an approving look. 'Phwoar!'

Ben was suitably flattered by her flirtatious comment, but he shook his head in jest, spraying the rain from his curly hair over Katie, who gave a little squeal.

'Oi!' She giggled again, turning inwards towards his chest.

Their faces were centimetres apart. Katie was grinning and the moment felt full of warmth, romantic even. He was looking at her lips and she was looking at his. Their eyes moved upwards and locked as Ben cleared his throat and stepped straight into another puddle.

'Urghh!' he said as the water seeped through his shoes again. 'Surely those clouds are going to run out of rain soon.'

With Katie scooped up in his arms, he began to stride quickly towards the magnificent entrance of the hotel, most likely to the amusement of the diners watching from the restaurant window.

Katie was still giggling uncontrollably. 'What must this look like?' she asked, secretly enjoying every second of being wrapped up in Ben's strong arms.

'It looks like a diva being carried from a car as she's refusing to step in puddles,' he teased, stepping over another large puddle. His feet were uncomfortable in his shoes and he was now wishing he'd left his socks on, but it wouldn't be long before he could strip out of the wet clothes, have a shower and enjoy a beer.

Katie swiped at him playfully. 'I think we look like a romantic couple in love. You are my knight in shining armour carrying me to the entrance of our castle to shield me from the treacherous storm.'

'And I think you have been reading too many romantic novels. You are a diva…end of.'

'Okay, maybe a little, but that's between you and me,' she admitted in jest.

'I much prefer it when you are sarcastic. Stop swiping my arm!' He reached the entrance and lowered Katie to her feet. 'Thank god for that,' he joked, shaking out his arms that had turned to jelly and stretched out his back.

'You don't mean that. You enjoyed carrying me. It makes you feel all chivalrous – some men can only dream about having me wrapped up in their arms.'

But before Ben could come back with a quick retort, Katie stood on her tiptoes and kissed him on the cheek. She had kissed his cheek jokingly in the past, usually to get a rise from him, but this felt different. Her eyes sparkled and she lingered there for a second. His heart was pounding. 'And what was that for?'

'Just to show you I'm not a diva and that I do appreciate that you carried me from the car.'

'Mmm, the jury is still out on whether you are a diva, but now I'm soaked through to the skin,'– he noticed Katie's eyes drop down to his sodden shirt – 'I may as well get the bags before we check in.'

With huge fat dollops of rain still falling from the sky, Ben looked at the car before making a run for it. He was going to have to make a least one extra trip to the car with the amount of luggage that Katie had brought with her. He threw the boot of the car up and began to grab all four of her bags. With his hair flat against his forehead and the rainwater dripping in his eyes, he hurried back to the entrance with the bags banging uncomfortably against his legs.

Dropping them at Katie's feet, he looked back towards the car. With only a slight hesitation, he set off again for the rest of the luggage. The warmth of that shower couldn't come soon enough.

Hearing a roar of an exhaust, Ben glanced over his shoulder to see a two-seater red sporty convertible hurtling towards him at a tremendous speed.

The car was within inches of him.

'What the—' He dropped the bags and jumped backwards onto the sodden grass verge. He froze as the sports car threw up a tidal wave of cold muddy water over his entire body.

'Bloody marvellous!' exclaimed Ben, losing his cool. Aghast, he stared at the ground. His suit carrier, now imprinted with tyre marks, was lying in the middle of the muddy puddle. Swiping the water from his bare arms, Ben was livid. What idiot drives at high speed down the hotel driveway in this weather?

The engine of the sports car cut out and the door swung open.

'You could have killed me!'

'Well, look who it is!' The sound of Eddison's voice

boomed out and his now portly figure stood in front of Ben. The smirk on his old flat-mate's face riled him even more as he strode towards him. He shook Ben's hand in a vice-like grip, taking him by surprise.

'You are an absolute lunatic; you could have killed me.' Ben pulled his cold wet hand away from Eddison's crushing handshake and was taken back by his appearance. Reality was telling a very different story from the recent photographs Eddison had posted on social media. He'd piled on the pounds and his belly showed through the burst button on his shirt. The sweat patches under his arms were very undesirable.

'At least there would have been a few doctors in the house to take care of the body,' he roared. 'Come on, loosen up! What's up with you? It's just a little water. Why are you walking in this weather anyway? Couldn't you afford a taxi from the station?'

'We've driven here.' Ben looked back towards Baby Spice, who was looking as sad as him – lopsided with a flat tyre, abandoned in a puddle.

'No way! Surely not? Is that Baby Spice? Old Spice by the looks of her.' Eddison was guffawing at his own joke, which Ben did not find amusing. 'Is life that bad you can't afford a new motor?'

Ben wasn't going to dignify him with a response and he was beginning to remember why he never really got on with his flat-mate. He was loud and crass and life had always been about himself.

'Possibly the only girl that you could ever pull, eh?' Eddison was still laughing at his jokes and Ben was beginning to wonder how the hell they had ever shared a flat together.

'I doubt that very much.' Ben glared at him. He really wasn't in the mood to be ridiculed and he knew exactly who Eddison was referring to – Katie.

'Whatever you say. If I was you, I'd think about getting yourself cleaned up.' Eddison turned and walked away. 'I'll see you in the bar.'

He opened the car door and Ben watched as he struggled to squeeze behind the wheel. Eddison looked through the passenger window and smirked. The roar of the engine sounded and Ben watched in horror as Eddison reversed the car back over the puddle and his suit carrier before shooting forward and racing towards the vacant car park space.

Bending down to pick up his suit, Ben muttered expletives. He was feeling agitated, never mind soaked to the skin. He was in the mood for driving straight home, but Baby Spice wasn't going anywhere until the tyre was replaced. Nothing seemed to be going right today. He looked towards the entrance but thankfully Katie had disappeared inside, no doubt checking them in. Gathering the rest of the bags with his feet squelching inside his shoes, he trudged the last few hundred yards to the hotel entrance.

As he stepped inside, he searched for Katie amongst the guests and noticed she was in conversation with the receptionist. He took a breather and placed the bags on the floor. Inside, he was still fuming and was convinced Eddison had reversed the car over his suit on purpose. Now he had no clue what the hell he was going to wear tonight if the suit inside the carrier was as sodden as the outside.

Ben clocked a few funny looks in his direction as he waited patiently for Katie. Hopefully, she was kind enough to check him in too whilst she was at the front of the queue. He looked around. The foyer was lavish, with a crystal chandelier hanging from the ceiling; the marble floor stretched out towards a regally arching stairway. There were gigantic windows that ran from floor to ceiling at the far end of the reception that looked out over the freshly cut lawns of the golf course. If it wasn't still raining, Ben would be hiring a set of golf clubs and thrashing his way around the course to relieve some of the frustration from the last five minutes. He took a swift glance towards the glass door to the right of the reception. Eddison had already surrounded himself with a group of people drinking at the bar, his voice booming above everyone else's.

'What kept you?' Katie was now standing in front of him. Horrified, she looked Ben up and down, then her gazed dropped towards the dripping wet suit carrier. 'What the hell has happened to you?'

'Eddison is what happened to me, but never mind about him. I need the key to my room and a warm shower followed by a drink. Did you check me in?'

Katie scrunched up her face.

'What is that look for?' Ben had an uneasy feeling.

She exhaled. 'I don't know how to tell you this…'

'Just tell me.'

'They haven't got a booking for you.'

'What do you mean? Of course they have. There must be some sort of mistake. I booked the hotel rooms at the same time and you have yours. I have confirmation on my emails.'

He whipped out his phone from his pocket and stared at it in dismay. The battery was flat. 'Marvellous.' Ben blew out a breath then strode towards the reception.

The receptionist's voice was bright and cheery; exactly the opposite of how Ben was feeling. 'Can I help you?'

'I hope so,' Ben said as he explained the situation.

The receptionist tapped away on the computer in front of her. 'Sir, there is no booking under your name. I'm so sorry.'

'Impossible, there must be a mistake. I booked it at the same time I booked for my colleague, Dr Katie O'Neil. Maybe there are two bookings under that name?'

The receptionist was still staring at the screen. 'I'm afraid, according to our records, there is nothing.'

Feeling even more frustrated, Ben was shaking his head in disbelief. All he wanted to do was go to his room and have a shower. 'Your records must be wrong. Please can you check again?'

'Of course, sir.' The reception checked one last time but

again only came back with the same response. 'We have no booking for you. I'm sorry, sir.'

The receptionist was still looking at him. There was nothing more she could say and Ben was fully aware there was a queue forming behind him.

'Okay, if you could book me into another room…'

'I'm afraid the hotel is fully booked, sir, and we don't have any other available rooms.'

The words hung in the air.

They were not the words he wanted to hear. In disbelief, his eyes widened. He was standing there wet and cold and all he wanted was a warm shower. He forced a smile. 'But you must have a spare room. All I'm asking for is one room with a bed and a shower.'

'We have various functions on over the weekend and, unfortunately, we are full. I do know there are spaces over at the hotels on the other side of town if you would like to try there. It's just a short drive.'

Ben really wouldn't like to try there. Apart from the fact that Baby Spice had a flat tyre, he just wanted a room in this hotel. As he stepped away from the reception, he cast his mind back. He could remember booking Katie's room and emailing her the confirmation, but now he had a niggle in his mind that he'd been distracted and forgot to book his own. He exhaled and swung a glance towards the hotel bar. Eddison looked over in his direction and held up a pint of beer with a huge smile on his face. In a moment of madness, Ben considered asking Eddison to share his room, just like old times, but as Eddison swigged back his beer, Ben decided he'd prefer to sleep in the car.

Ben's face looked as black as the dark thunderous clouds in the sky as he walked towards Katie.

'Well?' she asked.

'There's no room at the inn,' he replied. 'It seems I need to try the hotels on the other side of town. I'll need to book a taxi.'

'But I thought you'd booked your room when you booked mine?'

'I thought I did, but it seems not. I'll just have to try the other side of town. I was just looking forward to staying here, but it seems…' he exhaled. 'Could you just ring me a taxi? My phone is dead.' He sank down onto the plush leather chesterfield in the lobby.

'I've got a better solution,' said Katie with a smile.

'If you are about to suggest I share a room with Eddison, then please don't. That thought had already crossed my mind.'

Katie laughed. 'I'm not sure things have gotten quite that bad. I wouldn't wish that on my worst enemy,' she said, picking up Ben's suit carrier. 'You'll just have to share my room.'

Ben raised an eyebrow. 'What? I can't do that.'

'Why not? I've got a double room, and it's not as though I'm a stranger. It's only one night and it saves you traipsing across town looking for a room. You could be in the bath within ten minutes and have a beer in your hand within the hour.'

That thought was very tempting to Ben. Katie waggled the key card to her room in one hand and her phone in the other. 'A warm bath or shall I ring you a taxi?' She tilted her head, waiting for his answer.

'A warm bath,' he answered. 'Thank you.'

'You're welcome but, just so you know, if you snore, you're out.' Katie was already walking off towards the lift. Grateful, Ben picked up the rest of the bags and squelched after her in his sodden shoes. 'And you better keep to your side of the bed.'

As the lift moved towards the fourth floor, Ben began to relax. A bath and a pint were finally within reach, and Ben was thankful to Katie for saving the day.

Chapter Sixteen

O nce they stepped out of the lift, they set off through a maze of corridors until they found their room. Katie struggled with the key card but, thankfully, after hearing a click, the green light flickered and, much to Ben's relief, the door opened.

The room was elegant with modern décor, and the view overlooking the rugged Scottish coastline was scenic. It had a flat-screen TV and fluffy bathrobes hanging on the door with complimentary slippers, along with a huge bowl of fresh fruit. There was a huge four-poster bed dressed in crisp white ruffle linen adorned with a green tartan throw, a leather armchair, a coffee table with a bottle of wine, two small whisky bottles and a welcome pack. The bathroom was also a good size with white tiles and equipped with an oversized bathtub and a basket of expensive designer toiletries.

'This is the life,' Katie murmured, placing the plug in the bath and beginning to run the water. She gazed at the luxurious products and whipped the top off one of them and inhaled. 'Oh my, that smells divine.' She squeezed the product into the water.

Ben was watching from the doorway, holding two crystal glasses filled with whisky.

'Drink?' he asked, handing Katie a glass. Even with just the slightest touch of her hand, the skin on the back of his neck stood on end. How the heck did she have such an effect on him? He shivered.

'You are cold,' she said.

Ben didn't tell her the truth – he might be standing there in wet clothes, but that wasn't why reason he shivered and why his heart was racing. He had never expected them to be in the same room and, even though he knew it was just because of the circumstances, there was a tiny part of him that was glad that his room hadn't been booked. Was it wrong of him to have those thoughts?

'We need to get you out of those wet clothes,' she said, taking a sip from the glass and peering over at him with a playful sparkle in her eye.

'Those are words I didn't expect to hear today.' He grinned, watching Katie swirl her hand in the water of the bathtub to lather up the bubbles.

'You know what I mean,' she replied, rolling her eyes. 'I think your bath is ready.'

'Gosh, I could get used to this. Whisky, a fabulous hotel

room and having a bath run for me. I don't think anyone has ever run a bath for me.'

'Really?'

'Really and thank you for this. It is much appreciated.'

'You're welcome,' she replied with a smile and clinked her glass against his. 'I couldn't have you staying on the other side of town. What fun would that have been?'

'No fun at all,' he said, looking over towards the bed and then suddenly panicking about the sleeping arrangements. He glanced at the chair. It didn't look comfortable but he had to at least do the gentlemanly thing and offer to sleep on there, leaving what looked like the most comfortable bed in the world for Katie.

'And don't worry about tonight. I'll sleep on the chair.'

'I wasn't worried about tonight and why the hell would you want to sleep on the chair? There are other ways to put your back out, you know. Joking!' She grinned. 'There's a perfectly good half of the bed that can be used.'

'As long as you don't mind,' he replied, watching Katie hang up the sodden suit carrier. She pulled on the zip to reveal that the muddy water had indeed soaked through to the contents. The white shirt was crumpled and stained, and water was dripping off the jacket and trousers. He looked at Katie's luggage and wished he hadn't decided to pack so light. What the hell was he going to wear now?

'And exactly what other clothes have you brought with you?' Katie was looking at Ben's small rucksack.

He placed it on the bed and opened it. 'For tomorrow, I

have a spare T-shirt and a fresh pair of underpants.' He took out the folded T-shirt and placed it on the bed. 'And my toiletry bag along with a pair of socks.'

Katie peered inside the bag. 'Is that it?' she asked, reaching inside and putting the clean socks next to the T-shirt, then pulling out a pair of brightly coloured Y-fronts. She unfolded them and held them up with both hands to take a better look. 'What the…' Her eyes were wide as she turned them over. 'You really wear these?'

Ben snatched them out of her hands and placed the underpants on the bed.

'You have Mario Kart on your underpants?'

'I do, and what's wrong with that? In fact, don't answer that!' He gave her a wolfish grin. 'If it's okay with you, I'm going to get in the bath.'

Katie was still staring at the pants. 'You fill your boots… they are a joke, aren't they?' she asked, picking them up again.

'They are my comfy pants. Keeps everything in the right…'

Katie raised an eyebrow.

'Too much information, I know.' He was grinning as he undid his shoes and shook them over the sink to remove the excess water inside. 'Actually, what the hell am I going to do tonight?'

'Don't you worry. Just get in the bath, relax and leave it in my capable hands.'

Katie sat down on the armchair with her drink and

watched Ben struggling as he attempted to wriggle out of his skin-tight wet jeans. She took a swig of the whisky before taking matters into her own hands.

'For God's sake, that bath water will be cold by the time you get into it.' She gently pushed him backwards onto the bed, and with Ben's legs flailing in the air, she grabbed the jeans from the ankles and whipped them off in record time.

'I can see you've done that before.' He gave her a cheeky glance.

'Oh my God, look at you, Clark Kent. What are those? They are worse than those ones. Just remind me how old are you again? Superman pants. Really?'

Ben was laughing heartily and stood up. Waggling his bum, he plugged his charger into the socket and attached his phone. 'These are my favourite pants and they had no intention of being revealed.' His grin was wide as he hot-footed it into the bathroom, pulling his wet polo shirt over his head. He flung it over his shoulder, narrowly missing Katie.

Before she could say anything else, he closed the bathroom door and wriggled out of his pants. Twirling them around in his hand, he opened the door and flung them in Katie's direction.

'Ew! Behave! You aren't at uni now, you know!' She grinned, catching his pants and tossing them towards the rucksack. 'Traumatised is what I am.'

'You should see a doctor,' he joked, sliding into the warm bathwater and lowering his shoulders until the bubbles were up to his chin. Finally, he began to relax. The drive had been long, the weather atrocious and it had been a hell of a day so far, but Ben knew it wasn't over yet. What exactly was he going to wear to the black tie event tonight? The trousers could possibly be sponged down, then dried off with the hotel hairdryer, but the shirt was a no-go. Damn Eddison.

The more Ben thought about Eddison, the more he realised Eddison must have known it was Baby Spice that had broken down on the road. Eddison had been in that car umpteen times. There was no way he wouldn't have recognised it. As Ben thought about his medical school days, the more he remembered. Eddison always took his jokes too far, he drank to the max and was always belittling people in public for his own amusement. Tonight, Ben had every intention of staying out of his way as much as possible.

He closed his eyes and before he knew it, he woke up, startled. It took a second to remember where he was. The bath water had dramatically cooled and his fingers were all wrinkly as he picked up his watch, which he'd left on the side of the bath.

'Bugger,' he said out loud. He'd been asleep for nearly two hours, and now there was no time to go into town to sort out a suit and shirt for tonight. 'Double bugger.'

Standing up and grabbing a towel, he wrapped it around his waist and looked at his reflection in the mirror. He only had one option and he didn't relish the fact that the only way out of his dilemma was to ask Eddison if he'd brought a spare shirt and a pair of shoes.

'So sorry Katie, I must have fallen asleep. You'll be wanting to get ready, and here's me hogging the bathroom.'

The hotel room was empty and there was no sign of Katie. She was no doubt socialising in the bar, which is where he should have been. Picking up the bottle of complimentary wine, he poured himself a glass and stood looking out over the famous golf course. Thankfully, the rain had finally stopped. He noticed that Katie had unpacked her bags. He smiled when he saw her PJs folded up neatly on the left-hand side pillow and all her beauty potions were lined up on the dressing table.

And that's when he noticed, in the middle of the bed, three cardboard boxes with a handwritten note laying on top.

To Ben, just for you, love from your Fairy Godmother xx

'What the…' He put down the glass of wine and picked up the first box. He instantly recognised the label on the lid of the box, which was from one of the most exclusive and expensive boutiques in town. This was a shop that didn't have price tags on the clothes. If you had to ask the price, you couldn't afford it and he really couldn't afford it – that shop was way out of his league.

Excited, Ben's hand trembled as he carefully opened the first box. Inside, the contents were hidden by light-grey tissue paper. He peeled back the paper and found a crisp white shirt, a black tie and a folded-up suit. Ben couldn't believe his eyes and let out a low whistle. He lifted each item out of the box and ran his fingers over the expensive cloth. Already he knew he was going to feel like a million dollars, and he wasn't even wearing it yet.

Intrigued, he quickly opened the next box and was amazed to discover a designer pair of black shoes and socks, and in the last box, a new T-shirt, a pair of jeans and – he laughed when he held them up – a pair of designer boxer shorts which put his Mario Kart underpants to complete shame. He took a sip of his wine. Katie's kindness was too much. All this must have cost an absolute fortune. Thanks to her extraordinary generosity, he was going to the ball and was about to give James Bond a run for his money. All he was missing was the Aston Martin.

Chapter Seventeen

Hearing the click of the key card, the door opened, and Katie breezed into the room.

'There he is. It's about time you finished in the bathroom. Do you know how long you were in there?' She looked Ben up and down, but he was only dressed in a towel wrapped round his waist. 'And he's still not dressed.'

'I fell asleep, but never mind that.' He swooped his hand over the clothes laid out on the bed. 'Did you do this for me?'

In a Cinderella-like moment, Katie lifted the suit jacket out of the box and held it up against Ben's body. 'You shall go to the ball,' she said with a grin. 'I couldn't have let you turn up to the ball in rags, now, could I?'

'I-I-' he stuttered, 'am actually lost for words.'

'Gosh, let me enjoy the peace and quiet,' she joked, kicking off her shoes and helping herself to a glass of wine.

'Katie, I'm being serious. This must have cost a fortune. I can't accept such lavish gifts, even if it has solved the problem of what I was going to wear tonight.' His eyes were still focussed on the suit.

'You can for one night only! I had many jobs when I was at med school, and one was working here at Shorters Row.' She held up her phone. 'Whilst you were snoozing in the bath, I gave a quick call to George, the owner, who couldn't believe I was back in town. I told him about our dilemma and here we are! The suit was delivered to the hotel within thirty minutes and all you have to do is hand it back to reception in the morning. The rest of the stuff…call it a present from me.'

'It really is who you know.' Ben was impressed.

'You should never burn bridges, as you really don't know when you might need someone. Just make sure it's returned in one piece.'

'I will, thank you. Come here.' Ben flung his arms open and attempted to give Katie a hug, who stepped back.

'Don't weird me out. You have no clothes on.'

'Oh yeah.' Swiftly, he dropped his arms and held up the designer underpants. 'I best put these on.'

'That is a good idea. Now, with only an hour to spare, have you finally finished in the bathroom?'

Ben pretended to ponder the answer. 'Of course! And where have you been? Have you bumped into anyone you know who will be going tonight?'

'The bar is packed with old familiar faces; everyone was

asking if you were here. Oh, and if Eddison makes it past the speeches, I'll be surprised. He's already drunk way too much.'

'I'm going to do my best to stay right out of his way.'

'Dr Henderson is also here. Our favourite lecturer. He's looking forward to catching up with you.'

'He was one of my favourite tutors.' Ben was looking forward to the night ahead and even more so now that he was going to dress to impress, thanks to Katie.

'Anyway, I need to take shower, wash my hair and get ready. I'll leave you to put some clothes on.'

Katie disappeared inside the bathroom. Ben unplugged his now fully-charged phone and sat down on the edge of the bed. He searched through his emails and stumbled on Katie's hotel confirmation, but there wasn't one for his room. It must have been his mistake, but hearing Katie singing away in the bathroom, he smiled. A part of him was thankful for that mistake.

With Katie in the bathroom, Ben took the opportunity to get changed. Once he was dressed, he looked at his reflection in the full-length mirror. The suit fitted perfectly, and Katie had done a terrific job. After patting his aftershave on his face and taking one last look in the mirror, he shouted through to her.

'I'll leave you to get ready in peace. Shall I meet you in the bar?'

'Perfect,' Katie shouted back.

Ben decided to visit the whisky bar. After ordering a

drink, he sat in the leather wingback chair overlooking the long drive. He watched as limousine after limousine turned off the road and travelled along the driveway towards the hotel. As the line of cars pulled up, chauffeurs opened the doors and people that Ben knew from the past stepped out onto the red carpet that trailed all the way up the stone steps towards the foyer, where they were met by waiters and a glass of champagne. Everyone was dressed to impress; their suits smart, their dresses stunning. There was no doubt tonight's reunion was going to be all glitz and glamour.

Feeling calm and sipping his drink, Ben relaxed for thirty minutes. Katie had had a hand in organising this event and she'd done a magnificent job in not only that, but taking all his stresses away. That's when he realised, sitting there watching everyone arrive, that Baby Spice was no longer blocking the driveway. She was gone. He stood up and walked to the window, then quickly pulled out his phone and texted Katie, 'Baby Spice is missing.'

Immediately, his phone pinged back. 'Don't worry, she's parked safely in the carpark with a brand-new tyre…your Fairy Godmother was busy this afternoon! X'

Ben was astounded. Not only had Katie solved his clothing problem, she'd taken care of Baby Spice too.

'You're a keeper!' he typed.

'I know! Now, stop gawping out of the window and look behind you.'

Ben spun around.

With a warm fluttery feeling rising up, he saw Katie. She was a vision of total gorgeousness and her smile lit up the room. She was practically edible and completely took Ben's breath away.

'You seem to be catching flies, Dr Sanders.'

Ben was fully aware his jaw had dropped somewhere near his knees. 'Wow! Just wow!' They were the only words that Ben could muster up.

Katie was breath-taking. She was standing in front of him in a simple but stunning dress made from a shimmering dusky grey satin, gathered at the waist with a satin band and floating elegantly to just below the knee. The cap sleeves and soft gathering around the scoop neckline oozed class. Katie had accessorised with a silver sparkly handbag and matching heeled shoes.

'You look stunning!' Ben could feel the wide smile stretching across his face.

'Why thank you – and look at you! You don't look too shabby yourself.' Katie admired his exquisitely cut suit, sharp and well fitted. The black satin lapels were perfect alongside his black bow tie. She took a step towards him and inhaled his woody aftershave. She lowered her voice. 'And you smell divine, but what I want to know is: are you going as Clark Kent tonight or James Bond?' She had a twinkle in her eye.

'That secret is all mine,' he whispered with a lopsided grin.

She held out her arm. 'Would you like to accompany me to the reunion ball?'

'Absolutely I would.' He linked his arm with hers and they began to walk out of the bar like the latest Hollywood couple, both looking like a million dollars.

It was only then that Ben realised how many people had arrived. The foyer was brimming with doctors who'd started their careers in this town.

'Look at everyone. Don't they look amazing?' murmured Katie, looking around at the hordes of spectacularly dressed people. 'I'm beginning to feel a little nervous. I've got to stand up on the stage and give a speech in front of all these people.'

'There's nothing to be nervous about,' Ben reassured her, slipping his hand into hers and giving it a little squeeze.

A cluster of photographers were hovering at the entrance of the function room. Katie could hear her name being called.

Katie and Ben headed their way. 'That's me,' she confirmed.

'You've done a fantastic job helping to organise this event. Would it be possible to take your photograph for *Scottish Life* magazine?'

'Of course,' replied Katie, smiling.

'And is this Mr O'Neil? What a gorgeous couple.'

Katie gave Ben the most heart-warming smile. 'This is Dr Ben Sanders and I'm sure he would love to have his photograph taken too.'

The photographers led them to the steps of the regally arched staircase and gave them each a flute of champagne. Katie leant in towards Ben. 'I feel like an international superstar.'

'You look like an international superstar. Never mind *Scottish Life*, it's the cover of *Vogue* for you next.'

All eyes were on them as the cameras began to flash. After a few more clicks, the photographers finished and they followed the cluster of people towards the function room. Katie's heels tapped on the slate floor as she walked. Ben held the door open and Katie stepped inside yet another glorious room. Ben couldn't believe the extravagance of this place. He felt like he'd stepped into the reception of a royal wedding, not a doctor's medical school reunion.

The view from the room was magnificent and the golf course stretched out for miles through the floor-to-ceiling windows. Ben was in awe as he looked up at the vaulted ceilings embellished with scallop edging and painted artwork. The curved observation balcony on an upper level was adorned with fluted columns with scrollwork and numerous tiered crystal chandeliers hung from the ceiling, glittering in the soft light. The glossy hardwood floor was suitable for dancing and a baby grand piano in the corner of the room housed a huge floral display. Each of the round tables were decorated with a pristine white linen cloth with a light grey tartan sash and a silver candelabra. There were framed mirrors spaced across the wall, a small stage area and the most impressive bar he had ever seen.

'I've never seen anything so magnificent in my life.' He looked around, then towards Katie.

'Me neither,' she replied, catching his eye.

The room was bubbling with excited chatter. The white-gloved waiters circled the room, offering canapés and champagne. Old medical colleagues with their champagne flutes pinched between their fingers air-kissed each other as soon as they recognised their old friends. Ben had forgotten about Eddison until he heard his voice boom out. His eyes darted around the room until he spotted him shaking the hand of a tall man who Ben didn't recognise. Eddison slapped him on his back and laughed. He then spotted Ben and started swaying over in their direction. The smile slid from Ben's face – Eddison was drunk and had obviously already taken ample advantage of the bar. If anyone was going to spoil tonight, Ben's money was on him.

Katie had left Ben's side for a moment and was chatting with one of her old university friends from the hockey team. On his way over to Ben, Eddison spotted her and veered off in Katie's direction. Ben felt uneasy and watched in horror as Eddison slid his arm around Katie's waist and pulled her in close to his sweaty drunken body. His face was flushed, his bow tie askew and already his suit jacket was abandoned, the sweat marks under his arms rapidly spreading down the side of his shirt. Katie took a step sideward to try and release his grip, but to no avail. Ben was observing his antics as Katie grabbed hold of his hand and pushed it away from her waist, but Eddison wasn't giving up that easily. Without hesitation, Ben strolled over and said, 'Three's company.'

Eddison smirked, waving his hand in a dismissive manner.

In the past, Ben had seen Eddison this way many times before, and the best thing was to try and not antagonise the situation, but it was a little difficult when he kept trying to grab Katie.

Ben kept his voice calm. 'Look, we don't want to cause a scene, we just want a peaceful night and to catch up with some of our old friends.'

Eddison swayed as he tried to slide his arm around Katie's waist once more. She looked uncomfortable and pushed Eddison's hand discreetly away as Ben stepped forward. Much to Ben's amazement, Eddison brought up his fist and attempted to punch Ben. Obviously, his aim was way off.

Ben felt like it was all happening in slow motion as Eddison swayed and tried to regain his balance by grabbing onto a nearby waiter carrying a tray of champagne. They all went crashing down, smashing the glasses to smithereens. The commotion caused everyone in the room to look in their direction. Ben tried to keep a straight face as he took hold of Katie's hand and stepped over Eddison, who was sprawled on the floor.

'Do you think he needs medical assistance?' asked Katie,

looking over her shoulder at two men who were trying to haul him to his feet. 'Do you know a doctor?

Ben smiled at Katie's joke, 'More like a pint of water to help sober him up,' he replied. 'How the hell has he managed to get in that state so early?'

'God knows. Shall we get a drink? It's speech time in five minutes, then this party can really get started.'

'That sounds like a good plan to me,' replied Ben, walking over to the bar.

'Tequila,' Katie said to the barman.

'Are you mad?' asked Ben. 'You are about to give a speech to all these people; you don't want to be half-cut.'

'Just one. It will help to steady my nerves.'

Ben watched as Katie threw the tequila down her throat and looked at Ben, who did the same. The alcohol zipped through his body. 'No more until after the speech.'

'You are such a spoilsport,' she said, about to order another.

'Dr Katie O'Neil and Dr Ben Sanders. Our very own power couple.'

They spun round to discover their favourite university lecturer standing behind them as he extended his hand.

'Dr Henderson, how are you?' Ben had a huge grin on his face. 'I never thought our paths would cross again.' He had such admiration for this man; he'd given Ben so much time.

Dr Henderson patted him on the back. 'It's good to see

you. I want to know all about where you are and what you're doing.'

'Would you believe I'm working alongside this one?' He tilted his head towards Katie, leaving Dr Henderson to blow out a breath.

'And you haven't put each other in an early grave yet? Never in my lifetime have I had two students battling to gain top marks in every assignment they were given. You did this'—he pointed to his grey wispy hair – 'and caused most of these wrinkles.'

Katie laughed. 'I'm so sorry if we put you through the mill, but I can confirm we have calmed down in our old age.'

'Glad to hear it. I still mention you two in my lectures. I believe our star pupil is kicking things off for the evening,' said Dr Henderson, pointing towards the stage where they were waiting for Katie.

'Just in case you were wondering, that's me.' Katie nudged Ben's arm playfully.

'And I'll catch up with you both a little more later.' Dr Henderson touched Ben's elbow as he made his way to his table.

Ben wished Katie good luck as she was ushered towards the stage.

Everyone began to take their seats for the speeches and Katie pointed to a table at the very front of the room.

'We are at that one,' she mouthed. Ben nodded and made his way to the table. Another one of Ben's old lecturers took to the stage and blew down the microphone. The loud noise quickly silenced the room.

'Welcome. Welcome back to your old university town of St Andrews. It's great to see so many students reunited this evening and I know you've all travelled from far and wide. The weather today has not been kind, so I'm glad you've arrived safely. At some stage during your time at the university, it was my job to educate each and every one of you sitting in this room, and I hope you all used my knowledge and wisdom to carve out the career you wanted and deserved. I have to say, I'm proud of you all.' The old lecturer began tearing up a little and took out a handkerchief from his waistcoat pocket to dab his eyes. 'Sorry, sorry. I still get emotional thinking about how many doctors we have sent out into the big wide world. Tonight is a chance to catch up, eat to your heart's content, drink and be merry.'

'Hear, hear.' The voices around the room echoed as they held up their glasses.

'And without further ado, I'm going to hand you over to Dr Katie O'Neil, who was one of our highest achievers ever; captain of numerous sports and social teams, and no doubt still winning at life. Please welcome Katie to the stage.'

The whole room erupted in applause, with Eddison whooping loudly and punching his arm in the air. Ben noticed a few disgruntled looks from the people sitting at his table. Was Eddison ever going to grow up? How had this man become a doctor?

The guy next to Ben leant towards him. 'There's always one,' he whispered and Ben nodded with agreement.

The whole room was mesmerised as Katie walked onto the stage. She reminded Ben of an Oscar-winning actress about to collect her award and give her acceptance speech. He was really looking forward to seeing Katie shine on stage, along with watching all the footage of the university grounds and old photographs from their time at St Andrews. Katie had worked hard collecting all the old photographs and short videos of favourite memories from the former students.

'Hello to you all! Can I just say all the men in the room look absolutely handsome.' Her eyes flitted towards Ben. 'And all you women look stunning. I honestly feel like I'm at a Hollywood party, not a medical school reunion.'

Ben noticed her hand shaking as she took a breath and picked up a couple of cue cards from behind her on the table. He knew she'd written down a couple of points that she wanted to include in her speech just in case her nerves got the better of her. 'Now here's a question for you all. Does an apple a day really keep the doctor away?'

'Only if you have good aim,' heckled a voice from the back, causing laughter to ripple around the room.

'Exactly that,' she continued, and went on to share a little bit of St Andrew's history before touching on their time at university. Katie's speech was humorous and kept everyone entertained. Even Eddison had piped down and was hanging off her every word. Katie relaxed into her speech and was an absolute natural up there on the stage. Ben thought back over the trying few years she'd had, and he admired her strength to keep going. She didn't let much phase her.

'At that brings me to the video of our time at St Andrew's University.'

The room cheered as Katie walked to the table at the end of the stage and picked up another cue card as well as the remote control. She took a quick glance towards the card. 'Before I press Play, I would just like to thank you all for coming this evening and to the hotel staff. Isn't this place amazing?' She swept her arm around the room. 'Now let's take a trip down memory lane.'

As the lights in the room dipped, Ben felt his phone vibrate in his pocket. It was a text from Helly. Normally, he wouldn't dream of checking it, but he knew it must be important and he hoped there wasn't any sort of emergency back home. He quickly opened it.

'Check your email! The DNA results are in! The bad news is I'm not related to Harry Styles, but I have found a couple of cousins in a nearby town and it seems I'm twenty-five per cent Irish with a smidgeon of Scottish thrown in. It's so interesting!'

Ben stared at the message, then back towards the screen of university photos flashing up in front of him. The guy next to him nudged him lightly. 'Put your phone away,' he whispered politely.

With his heart thumping nineteen to the dozen, Ben

quickly apologised then stood up and made his way to the back of the room. With his phone in hand, he walked into the whisky bar and sat down in a leather wingback chair. He stared at Helly's message again. With a thumping heart, he took a breath and opened his email. There it was, sitting in his inbox – the email containing his very own Ancestry DNA results. He knew the second he clicked on that email, it could change everything.

With shaky legs, Ben stood up and stumbled to the bar. Ordering a drink, he chugged it back, then loosened his bow tie. Ben felt like he couldn't breathe.

'Are you okay?' asked the bartender, removing the empty glass.

'Could I have another please?' asked Ben, charging the drink to the room.

Feeling his phone vibrate in his hand again, there was another text from Helly. 'The suspense is killing me. Any famous relatives?!?!'

His legs felt numb as Ben sat back down on the chair and placed his drink on the table in front of him. He pressed the link on the email. He closed his eyes tightly for a brief second then opened them again.

This was it. The results showed that his ethnicity estimate was sixty per cent Irish and the rest English and North Western Europe, which took him a little by surprise. He clicked onto the relative filter and held his breath.

'Oh my…' Ben muttered under his breath.

There was a face staring back at him. According to this,

he had a full sibling with whom he shared fifty-six percent full DNA. Ben had a brother. He felt scared and excited; his heart was beating so fast he thought it was about to pound out of his chest. Then there were two more faces looking back at him. He didn't need to be a doctor to understand the percentage of DNA they shared could only mean one thing. Those two faces looking back at him were his parents. Ben could feel his pulse begin to race; he couldn't breathe and his mouth gaped open.

He loosened the top button on his shirt as he gulped in a huge breath of air. His hands shook as he tilted his head backwards and tried to gather his thoughts.

Trying to calm his beating heart, he stared at the photographs again. After taking a screenshot, he zoomed in. He looked over their names again. Niamh Clancy, mother. Connor Clancy, father. Daniel Clancy, brother.

This was surreal. Yesterday, he didn't know who they were, and now he had a brand-new family staring back at him. His resemblance to them all was striking. He shared the same nose and eyes, and his wild curly hair was exactly the same as his father and brother. There were so many unanswered questions swirling around in his mind that he couldn't think straight. He couldn't take his eyes off the photographs, reading the results umpteen times. He swallowed down a lump. Tears welled up in his eyes. What the hell did he do now?

Exhaling, Ben hovered over the message button. He had no clue what to write. How did you start?

Then, suddenly, he took the plunge and began writing from the heart. The words spilled out onto the screen as he blinked back tears. Before he knew it, the words had turned into sentences and paragraphs and staring back at him was his life history. Then he deleted it all. What was he doing? He had no clue whether they wanted to speak to him or the circumstances of his adoption.

Ben knew this was the start and that contacting those faces was going to change his life forever. He was ready for all the answers, even if it wasn't what he wanted to hear. He forced himself to breathe deeply and calm himself. His heart was racing, but he needed to think about this and not be impulsive.

Hearing a rapturous applause filtering out from the reunion, Katie's speech must have come to an end. Dinner was about to be served. But with his appetite completely diminished, he couldn't face going back into the room. As the light came back on, Katie would wonder where the hell he was, but he was hoping she would understand once he told her the news.

Chapter Eighteen

F ive minutes later, with his drink and phone in his hand, Ben couldn't wait to get back to the room, get changed out of his suit and take a closer look at the information on his phone. His head was scrambled. It was only a matter of time before his biological parents were notified of a potential match. Maybe they had already and were pondering what to do as much as he was.

Bloody hell, Helly, this is a hell of a birthday present, he thought walking up the corridor towards the room. Just as he put the key in the lock, he heard Katie shouting his name from the other end of the corridor. Spinning round, he tried to smile.

'Oh my gosh, what happened? You look awful.' Katie touched his elbow as the door opened and they stepped into the bedroom. 'Let me get you some water.'

Ben perched on the edge of the bed. 'I feel like I can't

breathe. My throat is getting tighter and tighter.' Ben knew he was having a mild anxiety attack; he'd often had them when he was younger.

Katie poured him an ice-cold water from the mini bar. 'Take deep breaths and control your breathing. In...out...' As soon as Ben's breathing was stable, she passed him the water. 'Now drink this.'

As soon as he felt calmer, he handed the empty glass back to Katie.

'Do you think you are having a panic attack?' She sat down next to him.

Ben shook his head. Through bleary eyes, he looked at her. 'I've found them. I've found my real parents.' His voice was barely a whisper.

Katie exhaled and rested a hand on his knee.

'It's certainly been a day of highs and lows.' He handed Katie his phone.

Now it was Katie's turn to stare at the faces on the screen. 'Just look at this. They really are your parents and brother. You must be in shock. How are you feeling?'

'Scared, excited, unsure what happens now. I don't know what to do. I feel frightened,' he shared. 'I'm always the one in control and now I really feel like I'm not. I don't know what to do.'

'We can work out the next step,' Katie said, soothing him. 'We don't have to do anything right this second. Let's just take our time.' She extended her arm and hugged Ben tightly.

'Thank you for being here, but you need to get back to the reunion. They will be serving the food and I'm just not hungry. I'm just going to stay here. You should go back…'

'Don't be daft,' she replied, hugging him again. 'I'm not going anywhere. We can order room service if we feel hungry later on. You don't get rid of me that easily.'

'At the moment, I'm feeling lost and I'm not sure I want to get rid of you easily,' he replied as he slowly pulled back from her hug.

She took his hands. 'I didn't end up in Heartcross by chance, you know. I did come looking for you.' Her eyes fixed firmly on his. 'I knew from the first moment I sat next to you in that lecture theatre that there was something about you.'

Ben smiled at her; now his heart was beating fast for a totally different reason. He stretched his arms out and Katie snuggled into his embrace.

'Did you really come to Heartcross looking for me?' Ben asked softly.

'I did. I was always thinking about you after we went our separate ways.'

Ben could feel Katie looking up at him. He met her gaze, then dipped his head and brushed his lips against hers. It felt so right being with her. It had always been her.

'But I don't understand. We spent a night together and then it felt like you didn't want anything to do with me. It confused the hell out of me, if I'm being honest.'

Katie hesitated. 'Ditto. It seemed like you thought you'd made a mistake.'

'I did not. What gave you that impression?'

'Because you never said anything to me about that night, so I didn't think you were interested in me.'

'But you didn't either.'

'Because you didn't.'

They looked at each other for a moment. Ben was shaking his head in disbelief.

'But look at us now,' said Katie. 'Our paths have crossed again.'

'Yes, just look at us.' Ben took her hands in his. 'Katie, I need to take some time off work. I just need to get my head around all this.' He gestured towards his phone. 'And think about the next move.'

'Take all the time you need; I'll hold down the fort.' Katie glanced at the screen again. 'And a brother too. The resemblance is uncanny.'

'I know, but are they looking for me? Why are they on this site?'

'It seems like there's only one way to get those questions answered. Contact them.' Katie tapped the screen.

'But there's the slight niggle about my own parents. They chose not to talk about the reasons why I was adopted. Does that mean I wasn't wanted?'

'You've come this far, and I'll help you through it. I was rejected by my own family. To be family is about love, safety

272

and support – everything I never had. Things happen for a reason. That seems to be the gist of tonight.'

'And what a night it's been.'

'I think if your biological parents have registered on this site, there is a strong possibility they are looking for you. You have nothing to lose, only a family to gain.'

Katie was making sense. He would be no worse off if they didn't want contact, so what did he have to lose?

His email pinged.

Wide-eyed, he looked up at Katie. 'I have mail.'

Sitting in his inbox was an email from Daniel Clancy – his brother.

Ben could feel a churning in his stomach as he looked towards Katie. 'What the hell do I do?'

'You have two choices. Either you read it or you don't. Sleep on it. Read it in the morning. Don't do anything rash.'

'And you really think I'm going to get to sleep knowing there's a message on my phone?' Ben stood up and began pacing up and down the room. 'When I got up this morning, I didn't think my day was going to end in having a new set of parents.'

'Or a burst tyre or a sodden suit or sharing a room with me,' she said, trying to lighten the mood.

'There is that. And a brother I didn't even know about.'

'Stop pacing. You're making me feel dizzy.'

'Sorry,' Ben apologised. He lay down on the bed and rested his head on the pillow. He wiped a lone tear from his cheek. 'I can't even remember the last time I cried.'

'Probably when I won the last boat race,' she joked, kicking off her shoes and lying down next to Ben, who stretched out his arm.

'You are just not funny,' he said as Katie snuggled into his chest. Ben closed his eyes tight. The memories of his own parents flooded through his mind. Why would they not talk about the adoption?

'I'm going to read the message in the morning,' he said.

'And I'll be right here when you do.'

'I'm feeling exhausted. Is it okay if I just lie here like this tonight in your arms?' asked Ben, hoping the answer was yes.

Katie kissed the top of his head gently. 'It's okay by me.'

Ben peeled off his clothes and slipped under the duvet. Wrapped up in Katie's arms, he felt safe. The message was still going to be there in the morning and Ben was trying not to think about it as Katie lay her head on his chest and wrapped her arms around his waist. Holding onto Katie tightly, they were silent. Ben was lost in his own thoughts. He had no clue how tomorrow was going to pan out.

Chapter Nineteen

Slumped on the settee in his faithful trackies and his favourite Spice Girls T-shirt, Ben was half watching *Grey's Anatomy* while continually looking at the email he'd received from his brother. He'd been staring at the words over and over again for twenty-four hours and the revelation; that they had been looking for him all of his life, had shaken Ben to the core.

The Clancy family was situated in Ireland and, even though Ben hadn't had direct contact with his parents yet, he'd agreed to fly to Ireland that very afternoon to meet with Daniel. The whole situation was surreal, and Ben had no clue what he was going to unearth when he arrived. His bag was packed and his passport at the ready; all he needed to do was take a quick shower, then the taxi would take him to the airport. Truth be told, Ben didn't know what to think about any of it. All he could do was go and meet Daniel and listen to what he had to say.

Thirty minutes later, Ben stood by his suitcase and glanced at his watch. The taxi would pick him up any minute and he was beginning to feel nervous. He didn't even know how long he'd been staying in Ireland, but the surgery was in Katie's capable hands until he returned. Katie had been amazing in the last few days; they'd grown closer and she'd been by his side through the tears, excitement and confusion. He was extremely grateful.

Ben had mixed feelings; a part of him felt disloyal to his adoptive parents by taking this journey, but he had actually found his biological family and there was a chance to get to know them and discover the truth about who he actually was, which caused a twinge of excitement. Even though he still didn't know what to think about it all.

The taxi beeped outside his window. He looked at his reflection and took a deep breath. This was it; it was time to go.

Ben watched the scenery whizz by during the taxi ride, and, before long, he'd arrived at the airport, wheeling his case behind him with his rucksack over his shoulder. The blast of air conditioning inside the terminal building was a welcome relief after the warmth of the sun, but as Ben made his way through the revolving doors, he felt a wave of sadness.

In the pit of his stomach was an unsettling feeling – how had he not known the full story about his past? He checked his phone and saw a message from Helly, which made him smile. It read, 'This is another fine mess I've got you into.'

He needed to thank her. The birthday present she'd given him was a surprise all right – it seemed he'd gotten a brand-new family. There was no text from Katie, but he knew she would be run off her feet with patients.

Shoving his sunglasses high on his head, he looked up at the clock as he walked into the terminal building. He'd given himself lots of time once he'd checked in to settle his nerves about this evening's meeting, which was taking place in a hotel restaurant not far from where Ben was staying. Ben still couldn't quite believe his brother, who was two years younger than him, had always known about him. His adoptive parents had also kept the name his biological parents had chosen for him. The only thing that differed was his surname. Ben was not a secret in the Clancy household, so all Ben could wonder was why the terms of the adoption been a secret in the Sanders household.

Thankfully, according to the departure time on the plasma screen, his flight was on time, which meant he could relax, browse the duty-free and grab a bite to eat. Inside the terminal building, he followed the crowds of people across the grey tiled floor, pulling suitcases, checking their watches and tapping on their mobile phones. Ben couldn't help but notice that everyone seemed in a rush as he took one of the two glass elevators leading to the upper levels where the check-in desks were situated. Ben had to admit, while handing over his passport, the feeling of nervousness intensified in the pit of his stomach. Tonight, he had no idea what he was going to say to Daniel Clancy, and even though he had rehearsed many questions in his head, he couldn't remember any of them.

After waiting his turn, he answered numerous questions, his bag was tagged, placed on the conveyor belt and disappeared within seconds. Ben carried on through Passport Control and then into the departure lounge, where he purchased a coffee and seated himself on a blue fabric seat while he browsed a newspaper. For the next couple of hours, he tried to relax but everything was playing over and over again in his mind. Surprisingly, time passed quickly and Ben's flight was announced over the Tannoy.

He sent a quick text to Katie. 'Just boarding.'

He stared at his phone, but there was no reply. He was hoping she'd reply just to give him a tiny boost. He had just been swamped with a feeling of loneliness, which was daft when he was on his way to meet his brand-new family. Switching off his phone and stuffing it in the side pocket of his rucksack, he followed the masses down the air bridge towards the aircraft and checked his ticket. Making his way to seat 14A, he was sitting by the window and smiled broadly at the two passengers that were already seated in that row when Ben felt a tap on his shoulder. He turned to see a flight attendant standing there.

'Dr Ben Sanders?'

'Yes, that's me,' he replied.

'I hope you don't mind, but we've relocated your seat. Please can you follow me?'

'Of course,' replied Ben, following the flight attendant towards the front of the plane. She gave him a warm smile and indicated his new seat allocation. He couldn't quite believe his eyes.

'What the hell are you doing here?' Ben's face broke out into a huge grin as he exhaled and raked a hand through his hair.

'You didn't really think I was going to let you go through this on your own, did you?' Katie patted the seat next her.

'Who is looking after the surgery?' he asked, placing his rucksack in the overhead locker. 'Oh my God, I really can't believe you're here.' He was still shaking his head in disbelief.

'Dr Taylor jumped at the chance to come out of retirement for a few days and I know how anxious you've been feeling. I couldn't let you do this on your own.'

Ben looked at Katie with such warmth; his voice cracked with emotion.

'It means the world to me. Thank you.' He leant over and gave her a swift kiss on her cheek as he settled into the seat next to her. He grinned, stretching out his legs. 'And we have leg room.'

'We do, and sweets,' she said, handing Ben a packet of Fruit Pastilles. 'To suck on when we take off.'

'You really have thought of everything.' Ben couldn't

quite believe that Katie was sitting next to him. As he opened the packet of sweets, his hand was lightly trembling. He felt an overwhelming sense of relief that Katie was by his side; his load had been lightened. He popped a sweet into his mouth.

Over the course of the next ten minutes, the passengers began to settle in their seats; there was the constant sound of the overhead lockers being slammed shut and the clicking of seatbelts. Ben felt a sudden burst of jitters as the engines started and the noise increased to a roar.

The plane began to roll, slowly at first, but then Ben was pushed firmly back into his seat and, before too long, the plane lifted off the runway and soared into the sky. Ben and Katie watched as the houses and trees got smaller and smaller. Before they knew it, the plane had climbed high and all they could see was the intense blue sky.

'How you feeling?' asked Katie. 'Has Daniel given you any clues as to what happened all those years ago?'

Ben shook his head. 'All he said was it was better to tell me face to face.'

'And will you be seeing…' Katie hesitated.

'Niamh and Connor Clancy – my parents. They are young, you know.'

'I thought they looked quite young from the photograph.'

'Only sixteen years older than me.' Ben raised an eyebrow. 'I wanted to hear what Daniel had to say first before I committed to seeing them because I feel…'

'A little guilty,' added Katie.

Ben nodded, thinking about his own parents. 'I just need to prepare myself. They've been looking for me for most of my life. I'm still getting my head around it all.'

Katie rested her hand on his knee and gave it a reassuring squeeze. 'Whatever you decide, I'm here for you. Just do what's best for you.'

'Thank you,' replied Ben, dipping his head and kissing her on the lips, then entwining his fingers around hers.

Katie rested her head on his shoulder.

'I mean that. I'm really glad you're here.'

Katie squeezed his hand and tilted her head up to kiss him. Ben knew having Katie by his side made the whole situation a little easier to deal with.

It wasn't long before they announced 'Welcome to Ireland' over the intercom.

Ben's parents had moved him to Scotland when he was still a baby, but now Ben couldn't help but wonder about the real reason for the move. The landing was smooth and the pilot steered the plane towards the terminal and cut the engines. Ben's nerves were kicking in as he waited patiently for the doors of the aircraft to open.

He was lost in his own thoughts as he walked with Katie. It didn't take long to get through Passport Control and collect their luggage from the carousel. They grabbed a taxi from the rank outside the airport and, in no time at all, they arrived at the hotel.

'The thing is,' said Katie, as they stepped into the hotel

foyer, 'I may have been a little impulsive and booked my plane ticket, but in the hurry of it all, I forgot to book my hotel room.'

'It's a good job I've got a double room, then, isn't it? Care to join me?'

She linked her arm through his. 'That would be lovely!'

They walked towards the hotel reception. Within five minutes, they were checked into a clean basic room and Ben began to unpack his bag.

'Woah! Jeez! How many outfits have you brought with you?' Katie was amazed to see the amount of clothes that Ben had laid out on the bed.

'After the last time I went away, I can't be too careful.'

'I see you learn from the best,' quipped Katie with a cheeky grin.

'And what exactly is the dress code to meet your brother for the very first time and possibly your parents too?'

Katie picked up a couple of the T-shirts. 'Now, that is the question. Smart as in a shirt, or casual and comfortable. Do you know where you are meeting?'

Ben walked over to the window and looked out over the main street. He pointed. 'In that hotel, just there. Apparently the place where my parent's relationship blossomed, according to Daniel. That's where they met, but other than that, I don't know anything.' Ben's voice faltered and he could feel the emotion rising up inside him. He swallowed. 'I suppose all will be revealed very soon.'

'How are you feeling?' asked Katie, switching on the kettle.

Ben held out his hands in front of him. They were visibly shaking. 'Nervous.'

'A good old-fashioned cup of tea is always good in a crisis. And I'd go for a casual but smart look,' she suggested, laying an outfit out on the bed. 'What do you think?'

Ben nodded. 'Thanks,' he said, looking at his watch. 'Time is going to go so slow.'

'How about we drink this, grab some food and then you can get a shower and it will be nearly time to go.'

'Do you think they are nervous?'

'God, yes. They've been waiting for this day all their lives. I bet they can't quite believe it. I can't imagine how any of you are feeling.'

'There's one thing on my mind that I can't seem to shake...what if I don't even like them? What if they don't like me and I disappoint them after all this time?'

Katie handed Ben a cup of tea. 'My guess is that really isn't going to happen. How can anyone not like you?'

'It all feels so surreal. When I buried my parents, I never expected that only a few years later, two more would pop up. I don't mean to make it sound like that. It's just not what I ever expected to happen, and what I keep thinking about is...'

'Go on.'

'Surely, they must have had a conversation...' Ben took a

breath. 'There was always a possibility I would go looking or they would find me. Why wouldn't they want to prepare me for that?'

'I really don't know,' replied Katie softly. 'Maybe they were in denial. Try not to think about it now. Let's grab some food and—' Katie looked down at her phone as it beeped. A huge smile spread across her face.

'That's a look of smugness. What are you smiling at?'

'My team are out on the river and they've smashed their own personal best. The race is on, Sanders.'

Ben blew out a breath. In the last few days, the boat race had totally slipped his mind, and it was getting closer by the day. He quickly pinged a text to Drew. 'Get the team out on the water!'

'Yes, Captain!' came back the instant reply.

'Believe me, the race is still on.' Ben gave Katie a lopsided grin before glugging back his tea. 'Right, let's get some food.'

***

They sat in the hotel bar near the window for over three hours. The table looked over the busy high street, which had an array of striped awnings, colourful shopfronts and pedestrians strolling along. Ben was people watching through the window, but couldn't help it. He was looking for the faces of his parents and brother and wondered whether they had already arrived at the hotel opposite.

Time passed quite quickly, and Ben knew he wasn't the best of company, but Katie kept the conversation flowing about anything and everything. They chatted about their favourite bands, Netflix series and of course the boat race. Before he knew it, he was back in the room having a quick shower and a shave and it was nearly time to go.

'This is it,' he said, checking the time on his phone again.

Ben couldn't keep still. He was sitting on the chair in the room bouncing a knee whilst rubbing his hand on the back on his neck. He kept looking out of the hotel window towards the street. Katie took both his hands in hers.

'This is it,' she repeated. 'And I'm going to be waiting for you.'

Ben nodded his appreciation and hugged Katie with all his might. She held him tightly in her arms until he was ready to let go.

'Are you ready?' she asked softly.

In silence, Katie walked by his side to the entrance of the hotel where Ben would be meeting his brother for the very first time and hovered on the pavement outside.

'I feel hot,' Ben said, pulling at the neck of his T-shirt.

'Take deep breaths and try to stay calm.' Katie linked her arm through his as they both looked up towards the hotel sign above their heads.

'I'll try,' Ben replied. 'This time last week, I was merrily going along with life and now I'm scared witless.'

'You are going to be absolutely fine – more than fine.' Katie gave Ben one last hug and kissed him lightly on his lips. 'I'll be waiting for you in our hotel bar. If you need me, just ring or text. You've got this.'

Ben didn't trust himself to speak, so he nodded. Since the night of the reunion, they'd grown closer and were spending every spare moment they had together. Their relationship was blossoming into something special. She kissed him once more on the cheek before giving him a light encouraging shove towards the hotel foyer.

Ben's insides twisted as he glanced over his shoulder at Katie before disappearing through the entrance. His legs trembled, barely holding him as he made his way to the hotel bar. Numb, he gathered his wits the best he could as he scanned the bar, but he couldn't see his brother.

'Stay calm,' he muttered under his breath as he found a seat and sat down at a heavy wooden table. He looked up at the trendy chalkboard that listed cocktails and the local craft beer. There was a waitress clearing a table and a tipsy hen party weaving their way to the restroom.

Earlier, whilst getting ready, Ben had played this scenario over and over in his head, but it didn't come close to the reality of what he was feeling. He spent the next few minutes shifting in his seat, rubbing the back of his neck, and folding and unfolding his arms. Time felt like it had slowed down as he watched the second hand move around the clock behind the bar.

The door swung open and Ben's chest heaved. He swallowed hard. It was like looking at himself in the mirror. The likeness was uncanny: the same wild curly jet-black hair, the same nose, the same eyes. Daniel's smile lit up the room as he walked towards Ben. Daniel held out his arms and Ben didn't think twice about giving him a hug; it just seemed like the most natural thing in the world to do. The hug was heartfelt and tears welled up in his eyes. His brother hugged him with all his might.

They both pulled away slowly, their eyes bleary with happy tears. It was a feeling Ben had never felt in his life – one of euphoria. Ben immediately felt a connection. He had a brother, who was standing in front of him, and even though he had no clue about the past, he knew the second he laid eyes on Daniel that he was going to become a huge part of his life.

'Hello,' said Ben, taking in a lungful of air. 'This is so surreal.'

All his nerves disappeared in an instant. Daniel's warmest of smiles had immediately put Ben at ease.

'Hello, Brother.' Daniel grinned. 'This is so strange. It's like looking in the mirror.'

Ben exhaled. 'Where to begin? I have no clue.'

'Drink. I think we both need a drink,' suggested Daniel.

With drinks in their hands, they settled at a table in the corner of the room.

'This must be so strange for you. I've got so much to tell you. Not a day goes by that we don't think of you. Every Christmas, every birthday, we talk about you and wonder where you are, wonder if you're happy.'

'Honestly, I had good adoptive parents. I didn't want for

anything. But the part I'm struggling with is why I was adopted. I always thought I wasn't good enough.'

'You have to believe me when I say you have always been good enough.'

Hearing those words, Ben felt a sense of relief. He had been scared of rejection his entire life, but that was all he needed to hear.

'Do your parents know you are here?' asked Daniel.

Ben shook his head. 'My parents have passed away.'

'I'm so sorry to hear that. We all appreciate that this must have turned your world upside down.'

'How are your parents? Are they well?… My parents… I have no clue what to even call them.'

'Maybe start with Niamh and Connor.' Daniel gave Ben a warm smile. 'And they're doing great. Even better now I'm sat here with you, and in case you are wondering, they would love to meet you, but obviously in your own time. We don't want to overwhelm you. They have dreamt about this day for a very long time.'

Ben was listening and of course he was curious to find out about the people that had brought him into this world, but it still didn't make much sense to him. 'Why was I given up for adoption?'

'You weren't in the circumstance that you may think. It wasn't until my early teens that I began asking the same questions. They talked about you openly from the day I was born. You were never a secret and they spent a long time fighting to get you back through the courts. They didn't give up hope. They have lived a life of upset and loss, even though they had me. The family was never going to be complete until we found you.'

'Fought to get me back through the courts?' he repeated. This was news to him. Ben had no clue about any of this. It felt like he was sitting in a pub with a mate and they were talking about someone else's life. But here he was, sitting in a pub with his long-lost brother, who he didn't know was lost, and about to hear a heart-wrenching story. Ben could see the sadness in Daniel's eyes as he began to talk.

'They fell in love as teenagers and Mum fell pregnant only a couple of months into the relationship. They were fully aware of the scandal this would cause within their Catholic community, and they hatched a plan to run away to England to bring you up.' Daniel took a breath. 'They didn't tell anyone – not their own parents, not their friends. They just packed a bag and left for London. Maybe a little naïve, but they thought they could do anything. Mum and Dad found casual work and managed to rent a room together and you arrived six months later. They were happy, over the moon, but unfortunately the happiness didn't last when the landlady received complaints that there was a baby crying most of the night. She hadn't known they were keeping a baby in the flat and kicked them out. As you can imagine, suddenly finding yourself homeless and with a baby on the streets of London is not ideal for anyone...especially teenagers. At that point, they put your needs first. They had an agreement with an agency to place you in the care of a family – your parents – with the possibility of adoption if they couldn't find their feet. They didn't want to give you up in the short term and it broke their hearts, but they thought they'd get you back. That's what they believed would happen. After six weeks, both Mum and Dad found permanent jobs and a flat, but made a devastating discovery when they went back to pick you up. They were told you'd been staying with an affluent Irish couple and that it was best to leave you there. They'd applied for adoption and their only chance to get you back was to go to court, but the judge…' Daniel's voice faltered. He composed himself. 'The judge ordered that the adoption be finalised. My mum and dad felt devastated and betrayed.'

Ben couldn't believe what he was hearing. He swallowed, overcome with emotion as he listened to Daniel. He couldn't believe a judge ruled that he should be taken away from a family who loved him dearly. There was a part of him that felt angry. Who was that person to make a ruling on his life? He was utterly saddened for what his biological parents had gone through, but Ben could tell by Daniel's face that there was more.

'Mum and Dad got married in London at the age of eighteen, and after two years of trying to get you back, they returned to Ireland to face the music from their own parents. Mum fell pregnant again on their wedding night with Millie, our sister.'

Ben was dumbfounded. 'I have a sister too?' He couldn't

quite take it all in. This was the first he knew of a sister. 'Is she here with you?'

Daniel shook his head. 'When I was two, my parents suffered another heartbreaking loss. Millie was killed in a road traffic accident. I don't remember much from that time except hearing my parents crying night after night.'

'I'm so sorry to hear this, Daniel.' Ben was struggling for words, he didn't know what to say.

'They were still trying to find out what had happened to you. If your name had been changed, where had the couple that had been granted adoption taken you, but due to legislation, they weren't allowed to know. They have been searching for you the whole time.'

'And then a random DNA test solved the mystery,' added Ben, not quite believing that if he hadn't received that birthday present from Helly, none of this would be happening.

'How are you feeling about it all?' asked Daniel uncertainly. 'It must be a huge shock.'

Momentarily forgetting his own emotions, Ben couldn't believe the pain these two people must have gone through. He took a second. 'I can't quite put it all into words – anger that a judge can decide the path of someone's life. Anger that I was kept away from my real family and missed growing up with my brother, but grateful to my mum and dad, who loved, cared for, encouraged, and protected me through my whole life.'

It dawned on Ben why his own parents didn't want to

talk about the adoption. They probably felt guilty knowing that his real parents had always wanted him back. Things were becoming clearer – the reason why they were overprotective and barely let him out of their sight when he was younger. Even though his biological parents didn't know where he was, it still must have always been on their mind what would happen if they located him. Was he feeling bitter towards his adoptive parents? A little disappointed, maybe, that they hadn't shared their side of the story with him, but maybe they didn't know the Clancys wanted him back. Maybe they just thought they were giving a baby a home.

What he'd learnt in the past few weeks, ever since Katie had arrived in the village and shared her past, was to never judge any person or situation without knowing all the facts. He didn't know what his adoptive parents were going through and all he could deal with was the here and now.

'Even though it's taken all these years, I'm glad Niamh and Connor have finally had a huge weight lifted off their shoulders. They finally found me and can rest assured I've had a good life and I've got a good life.'

'Would you like to meet them?' asked Daniel.

'Of course I would,' Ben replied without hesitation, his heart hammering against his chest. 'Are they here?'

Daniel nodded. 'Are you ready?'

'I think so.'

Daniel picked up his phone. 'Mum, Dad, your son would love to meet you.'

Within seconds, the door to the bar opened and Niamh and Connor walked through holding hands. Ben stood up as Niamh dropped Connor's hand and ran towards him, her arms already outstretched. Ben was struck by how young they both were. He threw himself into Niamh's arms whilst Connor wrapped them both up in his. A tsunami of tears fell down everyone's cheeks as they hugged like their lives depended on it.

'I'm so sorry, I'm so sorry,' Niamh was saying over and over again.

'You have nothing to be sorry for,' reassured Ben softly, holding each of their hands in his. A decision made by a judge had devastated their lives for so many heart-breaking years.

'I'm here now and I'm not going anywhere. This is the beginning of our next chapter and I'm looking forward to the future.' Ben felt the warmth coming from the people by his side. There was so much to discover about each other, and he couldn't wait to find out about them.

As they sat down at the table, Ben was still holding Niamh's hand. He could feel her hand shaking and gave it a tiny squeeze. The moment was so surreal; he was looking into the eyes of the woman who gave birth to him. His biological mother. Her eyes gleamed with tears.

'I never thought this day would come,' she said.

Ben could hear the pain in Niamh's voice, but he couldn't ever comprehend the suffering that the two people sitting in front of him had gone through. Connor was wiping the tears away from his eyes and reached over to place his hand on Ben's.

'We are so happy to finally meet you, and I'm sorry about the hair. That's from my half of the family.'

Everyone laughed, which lightened the mood.

'I'm sorry if you ever thought we'd abandoned you,' continued Connor.

'It's okay, I know you didn't. Daniel has filled me in about everything. I really can't imagine what you went through when the judge ruled for the adoption to go ahead.'

'It shattered my heart. But, finally, our nightmare is over. I realise this is a huge shock for you, discovering you have a whole new family out there.'

'It's beyond mind-blowing. And I can't actually believe how much we look alike,' he said, looking at Daniel. 'It's like I'm looking at myself in the mirror.'

Daniel was grinning. Niamh reached inside her bag and pulled out two photographs. She placed them in front of Ben. 'This was the only photograph we have had of you all this time.'

Ben looked at the photograph of the baby laying in a Moses basket wrapped up tightly in a pale blue blanket with a mass of jet-black hair. Next to him lay a teddy bear. He picked up the photograph. 'Oh my gosh, I still have Bear.'

'Bear?' asked Niamh.

Ben tapped the photograph. 'I called that bear Bear... I know it's not very original, but wherever I went, Bear did too. I still have him. He's part of my family and sits in my bedroom at home.'

Niamh had grabbed onto Connor's arm. She was biting down on her lip as the tears cascaded down her face. 'We bought you Bear. It was our first trip out as a family. He was sitting in a window in a boutique shop in London.'

'This one' – Connor placed a hand on Niamh's knee – 'wanted that bear as soon as she spotted it in the shop window.'

They all took a moment looking at the photograph before Daniel suggested getting a bottle of the best stuff to toast to the future and family. He gestured to the waiter and, within moments, a bottle of the finest champagne was delivered to the table.

In the back of his mind, Ben cast a thought to his own parents. How would they feel about all this? How would they have reacted if they were still alive? Ben was guessing they would have found it difficult to talk about and come to terms with, but hopefully they would have embraced the situation if they knew he was happy.

Ben took the champagne out of the cooler and passed it to Connor. 'Would you like to do the honours?'

Connor popped the cork and, as the champagne fizzed into each flute, they held up their glasses.

'I'd just like to say I'm so sorry for your pain over all these years,' said Ben.

'Today just couldn't come soon enough,' replied Niamh.

'And can I ask – what did you become? For a job. I want to know everything.'

Ben smiled. They had a lot of catching up to do. 'I'm a doctor.'

Niamh gave a tiny gasp. 'You're a doctor?' She nudged Connor. 'He must take after me in the brains department.'

Connor rolled his eyes.

'I am. I work at a practice in a village in the Scottish Highlands. I really can't wait to find out everything there is to know about you all. Cheers to the future.' Ben held up his glass and they clinked them all together.

'There are so many questions I want to ask,' said Niamh.

'Ask away. We have a lifetime to answer them,' replied Ben warmly.

'Are you married? Any children?' she fired off quickly.

Ben shook his head but thought of Katie. Since arriving in Heartcross, she had become very important to him. Even though their relationship was still at a very early stage, it was the best stage. They were discovering everything about each other and Ben knew he was in the first flush of love. He hoped Katie was going to be in his future. 'I'm not married and I don't have any children, but would like children. How about you, Daniel?'

'Married six months. Jools and I have a four-year old daughter, Ruby, and another baby on the way!'

'Oh my gosh. I'm an uncle! This is amazing! Ruby, what a gorgeous name.' Ben extended his hand. 'Huge congratulations, Brother!'

Daniel hesitated. 'They are here too if you would like to meet them? We just didn't want to bombard you all at once.'

'Of course I want to meet them,' replied Ben as his own phone pinged.

He looked down to see a text message from Katie. 'I hope you're doing okay?'

He smiled and looked up.

'I am actually here with someone. It's early days, but I'm hopeful.' Ben crossed his fingers. 'Would you like to meet her?'

Niamh looked at Connor. Ben could see her swell with happiness. 'We would love to meet her.' She squeezed Ben's hand.

He quickly punched a text back to Katie. 'More than okay. Would you like to come and meet my family?'

'Yes! I'm on my way!' came the immediate reply.

'What a day,' Ben murmured.

It was five to midnight and only fifteen minutes ago, Ben had hugged his brand-new family before saying goodnight to them. The whole day had been a good day, yet unreal. They'd made plans for Ben and Katie to go over to their home for lunch tomorrow before they flew back to Scotland the following day.

Sitting on the edge of the bed, Ben kicked off his shoes, then rested his hands on his knees and took a breath. His day had been full of so much emotion: anxiety, sadness, joy and happiness, all rolled into one. Thinking back over the day, he smiled from ear to ear. His jaw was actually aching from all the smiling.

Katie appeared in the doorway of the bathroom. 'Look at that smile on your face!' she said, leaning against the door frame. 'You look so happy.'

'I am happy. What a story. What an ending. I think they liked me.'

'Of course they liked you.'

'I can't believe any of this has happened. Things like this only happen to other people, not me. If Helly hadn't given me that DNA test, I might never have been brave enough to do one myself and I'd be none the wiser.'

'Are you glad she did?' Katie asked the question that had been on Ben's mind at the start of the day.

'Yes,' he replied. 'Honestly, Katie, I thought my heart was going to beat out of my chest when I saw my mother and father for the first time. I can't even describe how I was feeling.'

Niamh and Connor's story was tinged with sadness, but the joy that surrounded them for the rest of the day didn't go unnoticed. He admired their strength and positivity, and they had never given up hope that they would be reunited one day. No one had wanted the day to end. Their conversation flowed so naturally and there were no awkward silences – only good conversation and laughter.

'I do wonder what my life would have been like if the judge hadn't ruled for the adoption to go ahead.'

'Try not to think about that. You have had a good life. You were taken on that path for a reason, and just think, if the judge hadn't ruled that, you would never have met me.' She gave Ben a cheeky wink before going back into the bathroom to brush her teeth.

When Katie returned to the bedroom, Ben was sitting up in bed with the covers pulled up to his chest. She slid into the space next to him and cuddled into him.

'You looked like such a natural with Ruby. She was so cute,' said Katie.

'When she called me Uncle Ben, it melted my heart.'

The moment Ruby had walked into the room holding Jools's hand, she had let go and ran towards Ben, then stopped in her tracks. She'd swung a glance towards Daniel, then back towards Ben. For a second, she was confused. The two of them looked like identical twins. Everyone had laughed as Ruby outstretched her arms towards Daniel, who'd lifted her into the air and held her in her arms. 'I want you to meet your Uncle Ben.'

For the first couple of minutes, Ruby had been a little unsure, but it didn't take her long before she was sitting on Ben's knee and attempting to pinch his crisps from the packet on the table.

Growing up, Ben knew, as an only child, he would never have nieces and nephews, but it was something he'd always wanted. He envied his friends with brothers and sisters, but overnight, that's exactly what Ben had, and he was going to embrace every second.

'Can you believe that Niamh and Connor were the ones who bought me my childhood bear? Honestly, that bear went everywhere with me, even to university. I never knew it was them who gave it to me.' Ben's voice cracked a little as he reached across and turned off the bedside light. 'Do you want kids?'

'Four,' replied Katie.

'Four!' Ben was startled.

'Love a big family. Can you imagine the scene at Christmas? Four children excitedly running around our farmhouse kitchen with the log fire crackling away, the turkey sizzling in the oven and the oversize tree in the corner. Perfect.'

'Our farmhouse?' asked Ben with a smile on his face.

'Just a slip of the tongue.' She kissed him swiftly on the cheek.

Ben loved the sound of that. Katie was talking about the future and she wanted him in her future just as much as he wanted her in his. 'Four is a good number. I really would like a big family.' He pictured the idyllic scene in his head.

'Are you getting all broody on me?'

'Maybe.' He kissed the top of Katie's head.

'Can I just say – thank you.'

'What for?' asked Ben, puzzled.

'For making me a part of today and letting me meet your family.'

'I couldn't imagine you not being there.' He turned his head towards her.

Katie's gigantic smile was caught in the moonlight. Feeling the spark, the chemistry and the raw attraction between them, Ben kissed her softly on the lips and Katie kissed him back. He pulled her in closer.

Wrapped up tightly in each other's arms, they kissed slowly and softly at first. Pressing her body against his, she ran her hands over the warm skin of his chest and basked in the pleasure of his touch as he gently removed her top. She wriggled out of her bottoms, her lips never leaving his.

'You are gorgeous,' he whispered, kissing her neck and making her gasp.

'Dr Ben Sanders, you are perfect too, but stop talking.'

'Are you sure you want to do this?'

'I said stop talking,' ordered Katie with a smile.

An overwhelming feeling of happiness gushed through Ben's body as they nestled in deeper into each other's arms. The bright lights of the clock said it was just around half past midnight, but neither of them had any intention of going to sleep just yet.

Chapter Twenty

B en and Katie had barely been apart since arriving back from Ireland. But last night, Katie had decided she needed a good night's sleep as there was a boat race to win, and she wanted to reserve every little bit of her energy to pick up the winning trophy.

Ben lay in bed smiling at how seriously she was taking it and how determined she was to win, but that hadn't deterred Ben. His team had been out on the water rowing hard and their times were just a little faster than Katie's team, beating them by a matter of seconds. The teams, it seemed, were equally matched. The banks of the River Heart were going to be packed.

The night before, they'd taken a stroll across the bridge and grabbed a coffee when Katie had pointed to the tents and tepees that were scattered along the riverbanks. Spectators of the race who wanted a ringside seat of the finish line were already marking their spot. On the way back, they stood in the centre of the bridge and looked out over the water.

'There's the finish line. Who will make it under the bridge first? Now that is the question,' teased Ben, but Katie was adamant it was going to be her.

'Let's have a wager. Obviously, the money will go to the charity,' she suggested, tilting her head to one side, then pulling her phone out of her pocket.

'What are you doing?' he asked.

'Looking at how much we've raised so far,' she replied. She suddenly grabbed Ben by the arm. 'Holy moly!'

Katie handed him the phone.

He looked at the screen and let out a low whistle. 'Stuart is going to be over the moon. Just think how much more we will raise tomorrow. This is amazing.'

'Just under one hundred and fifty thousand pounds. How is that even possible?' Katie was still staring at the phone.

'The radio show, the local TV, everyone has been plugging this boat race. There are posters everywhere and, according to the event on Facebook, there are at least a couple thousand attending to cheer me on as I'm first over the winning line,' he teased.

'Oh, you are hilarious. So shall we say...five hundred pounds each?'

Ben nearly spat out his coffee. 'Five hundred pounds. That's a lot of money.'

'Put your money where your mouth is. If you believe you are going to win, you have nothing to worry about.' She nudged his arm with her elbow. 'And it's all for charity.'

Ben thrust his hand forward. 'Five hundred. You're absolutely right, I don't have anything to worry about, but I really need to make sure that when I do win, you aren't going to go all moody on me like last night.' He rolled his eyes. 'I really can't believe you were that stroppy over a game of Monopoly.'

'You were cheating! I'm sure you were stealing from the bank.'

'You are such a sore loser,' he said, watching Katie shaking her head and striding over the bridge.

———————

Still lying in bed and knowing he needed to get up soon, Ben reached for his phone and began scrolling. The Facebook page for the village of Heartcross had hundreds of notifications and photos. Ben sat up straight in bed. He couldn't quite believe it. The banks of the River Heart already looked like a mini festival. There were numerous banners hanging from the bridge in between trees. Ben zoomed in and smiled. 'Team Making Waves to Win!'

Everyone was getting into the spirit of the day, and no matter who won the race, Ben was hoping they did Stuart proud. His phone pinged. Daniel had sent him a photo. He burst out laughing.

On the screen was a photo of Ruby holding up a banner. 'Uncle Ben to win!'

His family had just arrived at Starcross Manor. This was their first introduction to the village of Heartcross and Ben knew it was going to be a fantastic day. He couldn't wait to see them and he'd spoken to his parents and brother every day since returning from Ireland.

Three taps on the bedroom wall made Ben jump. It was the wall that linked to Katie's bedroom next door. He tapped back three times and waited.

He listened carefully as Katie began tapping a message on the wall and within seconds realised she was tapping in morse code.

.. .----. -- / - --- -.. .- -.-- .----. ... / .-- .. -. -. . .-.

As soon as she stopped, he laughed. Katie had tapped out the words 'I am today's winner.'

--- .... / -. --- / -.-- --- ..- .----. .-. . / -. --- -

He quickly tapped back, 'Oh no you're not.'

Ben could hear Katie laughing on the other side of the wall. Within a couple of seconds, there was a knock on his front door and he quickly sprang out of bed.

With a grin on her face, Katie was standing there already

kitted out in her team T-shirt and leggings. She held a plate towards him. 'Breakfast. I didn't want to be at an unfair advantage and you need all the strength you can get.'

Ben took the plate off Katie and looked down at the steaming sausage sandwich oozing with brown sauce. 'Just what the doctor ordered; you are an absolute keeper!'

'Let's hope you still think that after I whoop your backside today.' With that, Katie spun around, kicked her leg back in the air and gave Ben a smile over her shoulder as she disappeared down the stairwell.

'Are you off to the river already?' he shouted after her.

'You better believe it!'

Quickly, Ben shut the front door and shovelled in the sandwich before grabbing a quick shower. Within half an hour, he had pulled on his team T-shirt and headed down to the river.

The atmosphere was exciting. All along the high street, the triangular coloured bunting weaved between the lampposts and flapped in the breeze. He noticed enlarged photographs of Katie's team hanging from the bunting along one side of the street and, on the other side, his own team. With a spring in his step, he walked down the road and was instantly recognised. People began to clap and cheer. He felt like an international superstar and waved as he walked on by.

The weather was perfect, the sun was shining and only a few clouds dotted the sky. Walking towards the river, Ben was amazed. Hordes and hordes of people lined the banks of the river and the bridge was closed off to the public. He could hear a voice over a loud Tannoy and swung his head towards the bridge. There were TV cameras positioned and the radio station was broadcasting from the top of an open-air bus with the full view of the finishing line stretched out in front of them.

Ben felt the excitement zipping through his body. The atmosphere all around was electric. He beamed as the Tannoy from the radio station alerted the general public to his arrival.

'Please put your hands together for Making Waves team captain Dr Ben Sanders, who is making his way along the path towards The Old Boat House.' The presenter Kim Smith, alongside other presenters from the radio station, were flag waving from the top of the open-air bus.

Beaming, Ben stood still, waving both hands in the air and acknowledged the well-wishers in the crowd with a nod of his head. He searched the sea of faces, but they stretched for miles and he couldn't spot his parents or Daniel, even though he was certain they would have spotted him. The boat race was being televised and up on a huge screen erected in front of The Old Boat House, Ben could see himself. He weaved his way through all the spectators, who had lined a path for him. Ben felt like an Olympic champion as the clapping and cheers erupted all around him.

Katie was up ahead, along with Helly. Both teams were gathered together on a makeshift stage that had been erected in front of The Old Boat House. As Ben approached his team, they outstretched their arms to make an archway with their hands and Ben stooped over to run underneath them.

'Here he is! Look at the turnout,' Helly said. 'I really wish I was rowing now, but then I wouldn't want you pair fighting over me. Do you know what? Making all this happen, I think I really do have the best bosses.'

'And don't you forget it,' teased Ben.

'This is all down to you,' Ben said as he walked towards Katie and kissed her on the cheek. Then he stretched out his hand. 'Let the best man win.'

'Or woman,' added Katie quickly, grinning as she shook his hand.

Both teams stood and looked out over the crowd. Everyone was having a fantastic time, and Ben felt immensely proud of Katie for pulling it all together. He knew that Stuart and his family were over the moon with the amount of money that had been raised so far. He was just overjoyed to be a part of the day.

Even though the boat race was for charity, nerves fizzed in the pit of his stomach. Maybe it was excitement; the thrill of the race. There wasn't much difference between the teams and there wasn't a clear winner. The final leg was between himself and Katie and only time would tell who was going to cross the finish line first.

Helly checked her watch. 'Right, my job is to make sure whoever wins, wins fair and square and in case of a photo finish...' she joked, holding up her camera. 'I need to take my place on the bridge alongside the TV crew. Apparently, I am their eyes and ears. It's going to be so much fun! Good luck to everyone and I'll see you all at the finish line.'

With a spring in her step, Helly made her way through the crowd towards the bridge and soon disappeared out of sight amongst the crowd.

At that moment, Ben glanced over the sea of people and spotted Daniel with Ruby sitting on his shoulders, his parents standing next to them. Ben shouted at them and they weaved their way towards the stage. Ben hugged each one of them.

'You made it,' he said, attempting to take a bite of Ruby's gingerbread man. She was giggling uncontrollably.

'I'm sorry Jools couldn't make it, but she is exhausted with the pregnancy at the moment,' said Daniel. 'But she wishes you all the luck in the world.'

'Honestly, you don't have to explain. I hope she's feeling better soon.'

'It's such a lovely village and the hotel is absolutely stunning,' said Niamh. 'Connor is already a fan of Foxglove Farm sausages and we've only been here a matter of hours. He's already joking about living here. It has everything you need and look at that view.'

All of them glanced over to see Heartcross Mountain towering in the distance. Heartcross Castle was standing proudly on the hill and the river glistened in the mid-morning sun.

'Rumour has it that once you arrive in Heartcross, you never want to leave,' shared Ben, knowing he didn't have any intention of moving anywhere else.

'And I can vouch for that,' chipped in Katie, joining Ben and slipping her hand into his. 'It's a magical place and already captured my heart in more ways than one.' She nudged Ben lightly with her shoulder.

Ben smiled warmly at her before he tickled Ruby's stomach and pointed. There were jugglers, stilt walkers and a bouncy castle. Families had already claimed spots alongside the riverbank and were sprawled out on picnic blankets.

Feeling a tap on his shoulder, Ben turned around to find Stuart standing between them. His arms opened wide.

'I can't thank you two enough. I was never expecting this turnout at all. This is well and truly putting the dementia charity on the map.'

'You are very welcome,' replied Katie. 'We are glad to help.'

'Stuart, let me introduce you to my mum, dad and brother, and this is my niece, Ruby.' The words had left his mouth before he even had time to think about them. Ben noticed that Niamh had teared up and squeezed Connor's hand.

He realised she must have been waiting a long time to hear those words. Ben knew his adoptive parents would always be his mum and dad; that would never change, but the future was looking bright. Ben was at his happiest.

After shaking hands, Stuart nodded towards the stage. 'Are you guys ready? It looks like there's a boat race about to happen and we need to get this show on the road.'

'Ready as I'll ever be,' claimed Ben enthusiastically.

'Uncle Ben to win!' shouted Ruby, causing everyone to laugh.

Katie brought her hands up to her chest, pretending to look hurt. 'And what about me?'

'Auntie Katie, you can win next year.'

Ben slid his arm around Katie's shoulders and pulled her in for a hug. 'It looks like you have Ruby's seal of approval,' he said, kissing Katie softly on the lips as they walked towards the stage.

'It does, doesn't it? And what about you, do I have your seal of approval?'

'Without a doubt. Auntie Katie,' he repeated. 'I like the sound of that.'

'It makes us sound like we're a proper couple.' She caught his eye.

'We are a proper couple.' He kissed her again, then slipped his hand into hers.

Stuart was standing in the middle of the stage alongside Rory and Allie. Alana was safely back at the care home. Behind them was a magnificent backdrop that read 'Heartcross 1st Annual Boat Race.' The logo from the dementia charity was there, alongside a photograph of Alana.

Katie and Ben waited at the side of the stage whilst

Stuart switched on the microphone in his hand and looked out over the crowd.

'Folks, thank you all for coming here today to support Heartcross's very first boat race.'

Everyone began to clap.

'The boat race will commence in five minutes, but today, if I could just remind everyone why we are here and thank you all for your fabulous support and for your donations to the wonderful charity that we are supporting today.' Stuart's voice faltered as he talked about the charity and his wonderful life with Alana, but, like a trooper, he carried on with the support of Rory and Allie by his side.

'If you haven't had the pleasure of meeting Dr Ben Sanders and Dr Katie O'Neil, then please let me introduce to you to our new doctors in Heartcross, who are also our team captains today.'

Both of them bowed, then walked onto the stage with their arms up in the air. The crowd went wild and the cheers could be heard all along the riverbank. The crowd was one hundred per cent behind them. It was an amazing feeling to be standing up there in front of them.

Stuart passed the microphone to Ben and the crowd hushed.

'It's only a short time that I've been a part of this community. You have all made me feel so welcome. It's a privilege to be captain of my team today, Making Waves. Please welcome to the stage my team: Allie, Rona, Drew, Meredith and Flynn!' The team walked onto the stage waving their arms in the air and stood next to Ben, who passed the microphone to Katie.

'And please welcome onto the stage my team... Seas the Day! Martha, Rory, Isla, Julia and Fraser!'

As they all took their places on the stage, Katie shook a donation bucket and said, 'Please do enjoy your day and give generously. Are we ready? Here we go!'

The teams stepped down from the stage and began to make their way towards the speedboats at the end of the jetty, which was equipped with the team's kayak and paddle.

They walked under a giant balloon archway and Ben noticed a few stray balloons floating up in the sky. Most of the onlookers were recording them from their phones, and the TV cameras situated on the end of the jetty were recording their every move. They all waved to the crowds and Ben shook his head lightly as people began to throw confetti when they walked by. There were flags flying, banners and signs being held in the air, and air horns honking. Everyone had a smile on their face.

'This is just unreal,' said Katie, looking over her shoulder. 'I feel like an astronaut walking towards the space craft.'

The villagers and team's families carried on high-fiving them on their way and lined the edge of the jetty. Ben spotted his parents, Daniel, and Ruby. He grinned as he pointed to the front of their T-shirts, which had his team's name printed in bold lettering. He gave them the thumbs up until all of a sudden, they spun around to reveal Katie's team name on the back. Katie burst out laughing whilst Ben was shaking his head in disbelief.

He started muttering, 'Traitors,' but was taking it in good spirits.

'There's a pint waiting at the end,' confirmed Connor, patting Ben on the back as he walked by.

Hovering at the end of the jetty, the local press took photographs before the teams climbed onto the speedboat. Katie hesitated.

'You okay?' asked Ben, hanging back.

'I was just thinking of Ellis. He would have loved today.' Her voice wavered and she took a quick glance towards the sky. 'He'll be with me in spirit.' She swallowed.

Ben hugged her tight. 'Your brother would be so proud of you.'

'Do you know what I think is wonderful?' She looked up into Ben's eyes. 'That your new family are here for you. It's just so nice to see everyone happy.'

'I think they are here for you too,' replied Ben, knowing how difficult her own family situation was. He kissed Katie's cheek. 'I'll see you at the finish line.'

'Stop fraternising with the competition,' teased Flynn, hurrying Ben along. 'Let's get this race started!'

'Ben, there's something I need to tell you,' Katie whispered in his ear.

His eyes widened. 'What is it?'

She looked him up and down. 'You are not wearing your wetsuit!'

'Oh shit!' he said, causing everyone nearby to laugh. With everything that was going on around him, he'd forgotten to get changed. He sprinted as fast as he could towards The Old Boat House and within a matter of minutes, he returned wearing his wetsuit with his team T-shirt on top.

'This is it,' said Ben, checking over the team's kayak before it was loaded onto the speedboat. 'Are we ready, team?'

'Yes, Captain!' they all replied in unison and saluted.

After shaking hands, Ben and Katie climbed onto their team boat and fastened their life jackets. Both teams waved towards the crowd. The cheers rippled all along the riverbank as the engines fired up. With the sun reflecting on the water, darting fish below the surface and the gulls spiralling overhead, they made their way towards the start line.

With the breeze whipping through their hair, the speedboats travelled side by side until they reached the tiny bay a stone's throw away from The Lake House restaurant. Ben was amazed to see the number of rowing boats dotted on the water ready to watch the start of the race. There was a helicopter circling up above and water taxis full to the brim with passengers waiting to cheer them on. With TV cameras dotted along the shoreline, there was not one part of the race that was going to be missed. The excitement was growing in both boats and everyone was keen to get the race under way. As the engines cut on the speedboats, Ben spoke a few words to his crew.

'Give it your absolute all, but remember to have fun out there. You all know your route and who you are up against. Stay focussed! When you've rowed your leg of the water, remember to pass your paddle to the speedboat, then slip out of the kayak on the furthest side, and as soon as the kayak is on the way, we will pick you up and have a towel ready.'

'I hope there's gin in the tin waiting,' exclaimed Rona with a glint in her eye.

Ben bent down towards his rucksack and pulled out exactly that. 'Just for you, Rona!'

She leant forward to try and grab it. 'I'm thinking I'll row better fuelled with gin.'

'Not a chance! We don't want to be disqualified for being drunk in charge of a kayak!' teased Ben, stuffing the gin back in his bag.

Noticing another boat next to them, Ben was now fully aware of the TV crew filming up close, a commentator poised with a microphone. There was an air of anticipation all around as they listened to the reporter.

'Now is the moment the first crew member comes to the water,' he said.

Both crews waved towards the camera.

'We are watching the kayaks being lowered into the water and rowing first for Dr Ben Sanders's team, Making

Waves, is Allie McDonald. Isla Allaway is first up for Dr Katie O'Neil's team – Seas the Day. The two kayaks are identical and have been checked over by an independent adjudicator. Each team captain is to ensue all is fair in love and rowing. The sun is out with a moderate wind, the perfect day for this boat race. This, hopefully, is going to be the first of many annual boat races. These two teams are racing against each other for charity, the dementia charity, and so far, the donations are coming in thick and fast with just under a whopping one hundred and fifty thousand pounds being donated to this wonderful cause.'

In the distance and along the riverbank, the sound of cheers could be heard.

'How are we feeling?' asked Ben.

'I can feel the adrenalin pumping. Honestly, I'm raring to go!' declared Allie, high-fiving the team. 'Let's do this.'

Allie was up against Isla in the first leg of the thirteen-kilometre race. As the kayak was lowered into the water, Allie slipped off the edge of the boat then climbed into the kayak. Ben passed her the paddle. She looked across at Isla in the kayak next to her. She was grinning.

'Are you ready?'

'As ready as I'll ever be!' replied Isla as they began to paddle towards the start line.

Their arms were poised on the paddles, raring to go. Roman, the driver of the water taxi, had been given the job of starting the race. He was standing at the helm of the taxi bobbing on the water close by. Ben and Katie gave him the thumbs up and he brought the megaphone up to his mouth.

'Attention! On your marks, get set... GO!' A loud air horn sounded and they were off!

Allie and Isla were powering through the water. The engines of the speedboats began and each team followed their crew, continuously shouting encouragement.

The commentary from the TV crew could be heard through a sound system as they followed the race down the river.

'Allie McDonald is up by half a length – from an aerial shot we have a better view. Yes! Allie McDonald is in the lead. The kayaks are just approaching the Glensheil bend. Allie McDonald is not giving an inch and is still in front. Each crew member will be covering just over two kilometres of the river and the team captains, Dr Ben Sanders and Dr Katie O'Neil, will go head-to-head in the final race. Making Waves are at an early advantage but not by much. Isla Allaway is paddling strong with a long hard stroke. These are placid conditions with calm waters today and the support is magnificent. There's a gorgeous blue sky and big crowds are following this race. With another eleven kilometres to go, the finish line is Heartcross Bridge. Look at the crowds gathered there.'

The cameras panned towards the bridge.

'There are still busloads of well-wishers arriving. Such a great day for this boat race. There's been a huge surge in interest thanks to social media and Kim Smith, radio presenter, and of course all funds raised are going to the dementia charity. We can see people are watching from the hiking paths of Heartcross Mountain and spectators are watching from the tower of Heartcross Castle. We have a helicopter shot… Yes! Allie McDonald is still leading by two lengths, but Isla Allaway is only seconds behind as we reach the first swap over point.'

'You're up next, Rona, up against Martha. We are ahead but really not by much.'

'I've got this!' replied Rona, slipping into the river and pulling herself up into the kayak.

Ben passed her the paddle. 'GO!'

But Rona's grip on the paddle slipped and it fell in the water. It took her a moment to retrieve it and that's all Seas the Day needed to be out in front. Martha was paddling furiously and in the lead.

The atmosphere was electrifying. Shouts and cheers could be heard from the crowds' flag waving both teams from the riverbanks.

'Drew, I'm putting you up next, followed by Flynn. Meredith, you are going on the straight, and I'll take over for the last leg.'

'Yes, Captain!' they chorused.

Allie was sitting with a towel around her. 'That was so much fun! But so tiring!'

'You did fantastic. Well done,' said Ben. 'It was brilliant to watch. Honestly, my heart is pounding so fast.'

Seas the Day was out in front for the next couple of

kilometres and with Drew and Flynn closing the gap in their legs, Meredith was now on the straight. She was up against Julia.

'It's such a close call,' Ben said to his crew. He looked across towards Katie's boat.

They would be up next and even though Ben knew there was a possibility he had the edge on physical ability, Katie had mental strength, and whatever she put her mind to, she usually got.

Meredith and Julia were neck and neck the whole way, and as they passed the paddles and jumped into the river, Ben was already slipping into the water. As soon as he was in the kayak, he took a swift glance across at Katie, who was grinning at him. With their paddles hitting the water at top speed, they were off. Both crews were shouting at the top of their lungs, cheering their captains along every inch of the river.

The crowd went wild as the two kayaks came into sight.

The commentator could be heard over the megaphone and Ben could see from the corner of his eye that Katie was right by his side. They were rowing at the same rate and their paddles were close to colliding.

'Dr Ben Sanders has settled into a good rhythm, but Dr Katie O'Neil is giving it her all. Making Waves has got the edge and Ben Sanders has increased to half a length. If Ben can hold onto this position, he has the advantage. They are about to come round the last bend of the river and Katie O'Neil has closed the gap. They are on the crown of the bend and Katie O'Neil has taken the lead. Ben Sanders is giving it everything he's got. Katie has put on a new spurt – she's found a renewed strength but this race isn't won yet. Ben Sanders can still pull it out of the bag! It's going to be close!'

'Feel that burn,' Katie shouted towards Ben.

As they were on the home stretch, the crowd was deafening. The whole atmosphere spurred Ben on and with one almighty push, the crowd roared and they were neck and neck. The bridge was in sight. Ben took a swift glance towards the bridge. Helly was standing in the middle and he could see her jumping up and down. Standing next to her were his parents and Daniel with Ruby still on his shoulders.

Helly was holding a huge red flag. She was getting ready to wave it as they crossed the finished line.

'This is it!' bellowed Ben as he pulled the paddle through the water but as he looked at her, he noticed Katie's face had crumbled. Ben took another swift look in her direction. Something had thrown her off her stride. She'd slowed right down. Ben followed her gaze towards the bridge and he noticed Luke standing next to his family. Ben could see that Katie's lip was trembling.

'Luke's here! He's going to be so proud of you!'

Katie nodded and fought back the tears. All she could think about was Ellis and how her family had treated him and let her down. She swallowed down a lump and smiled up at Ben's brand-new family. They were here, cheering, and supporting him every inch of the way. She was delighted that everything had worked out for Ben, but what she would give, to have a solid loving family unit.

Ben edged his kayak closer to hers. 'What is it? What's going on?'

'I'm just being silly,' she replied, blinking back the tears. Her hands were shaking as she gripped the oar.

'Tell me. Let me help.'

'Why wasn't I ever good enough for my parents?'

Ben swallowed. He'd struggled with his own identity all his life and he knew what it was like to know that your family was out there, but in Katie's case, she didn't have the parents she so deserved.

'You are good enough. It's them that don't deserve you as a daughter.' He locked eyes with Katie. 'How about you share my new family? They already love you and I bloody do too.'

Katie couldn't stop the tears from flowing down her cheeks. Ben's offer was the kindest offer she had ever received.

'I mean it. They already think the world of you.'

'Do you know what? You are simply the best! Let's finish this race!' Katie shouted.

'You bet! Are you ready?' he asked.

'In a bizarre turn of events, the kayaks have slowed down.' The commentator's voice could be heard over the megaphone. 'But now they are picking up speed again.'

The crowd continued to roar.

Ben shouted towards Katie. 'Let's cross that line together!'

Katie pulled the paddle through the water; both kayaks were aligned with each other as they sailed through the finish line. Helly waved the flag as a burst of fireworks shot into the sky. All the boats following the race sailed across the finishing line, following the kayaks. Katie and Ben were side by side as they stood up on their kayaks.

'One...two...three...' said Katie as the pair jumped into the water and swam towards each other.

'You had me worried there for a minute. Are you okay?' asked Ben, throwing his arms around Katie and hugging her tight.

'I will be, and I'm so sorry. My thoughts just threw me into a complete meltdown for a moment. You should have just won the race.'

'Don't be daft. You're more important to me than any race.'

'And for a second there, I thought you said you loved me,' Katie said.

'That's exactly what you heard.'

'I love you too,' she whispered back as she took Ben's face in her hands and planted a huge kiss on his lips. The crowd erupted in applause and the pair of them threw their heads back and laughed.

As they began to swim back towards the bank, she asked, 'Do you think all these spectators feel they've been cheated that we crossed the line together?'

'Do they look like they've been cheated? Everyone looks like they are having a fantastic day. Come on, we have a speech to make and there's a trophy to collect. Let's see how much money we raised,' said Ben, pulling himself up on the bank. 'And then we can face the world together.'

'I like the sound of that,' she replied, holding out her hands as Ben pulled her from the water into the arms of her team, who cheered and hugged her tight.

'We won!' joked Katie, smiling.

'And we won too!' exclaimed Ben with a grin as they were handed an aluminium foil cape to wrap around their shoulders.

As both teams walked towards the bridge with their arms in the air, they received a hero's welcome. Everyone was cheering and clapping. 'We are the Champions' was blasting out from the radio station as they walked on by and Ben took Katie's hand.

'Teamwork, this is.' He bumped her shoulder.

Katie looked up ahead and Luke striding towards her with his arms open wide. 'You were amazing. You were both amazing.'

Katie fell into his arms.

'All this is because of you. You are an absolute superstar. I'm so proud of you.'

'Thank you,' she replied, giving him an extra squeeze.

'Ben, let me introduce you to my brother, Luke.'

They shook hands. 'Fantastic to meet you Luke,' said Ben. 'And I agree your sister is amazing.'

'She might be amazing, but I'm not being funny, Sis – you do stink to high heaven.' Luke grinned.

'I was wondering what that smell was,' agreed Katie, taking a whiff of her hair. 'Eau du river! Are you coming up onto the podium, Luke?'

'I'd love to,' he replied. 'And just so you know, Ellis would be so damn proud of you too.'

Katie swallowed down a lump at the sound of his name. 'I know.' She took a second to compose herself, then noticed the team members were beckoning them over. 'Come on,' she said.

On the way towards the small podium that had been erected in the middle of the bridge, Ben was met by his family, who were all beaming.

'What an absolute brilliant race! We were on the edge of our seats,' said Niamh.

'Grandma, that's not true. We didn't have seats, but Uncle Ben, you are a proper champion. I saw you on the telly and everything!' Ruby pointed towards the big screen.

Everyone laughed. Ben stretched out his arms towards Ruby, but she shook her head and grabbed onto Daniel.

'You smell,' she said, wrinkling up her nose.

'Just this once, you are forgiven for not wanting a hug, but after I'm showered, it's not up for discussion.'

Ruby smiled as Daniel hoisted her on his shoulders once more.

'Fantastic, Son. What a race!' said Connor, beaming at them both.

'Thank you! Can I introduce you to Luke? This is Katie's brother.'

After a hearty handshake, Ben announced they needed to go and collect the trophy. He slipped his hand into Katie's.

It meant the world to Ben that his family had flown over to share this day, and even better, they were staying for the next few days so he could properly spend some time with them before they flew back to Ireland. He meant every word when he told Katie that she could share his family; it was the greatest feeling knowing that all the people he cared about were standing right here, supporting them as they stepped onto the bridge. Every phone and TV camera was facing in their direction.

'Please put your hands together for our team captains, Dr Ben Sanders and Dr Katie O'Neil,' announced Helly, who started off the applause. Ben and Katie walked towards the small podium. Stuart was waiting for them and standing behind the microphone stand alongside Rory.

Ben and Katie looked out over the banks of the river and took in the view. They were astounded. The crowds stretched for what seemed like miles. The scene in front of them was magnificent.

'This is surreal,' murmured Katie.

'Unbelievable,' replied Ben. 'How are you feeling?'

'Actually, on top of the world. Luke is here and I'm with you, but I'll tell you one thing: I can't wait to get out of this stinking wetsuit.'

All the team members were chattering excitedly and standing in a long line with their arms slipped around the shoulder of the person standing next to them. Ben and Katie squeezed into the middle.

Stuart picked up the microphone. 'What a race!'

He turned towards the two teams and applauded them all before turning back towards the crowd. 'It was only a few weeks ago that I turned up at Peony Practice asking for fund-raising ideas for a charity very close to my heart. I wanted to increase awareness around dementia and raise money for the nationwide charity. It was at that moment that Dr Katie O'Neil suggested a boat race along the River Heart, and wanted the whole community to get involved, and that's the reason we are here today. I know a lot of families have been affected by this terrible disease, including my own wife, Alana. I can't thank the community of Heartcross enough for helping our family through such difficult times.'

Stuart looked towards Rory, who placed a supportive hand on his dad's shoulder before he continued. 'We are sorry that Alana couldn't be with us today to see such a fantastic turnout, but she will be over the moon to hear this news. After today's success, I'm pleased to announce that, thanks to the generous sponsorship of Kim Smith from the radio station and Flynn Carter, owner of Starcross Manor, this will be an annual event! Yes, that's right. I'm pleased to announce the Alana Scott Boat Race will take place at the same time next year. Today's boat race will be the first of many.'

Cheers erupted from the bank of the River Heart whilst Stuart dabbed his eye with a handkerchief before stuffing it back into his pocket. 'I told myself I wasn't going to get emotional, but...' He paused for a second whilst he composed himself. 'Today was all about fund-raising and putting this race on the map, so please welcome Dr Katie O'Neil and Dr Ben Sanders, who are going to give us an update on the amount of funds raised so far.'

Katie and Ben stepped forward and Stuart handed Katie an envelope. 'If you would like to say a few words.'

Everyone began to clap. Katie held up the envelope and the crowd fell silent. 'We can't thank you enough for such a wonderful turnout and the support that has been given by everyone here on the banks of the river today. My family, too, has been affected by this disease...' Katie's voice wobbled and she took a breath.

Ben squeezed her hand. 'Do you want me to continue?'

She shook her head. 'I've got this,' she replied softly as Ben put his arm around her shoulder. 'My brother Ellis was diagnosed with dementia at an early age.'

Katie looked towards Luke and smiled. 'My brother was taken way too young because of this disease and our family was torn apart in more ways than one. I loved him dearly.'

The tears slipped down her cheeks as Ben pulled her in tightly.

'I've got you,' he whispered. He took the microphone.

'It's an absolute privilege to work alongside Katie every day. She is a fantastic doctor, a great asset to our community and is always putting others before herself. This race was her idea and what a success it has been. And now for the reason we are here today.'

Ben gestured towards the envelope, which Katie began to open. She pulled out a card. Ben and Katie looked at each other. They couldn't quite believe the amount written on the card.

'Wow! I can't quite believe it. Thanks to these guys,'– he swept his arm towards the crew members – 'and you all' – he swept his arm towards the crowd, then nodded towards Katie.

'We have raised just over one hundred and seventy-five thousand pounds!'

The crowd went wild.

Stuart and Rory hugged each other whilst Ben lifted Katie off the ground and spun her around, then planted a huge kiss on her lips.

'That is a huge amount of money! You did that. You are a superstar,' Ben said.

'No, we did that. A race isn't a race without two team captains.'

Ben and Katie hadn't noticed, but Helly had hijacked the microphone. The press was on the bridge with their cameras poised. 'It is my greatest pleasure now to announce the winner of this year's Alana Scott Boat Race. It was a photo finish and after checking the footage…the winner is…'

Thinking they had crossed the line at the same time, both Ben and Katie stepped forward.

Helly had a glint in her eye. 'Dr Katie O'Neil!'

Katie punched the air as Ben looked flabbergasted. He was shaking his head in disbelief. 'How did that happen? We crossed that line together!'

'You win some, you lose some.' The beam on Katie's face said it all as she bent her knees and pretended to curtsey. Helly presented her with a trophy and soon Katie was joined by the rest of her team, who were jumping up and down and hugging each other.

Ben knew he was never going to hear the end of it. Up on the big screen, they replayed the end of the race and Ben watched as Katie's kayak just edged across the finish line first.

'Don't you forget our little bet.' Katie gave him a wink. 'But don't worry, I'll match it.'

The photographers' cameras were clicking away as Katie and her crew posed for photographs.

The champagne was flowing on top of the bridge and Ben took to the microphone. Katie narrowed her eyes at him.

'I have to say when Katie O'Neil turned up in the village, we got off to a shaky start, but in the past few weeks she has been worth her weight in gold and is indeed a worthy winner…'

Katie brought her hands up to her heart.

'To pull off an event like today takes some organising and it starts with a nugget of an idea that has grown thanks to Katie. Now the Alana Scott Boat Race is going to be an annual event.'

Ben raised his arms in the air and, once more, the crowds on the bank of the river erupted with applause and Katie thrust the winner's trophy high in the air. Ben looked over towards Isla and gave her a nod. She hurried towards him, carrying a stunning bouquet of large pink roses tinged with crimson, hand-tied with eucalyptus.

'These are for you – for just being you,' he said warmly, looking at Katie.

She handed the trophy over to Helly and fanned her hand in front of her face.

'These are beautiful,' she said taking the flowers from Ben. 'Thank you!'

'You are very welcome,' he replied, leaning forward and kissing her lightly on the lips. 'Now there are just a couple of things left for me to say.' He turned back towards the crowds on the riverbank. 'Same time next year and let's see if Making Waves can steal that trophy away from Seas the Day! And finally…thanks to Kim and the radio station, both crews and all of you for coming out to support us today. Please enjoy the rest of the day!'

With the speeches wrapped up, Katie stepped straight into Ben's arms.

'I'm sorry for winning.' She looked up at him and smiled.

'Are you really, though?' he teased.

'Absolutely not,' she replied, laughing.

Still wrapped in each other's arms, they were the last ones left standing on the bridge. They looked out over the river and stared at the beauty of it all.

'It's been a roller coaster of a few weeks, hasn't it?' Katie murmured, leaning into his chest. 'But can I just say – we really need to get out of these wetsuits. They are so damn gross.'

'We do,' he replied, kissing the top of her head, then pointing up to the sky. 'Look!'

Katie swung her gaze up towards the small Cessna plane flying up above, trailing a long pink banner through the sky that said: Dr Katie O'Neil winner of Alana Scott Boat Race 2021.

'Just look at that! I'm a winner!'

'I think we are both winners today.'

Katie kissed him one last time before handing him the trophy. 'Here's what you could have won,' she joked.

'There's always next year!'

They stared out across the water for a moment longer before Ben's family and Luke ran onto the bridge and began to spray them with champagne. They lapped up the glory.

Ben had loved every second of the day; it was the happiest he'd been in a long time.

'Do you think you'll be sticking around in Heartcross?' Luke asked his sister.

'Once you arrive in Heartcross, you never want to leave,' she chorused along with Ben.

'And I really don't want to be anywhere else,' Katie added. knowing that Ben had given her the greatest gift, she didn't need a trophy, she had him and was very much looking forward to becoming a part of his life and family.

The last few weeks had been a complete roller coaster for Ben and he couldn't wait for the rest of his life to begin. The village of Heartcross already held a special place in his heart and, despite his initial reservations when Katie had arrived in the village, he had fallen for her hook, line and sinker. Giving him a new zest for life, he was excited for what the future held for both of them.

Acknowledgments

Hugest of thank yous to my fabulous editor Emily Ruston – I have so enjoyed working with you on the latest book from the Love Heart Lane series. This extends to the wonderful team at One More Chapter and especially the brilliant Charlotte Ledger, who without a doubt the nicest person you will ever meet in the world of publishing.

A massive thank-you to my children, Emily, Jack, Ruby and Tilly who now believe I'm a proper author after having fifteen books published!

Much love to Woody (my mad Cocker Spaniel) who so far has been by my side throughout the whole of my writing career and to Nell (my bonkers Labradoodle) who is always by my side, whether I like it or not!

Much love to my epic friend Anita Redfern of over thirty years. Friends are the family we choose and I'd definitely choose you every day of the week.

Julie Wetherill what can I say – we stumbled across each other by chance and you are gintastic!

A big thank you to Nicky Chisnall who throughout the pandemic checked up on me every single week. I really appreciate you being my friend and I wished we lived closer!

A special mention to Kim Smith, Sam Newey and Ashley Costello. There is no limit to what we as women can accomplish and I am in awe of you all. You are all amazing!

High fives to my fabulous and slightly bonkers writing friends, you know who you are! Writing can be a lonely job but you all bring a smile to my face on a regular basis – thank you.

Big shout out to everyone in the book blogging community especially Rachel Gilbey who always champions my books and takes them on tour.

Deep gratitude to all my readers, reviewers, retailers, librarians and fellow authors who have supported me throughout my career. Authors would be lost without you, and I'm so grateful for your support.

I have without a doubt enjoyed writing every second of this book and I really hope you enjoy the latest instalment from the Love Heart Lane series – *The New Doctor at Peony Practice*. Please do let me know!

Warm wishes,

Christie xx

Christie Barlow

New Beginnings at the Old Bakehouse

'Full of warmth, fun and feel-good factor'
Katie Fforde

Don't miss *New Beginnings at the Old Bakehouse…*

The next heartwarming instalment in the Love Heart Lane series by Christie Barlow!

Where friends are there for you no matter what…

YOUR NUMBER ONE STOP
ONE MORE CHAPTER
FOR PAGETURNING BOOKS

One More Chapter is an
award-winning global
division of HarperCollins.

Sign up to our newsletter to get our
latest eBook deals and stay up to date
with our weekly Book Club!
<u>Subscribe here.</u>

Meet the team at
<u>www.onemorechapter.com</u>

Follow us!
@OneMoreChapter_
@OneMoreChapter
@onemorechapterhc

Do you write unputdownable fiction?
We love to hear from new voices.
Find out how to submit your novel at
<u>www.onemorechapter.com/submissions</u>